Beecher

Beecher

Virginia O'Neal

Cliffhanger Press
Oakland, California

Acknowledgments

I wish to thank Ruth, Lee and Gail for artistic support; Ramona, my typist; David and Marsha Meece, whose expertise brought *BEECHER* into the computer age; the reference staff of the New Albany-Floyd County Public Library; Al Smith for a jacket design that captures the spirit of the book; Martha and Joan, for their unfailing support; Bruce Bell,. whose literary career inspired me to start writing; and especially Jim, who took me on the fabulous trips to Italy that made this book possible. I am grateful for the support of family members and friends too numerous to mention here. Finally, I owe a special debt to my editor and publisher, Nancy Chirich, for her editorial assistance, encouragement and belief in *BEECHER*.

Virginia O'Neal

Published by
Cliffhanger Press
P.O. Box 29527
Oakland, California 94604-9527

Manufactured in the United States of America

Library of Congress Cataloging-in-Publication Data

O'Neal, Virginia.
    Beecher / Virginia O'Neal
    p. cm.
    ISBN 0-912761-31-8 (alk. paper)
    I. Title.
PS3565.N44B44 1990
813".54–dc20
                           90-31496
                           CIP

First Edition

For Jim, my husband,
who helped bring Beecher to life.

Prologue

Beecher crossed the crowded Piazza di Spagna and stopped beside a flower vendor's cart to light his pipe. He shifted his sketch pad, placing it under his left arm as he lit a match. He glanced around the ancient and beautiful plaza, breathing in the essence of Rome.

Trees had begun to bud, and the late afternoon sun cast purple shadows on the magnificent Spanish Steps, ablaze with azaleas and crowded with the disenchanted youth of several nations. Tourists rested, recouping their energies for a fresh onslaught on the next cathedral, the Pantheon or the leather shops on the Via Condotti. Even now, in the early spring, Rome was swarming with visitors. Dapper Italian men in dark business suits sidestepped hirsute dropouts as they briskly ascended and descended the steps. The bells in the church of Trinitá dei Monti's twin campaniles pealed the hour, drowning out for a moment the honking of auto horns, the babble of diverse languages and the voices of hucksters of souvenirs, post cards, cameos and fake Rolex watches.

Beecher had been strolling and sketching all day, getting ideas for his Italian Series, fascinated by the golden patina of this city of the Caesars. Was it the Mediterranean light, Beecher wondered, or the coloration of the buildings that gave Rome its unique look—so different from the clearly delineated values of his native Indiana. It was a different world. A whole new set of esthetics was involved in capturing this peculiar golden ocher light of Rome in watercolor.

He was studying the intricate play of sun and shadow on the steps when he saw the woman turn, and caught a clear glimpse of her profile beneath the brim of her hat. It was Myra.

The woman turned back, reached for her companion's arm, and they started on up the steps. For an instant the burning sensation that filled Beecher's chest threatened to stop his breathing.

What was happening to him? Was he losing his mind? His wife Myra had been killed five years ago.

He ran up the steps, dodging tourists, knocking over an easel on which a painting was displayed, and caught sight of her again for only a second, just long enough to see Myra's lush black hair beneath the teal blue hat and the familiar line of her shoulders before he was cut off by a group of German tourists in Alpine hats and long raincoats. Their leader's face grew red with Teutonic rage as Beecher pushed him aside in his attempt to pass. When he reached the top the woman had disappeared.

Maybe she had entered the Church of Trinitá dei Monti, he thought desperately. The cool gloom enveloped him as he stood at the back. In an instant his eyes had adjusted to the light and he could see that she was not there. Two elderly Italian women in black kerchiefs were praying and a small group of tourists were gazing raptly at the frescos. Otherwise the church was empty.

Beecher dropped into a pew, too stunned to go further.

He was assailed by doubts of his own sanity. What he had seen was beyond reason. Myra was dead. He had identified her body. But had he seen what he was told he would see, what he had expected to see? He had heard of this kind of testimony in courts of law too often to believe it could not happen to him. Or was he falling victim now, five years later, to hallucinations, in the city which had a way of lulling and seducing even the most wary of visitors?

Only the other night, as he lingered over a glass of wine in a sidewalk *caffè* and watched the eternal parade of strollers in the Via Veneto, he had become aware that during these days in Rome he had been overtaken by a delicious idleness, a feeling all the harder to resist because it was so new and foreign to his nature. Surprisingly, he had no desire to fight it.

Myra had often chided him, "You never learned to relax. You may not be conscious of it, but you are a product of the Protestant work ethic." What if she could see me now, he had thought, as he tasted again this vintage that made him think of sun-drenched hillsides and dusty fruit bursting with ripeness. The wine had a hint of dry harshness, like this land.

Now, as he sat in the dim light of the church, he asked himself if Rome had captivated him with its visions of past glory and its strange insinuating beauty until his sense of the here and now had begun to fade. Had he only imagined that he had seen Myra on the Spanish Steps, dredging up her image from the long-buried depths of his desire?

And now he could resist the memories no longer and they came rushing and crashing in upon him like huge waves. He was too dazed to struggle further, and the undertow pulled him out... out... far out to sea...

Part I - Sparta, Indiana

1.

The phone rang at five-thirty Monday morning. Not the most ideal way to be awakened, thought Beecher, as his neighbor Hollis Franke bellowed at him through the phone. Hollis really didn't need AT&T. A megaphone would have served him just as well.

"What's the problem, Hollis?"

"Your dern black bull is in with my Hereford heifers. If I'd wanted my herd intergrated, I'd a bought a black bull in the first place."

"Well, Hollis, I think it would be an improvement over what you've got, but if you feel that way about it, I'll be right over to get him." Cantankerous old coot, thought Beecher. Hondo was a prizewinner, and new blood could do nothing but improve Franke's herd.

Beecher hung up the phone and called Cassie. "Come on, little girl. Let's go and collect Hondo. I wish you knew how to start the coffee." Cassie, the sturdy little Cairn terrier, gave him an apologetic look. Beecher struggled into his pants, flannel shirt and Redwing boots. He put on

1

his insulated jacket, the one Myra had always referred to as his Chinese communist gear, and stepped out into the frosty morning air.

During the entire month of March the weather had been unseasonably warm, causing trees and shrubs to bud out early, and crocus and tulips to push up through the warming soil, but it had all been premature, like the opening of a play on Broadway before the out of town run.

During the afternoon snow had started to fall, bringing with it the heaviest accumulation of the winter. Flakes the size of silver dollars had drifted down all night, and now Beecher stepped out of his door into a magical white world.

The branches of the Norway spruce, Beecher and Myra's first live Christmas tree, were bent under the weight of a wet eight-inch snowfall. Together, they had planted the little spruce eighteen years before, and now it was taller than the house. Beecher had dug the hole during the first January thaw that year, while Myra stood by in her parka with the fur-trimmed hood, plucking off remaining bits and pieces of silver icicles and tinsel.

Everywhere he looked, there were reminders of her. He sometimes felt that if he traveled to the ends of the earth in the hope of forgetting, he would encounter some reminder of Myra.

The day before this late March snowfall, the forsythia bushes had been in full bloom. Now only hints of bright yellow peeked out here and there. Beecher had the distinct impression that during the night a puffy white down comforter had been drawn up over the entire earth, covering all imperfections and flaws. This pristine whiteness spoke to him of nature's forgiveness, eradicating much of the ugliness that man imposed upon the earth with a blanket of beauty and peace.

Beecher plodded through the snow to Hollis's adjoining farm, planning his strategy for capturing Hondo. Cassie carefully followed in his tracks on her short legs, her low little belly dragging in the snow. Cassie had a strong sense of duty, probably picked up from Beecher.

Usually Hondo was easy to manage, but one of Hollis's heifers was in season. Beecher tricked the old fellow by maneuvering the heifer over to the gate, then he slipped the halter over Hondo's head and eased him out. Cassie nipped at the bull's heels to get him moving and Beecher led him back to the farm and into the barn.

He threw six bales of hay down to the cattle. His breath frosted in the icy air inside the barn, but suddenly it was July and Beecher could see Myra and hear her say, "I'll wear a white eyelet peasant blouse. It will slide off one shoulder." His eyes misted over.

Beecher called gruffly to Cassie, who was burrowing in the hay for a mouse. The sound of Hondo's satisfied low-keyed bellow followed them as they tramped through the snow to the house. Smoke drifted from the chimney. The remains of last night's fire still burned in the fireplace.

The white frame farmhouse sprawled comfortably on the land like a plump matron, slightly past her prime. Dark green shutters framed the windows, and ice etched delicate patterns on the glass to match his mother, Sara's, old lace curtains, barely visible at the upstairs dormer windows.

The sun porch, which Myra had designed, jutted out on the left side of the house—at odds with the older construction, just as Myra's eccentricities had caused consternation in conservative Sparta, Indiana.

The custom of meditating in the nude had not reached the heartlands until Myra showed up. "When reaching for the infinite, it's necessary to get down to the bare fundamentals," she told Beecher. He was never sure exactly who or what Myra was trying to contact. He preferred not to inquire into it too closely. She did yield, however, to Beecher's suggestion that she have a robe handy in case someone came to the door.

"Hollis is getting on in years, darling," Beecher chuckled, "his old ticker might not survive the shock of seeing you appear at the door in the altogether."

Myra's sudden trips to New York gave rise to the rumor

that Beecher Hornbeck's wife had grown tired of rural life and had probably taken off for good this time. Beecher realized that he had more chance of holding on to Myra if he gave her the freedom she needed, and she in turn responded to his trust with a tenderness and passion that filled every corner of his reserved nature.

As Beecher approached the house, he reminded himself that it was time to have it repainted. He would attend to that later in the spring—after he returned from his exhibit in Rome. Since Myra's death, house repairs didn't seem as important. He still planted bright red geraniums in the window boxes every summer because he knew she would expect him to.

Beecher loved this farm. It had sustained him during all those years he had worked and struggled to establish himself as an artist.

He painted his beloved fields and streams in all seasons. The subject of his most famous painting, the old stone chimney, reminded Beecher of an ancient monolith. It stood at the far end of the four-hundred-acre farm. In the early years of their marriage, he and Myra had often picnicked in the woods, near the chimney. They ate their lunch under the huge spreading oaks and then made love afterward.

Before they married, Beecher had worried about his and Myra's prospects of happiness together. They came from totally different backgrounds and their personalities were nothing alike. Myra had said to him, "Beecher, don't you know that love is the most practical thing in the world to build a marriage on? It's the only thing that lasts. It will outlast anything, darling. Try it and see."

Beecher took off his boots on the small braided rug inside the kitchen door and admonished Cassie to wipe her feet. "You know, Cassie, the old dragon will wipe up the floor with us if we make a mess." He made coffee, scrambled eggs and fried bacon. There were also donuts, which he shared with Cassie, who loved sweets.

It was after nine when Beecher left the house and

walked the short distance to his large studio near the pear orchard. He never failed to notice the beauty of the hazy blue southern Indiana knobs in the distance.

Cool northern light flooded the studio. Beecher had allowed himself the extravagance of a skylight when he had the studio built some twenty years before. Sketches and paintings—both his and Myra's—hung on the walls, and a large built-in console held paints, brushes and other supplies. One wall had slots for storing canvases.

Beecher preferred to stretch and prime his own canvases, using the finest linen canvas available. The familiar odor of the studio–gesso, oil paint and linseed oil,–mingled together, always had a calming effect on Beecher. Relics of his art school days were scattered about the large room: the plaster hand and foot and Michelangelo's statue of David. All of these he had sketched from dozens of angles in his first anatomy class.

His easel and palette were bathed in light in the center of the spacious room. The easel stood apart from the homey clutter of the studio just as the artist at times must stand aloof from the rest of life in order to distill his unique vision and convey that vision to others.

Myra's easel still stood in the corner with the half finished portrait she had been working on when she died. Somehow, that didn't bother him. In fact it gave him the strange feeling, at times, that it had all been a bad dream and that he would go out to the studio to paint and would find her working on the portrait as he had so many times before.

The desperation with which Myra had pursued her painting after her failure to become pregnant had worried Beecher. He could understand her disappointment—he longed for children too, but there was a frantic quality in Myra after that which frightened him.

She would be her usual self for months at a time; enthusiastically redecorating the house, painting portraits, flying to New York to meet her mother for shopping and the opera. And then she would suddenly lapse into a depression and anguish that disrupted their life together. Beecher felt helpless when he tried to comfort her, and her anger erupted when he suggested they seek counseling. These black moods would leave as suddenly as they came on. Myra's return to normal always convinced Beecher that there would be no reoccurrence—that there was nothing to fear after all.

Today he hoped to finish the canvas he had been working on for the past two months. He planned to spend the next week framing pictures and getting his paintings ready to crate and send to Rome for his exhibit at the Brazzano Gallery in May.

He looked at the large oil on his easel with a fresh eye and immediately saw several small touches that needed to be added. Often he left a picture when he became frustrated—at a loss to know what to do next. After a day or two of farm chores, he came back to his painting with renewed vigor, his mind fresh, his creative processes operating at full capacity.

His painting was of one of Myra's favorite places on the farm, an old stone spring house that had lost its roof. The walls were crumbling, but the spring still ran pure and crystal clear. A gnarled elm struggled to prop up the remaining wall of the spring house. This, like so many of Beecher's recent paintings, gave the viewer the feeling of strength in loneliness, a feeling of tranquility.

He painted all day, stopped only for lunch, and finally laid down his brushes when the light faded.

As Beecher stepped back a few feet and studied his work, his whole being was flooded with the knowledge that this one was good—a work of real depth and creativity. Was there any feeling in the world to equal this, he wondered? That is what kept an artist going, even in the face of disappointment and rejection.

The corners of the studio were filled with shadows. Myra's easel was barely visible in the fading light, her old paint-dabbed smock hanging next to it with the wide brimmed straw hat she had worn when sketching out of doors in summer.

Beecher slowly began to clean his palette and brushes, the final ritual of creation.

2.

Beecher put another log on the fire and sat back and watched the dancing flames—orange and blue—casting shadows on the bookcases and paneled walls. The old farmhouse had been in the Hornbeck family for three generations, but he and Myra had done some remodeling after his mother Sara died. In this room they had retained the massive fireplace, beamed ceiling and brick floor, but had added mellow rubbed cherry paneling, a large, bay window and ceiling to floor bookcases on both sides of the brick fireplace. Even so, they never seemed to have enough room for their books, which continued to overflow into every room in the house. Every end table was piled high with art books and novels, classics, volumes on gardening and veterinary medicine.

This had always been Beecher's favorite room. So many ideas for paintings had come to him as he sat in front of his fireplace and stared into the bright flames. Now he reached for the package of tobacco on the table at his side and filled his pipe, never taking his eyes off the fire. His pipe was as normal an appendage of his person as his hands and feet and certainly necessary to the operation of his thought processes. He had tried a few times to give up his pipe, but he had discovered as C. S. Lewis did, that not smoking was a full-time job. Now he merely suffered the slights, disgust and hysterical coughing of reformed smokers with the quiet tolerance that was so much a part of his personality.

There was nothing about Beecher Hornbeck's appearance to draw special attention, at least not at first glance. He had a knack for blending in with his surroundings, when the situation demanded it: medium height and build, light brown hair, which the sun turned blond in summer, regular features that didn't register a lot of emotion.

He was good at hiding that, especially now that Myra had gone.

He had inherited the Beecher looks, along with his Anglo-Saxon genes, from his mother's family, and according to the locals was the "spittin image" of Sara Beecher Hornbeck. Beecher was one of those few extraordinary people who had a chameleon-like quality which enabled him to look at home in many diverse settings. In London, he looked very much like a middle-class British accountant getting off the train at Paddington Station, and he had once been mistaken for a Finn at the Intercontinental Hotel in Helsinki.

An astute observer would not be deceived, however, by the apparent blandness of his features. This observer would realize that there was an unusual intelligence in the light blue, deep set eyes; would note the hint of silent amusement at the corners of Beecher's mouth, but would be, at the same time, perplexed by the shadow of some deeply hidden sadness, more than merely a meditative quality, that sometimes passed over his countenance like a fleeting cloud over the summer landscape. Beecher had the gift of observing the smallest details and cataloging them in his mind for future reference. It was his artist's eye, developed over the years of looking into the depths of his subjects' personalities, studying every nuance of nature, every subtle change of light that would give meaning to his painting.

Mrs. Daily entered the room and spoke to him twice before Beecher even noticed her presence. He was poking the blazing fire, and Cassie was standing by hoping to pursue any stray spark that might escape from the fireplace.

"Mr. Hornbeck, I'm leaving now. Your shirts are all ironed and hanging in your closet. I finished the cleaning while you were out in your studio this afternoon. I checked on your soup, like you asked me to."

"You didn't add anything, did you Mrs. Daily? Be truthful now." He couldn't resist teasing her. Mrs. Daily swelled up like an officious toad at any hint of criticism.

"No, I certainly didn't. It's your stomach and if you want to ruin it with that strange foreign stuff, that's up to you, I guess. But I did bake you a cherry cobbler for your supper. It's in the oven."

"You certainly know the most direct way to a man's heart, Mrs. D." Beecher had often remarked to Myra that if it weren't for cobbler, art and women, not necessarily in that order, he added with a leer, he would just check out of this tired old world.

But no amount of flattery could long deter Mrs. Daily from the mundane, which was her stock in trade.

"Just look at the snow you tracked in, Mr. Hornbeck. I don't know what good it does me to clean this place up for you. If you would only be careful with your pipe and carry your dirty dishes to the kitchen, things would stay real nice till I come back on Friday."

"I will Mrs. Daily, really I will."

"Promises, promises," muttered Mrs. Daily as she picked up another of Beecher's slimy pipe cleaners as though it were a dead rat and stalked belligerently to the kitchen. Minutes later she reappeared in her coat and hat, carrying her enormous purse.

"If that's all you need, Mr. Hornbeck, I'll be leaving."

"Thank you, Mrs. Daily, I'll see you on Friday."

"Be sure and put the sheets on the couches tonight. That

little beast is ruining all of Miss Myra's lovely furniture."

"I'll be sure to do that," said Beecher, trying hard to keep the impatience out of his voice.

Mrs. Daily sighed and peered out from under her ancient millinery, an elderly, stout midwestern martyr with a carpet bag. She didn't believe him for a minute. As soon as she left, he would allow Cassie to jump up beside him in his favorite chair. He would eat cobbler in the den and leave the mayonnaise jar out of the refrigerator all night. She sighed again and headed for the front door.

Beecher had borne Mrs. Daily's lecture on his sloppy habits with good grace, even though he hadn't been in the mood to listen. It had been a long day, beginning with Hollis Franke's frantic call about the amorous Hondo. Eight hours of intense concentration on his painting had taken a lot out of Beecher, and he still hadn't finished the picture, as he had hoped he would. Even though Beecher had now become a well known painter, art would always be a dilettante pursuit to most of the folks of Sparta, Indiana—just something extra he did in addition to farming.

After Beecher heard the door close, he poked the fire again. "Cassie, why do we put up with her bullying?" he addressed the little Cairn. He was quite sure Cassie understood every word. She looked up at him with her soft, shiny little black eyes. Cassie knew all of Beecher's moods as well as being able to discern the day's activities by the clothes he wore. On the mornings that he got up and put on his farm clothes, Cassie's excitement knew no bounds. His painting clothes failed to interest her. He was no fun when he stood in front of his easel for hours, often not even stopping to eat. Cassie couldn't understand why he never talked to her when he painted.

Beecher's years of studying art and patiently pursuing his craft were finally paying off. The pendulum in the art world was swinging in the opposite direction and Beecher was basking in the sunlight of artistic recognition. But recognition has been a long time coming, too late for him and Myra to enjoy it together.

Myra had always believed in his talent. "Beecher, the art critics have conned the public into thinking that these mindless blobs and dribbles have some deep hidden meaning, visible only to the initiated—the elite. It's simply a case of the Emperor's New Clothes. The whole thing is a fraud. Your painting is growing stronger and more intense, and one day you will be recognized. You are the strongest definitive painter in the midwest."

And so it had happened, just as Myra said it would. After Myra had been killed, Beecher had thrown himself into his painting with an almost fanatical single-mindedness. He often stayed in his studio for twelve or fourteen hours at a stretch, stumbling into the house late at night and falling asleep on the couch in the den with his clothes on. Outwardly, his friends and neighbors saw little change in his demeanor. But, then, as they observed, Beecher Hornbeck was never one to wear his feelings on his sleeve. Myra had been emotional and full of enthusiasm. Sometimes she fell prey to dark moods, but Beecher could usually talk her out of them. They were a perfect foil for each other.

He avoided their bedroom for the first few months after her death and started sleeping in the guest room, those nights he didn't spend on the couch in the den. At first he just couldn't bring himself to sleep alone in the king size bed or to have her clothes removed from the closet or her perfume and brushes from the dresser.

Meanwhile, Beecher's painting took on a power and authority it had never had before. His stark painting of the old stone chimney, standing in the middle of a snow field, won him a coveted first prize and was purchased by the St. Louis Art Museum for their permanent collection. Beecher Hornbeck was described in the reviews as, "The most powerful painter of the American scene in the past fifty years," "and as "The midwestern Andrew Wyeth.". He accepted the praise calmly and kept on painting. His reputation was firmly established.

Many clichés are true. He found that time was the great healer, and that while his life would never be the same again, he had re-entered the land of the living.

3.

Sara Beecher Hornbeck's sole ambition had been to obtain the finest education possible for her artistic son. The boy had shown unusual talent. He spent all his spare time sketching the farm animals and painting in watercolor.

The farm operated at a fair profit. Sara ran it with the help of a hired hand and extra part-time workers at haycutting and harvesting time. She had been widowed when her son was ten years old.

When Beecher finished high school, he took over the running of the farm and studied with a local Indiana landscape painter. After a year, the artist realized that he had taught Beecher all he knew, and that the boy had a great future ahead of him as a painter. "You need to enroll him in a first-rate school. Beecher has too much talent to waste on the farm," Harold Robards told Sara.

Beecher enrolled in the Art Academy in Cincinnati, a fine old school where he studied life drawing and anatomy, spending many hours a week on each large detailed charcoal drawing of the human figure. But his real love was oil painting—landscape painting in particular. He longed to be able to convey his feeling about nature to others. The school was connected to the Cincinnati Art Museum in Eden Park and provided a wonderful place to study the old masters. Beecher was already discovering a unique style of his own.

During his fourth year at the Art Academy, Beecher was given an opportunity to spend a summer studying with Leland Randolph, the real master of landscape and marine painting. Randolph taught at the Art Students' League in New York in the winter and held summer classes at his studio and summer home in Noank, Connecticut.

It was at Randolph's summer class that Beecher met Myra, who was also an art student. It was a case of the attraction of opposites in many ways, and yet these were superficial differences. Myra's dark Mediterranean beauty was as sharp a contrast to Beecher's pleasant but rather ordinary Anglo-Saxon features as her emotional temperament was to his more temperate dependable nature.

Myra fell in love with Beecher almost immediately. With her deep intuitiveness, and in spite of Beecher's natural reticence, she knew that this was not only a man of rare talent and potential as a painter, but that his mind was philosophical and subtle and that his passions would run deep.

On this particular afternoon, the painting class had been cancelled. Randolph was in New York supervising the hanging of his exhibit at the Rollins-Laurence Gallery. Myra had prepared a picnic lunch and had lured Beecher away from his painting.

"You can't work all the time. You need a little inspiration occasionally," she said, turning on him that direct gaze of hers that was so feminine and at the same time so free of artifice. Obvious flirtatiousness had always turned Beecher off, for he sensed in it the implication that a man was a fool to be exploited and manipulated. Myra had no bag of tricks. Her sensuality was so much a part of her nature that she was totally unaware of its effect on him.

It was a glorious summer day and they drove along the Connecticut coast road in Myra's convertible, enjoying the view of the ocean and this unexpected mid-week freedom from class. Beecher found just the right spot for their picnic. After a steep climb, they reached a secluded plateau among the rocks large enough to spread out the blue and white checked table cloth and cushions. A gnarled tree sheltered them from the wind.

They feasted on the fried chicken, deviled eggs and salad that Myra had packed. She had included a loaf of French bread and Roquefort cheese—Beecher's favorite—and a bottle of dry red wine. Myra tore off pieces of crusty French bread and threw it to the gulls, who wheeled and screeched overhead.

The remains of their lunch was spread out on the cloth and Beecher lay back against the cushions, staring at the sea. He decided to come back to this spot and paint a seascape, to try to capture the incredible beauty: the crashing waves and screeching gulls, the irregular rocky coastline and forbidding cliffs, a ship on the horizon—only a speck, about to fall off the edge of the world.

Myra had been silent for several minutes but she spoke now with an urgency that startled Beecher. "What are we going to do in September when the class is over? I've been wondering if you care as much as I do—hoping that you would bring it up first." In spite of the overwhelming attraction that Beecher felt for Myra, he could think of several reasons why marriage might not work.

"I've been trying to picture you in Sparta, on the farm, Myra. Frankly, it's difficult. Swiss finishing schools don't mix too well with the Moose Lodge. Main Street is pretty far from Broadway, you know. I'm crazy about you, but I'm trying to keep a level head."

"Don't use those old clichés on me, Beecher. Just what's so special about a level head?" she asked with a touch of anger in her voice. Myra's emotions were close to the surface—ready to flare up. "And just how am I supposed to know that you're crazy about me?" she added.

Beecher ran his finger gently down her cheek and across her lips. "Please, darling, calm down a minute and listen to me. The farm and the countryside are the inspiration for my painting. That's where I need to be if I'm ever going to amount to anything as an artist. I just can't imagine you being happy there."

The irritation passed from Myra's face, leaving no shadow, and was replaced just as suddenly by enthusiasm.

"I know I'd love the farm. I'll wear a blue and white checked apron and make homemade bread and those cherry cobblers you're always talking about. We can frolic in the haystacks. Can't you just imagine it, Beecher, frolicking in the hay? I'll wear a white eyelet peasant blouse. It will slip off one shoulder."

Beecher just looked at her in amazement, trying to figure out why this goofy, romantic, almost childlike streak in Myra appealed to him so much. Could it be because he came from a long line of practical people, he wondered. Myra's impression of life on the farm seemed to Beecher to be based on the idyllic scenes depicted on French toile wallpaper—a shepherd boy plays the lute for his lady love whose ample bosom overflows her tightly laced bodice while gentle lowing cattle are driven home from the fields, and swans glide across a glassy lake.

"Your grasp of farm life, Myra, is really amazing." He smiled, thinking that Sparta, Indiana, had never seen anything like Myra before.

"Why are you smiling, Beecher? What are you thinking?"

"I'm wondering how the staid Wellingtons you've described to me ever produced you. Are you sure you're not adopted?" he grinned back at her.

"No," she said shaking her head, "on Harry's side—that's Mother—several generations back, there was an Italian in the family. Apparently, I'm a throwback, or something. Oh, Beecher, can't you see how great we'll be together? We both have our painting. I need you—your stability. With you I'm longer afraid of myself, afraid of going off the deep end. And without me, you might become a stodgy old farmer."

Beecher's voice was husky as he said, "You may be sorry you accused me of being stodgy."

He entwined his hand in her long black hair and pulled her down beside him.

She kissed him gently, but her eyes were veiled and sad as she said, "This thing can work two ways, darling. You really hardly know me. Maybe you'd be getting some things you hadn't bargained for. Have you ever considered that possibility?" Myra's mercurial emotional changes never ceased to surprise him.

"I have no doubt that I'd be getting a hundred times more than I bargained for," he said. "That's what fascinates me about you."

She lowered her head, and her hair fell like a dark wing across his cheek. Myra's hair smelled of lemons, and when he kissed her shoulder, her skin tasted of sunlight and salt.

"I'm tired of talking," Beecher whispered. "I'd rather explore the possibilities." He pressed his mouth against hers with an urgency that parted her lips in astonishment, as his fingers traveled down her face and neck, pausing for an instant at the throbing pulse at the base of her throat. She realized then, that there was an eloquence in his touch that his words lacked. She lay trembling in his arms.

"I thought New Yorkers were supposed to be cool and in control," he said.

"And I thought you were tired of talking," Myra whispered. He held her close, and the rhythms of the sea took possession of her entire being. The world around them no longer existed....

The passion and tenderness that she evoked in him, feelings that came from the depths of his being, that afternoon by the sea, were far more of a revelation to Beecher than they were to Myra, who instinctively sensed his true nature. It was the contrast that excited her, between his controlled, slightly aloof exterior and that part of him she thought of as the other Beecher, the side of his nature she knew she had the power to call forth. There were hints of it in his painting, a controlled sensuality that was all the more alluring to her because of its subtlety and all the more potent because of its innocence.

So the love they experienced, accompanied by the crashing waves and the crying of the gulls, was indeed a revelation to Beecher. Not to Myra, for the seaside interlude turned out as she had hoped. Beecher's doubts about their compatibility and divergent backgrounds were consumed in the bright flames of tenderness and desire.

Myra could have been a Montague and he a Capulet. It made no difference now.

4.

Beecher would never forget the first time he met Harriet and William Wellington. Their home near Westport was very much as he had imagined, the kind of place that didn't have a yard, but "grounds", tended by Fred, the elderly gardener. It was late July and Myra drove Beecher down the shady lane in her red convertible. Fred's flower beds with their profusion of color turned the lawn into an English garden.

William was almost a stereotype of the Wall Street broker, but Harriet was a real surprise, not at all the society matron that Beecher had expected. Harriet Wellington was a small-boned aristocratic tomboy with red hair, in a classic tailored silk shirt and slacks. There was an austere spareness about Harriet that Beecher admired. He sensed in her a kindred spirit.

In a charming dining room, they dined by candlelight, on lobster bisque with dry white wine, followed by rare roast beef and hot house asparagus—courtesy of Fred—in hollandaise sauce. The cook had whipped up Myra's favorite, chocolate mousse, for dessert.

William's manner was outwardly friendly, but his grey eyes were cold and distant the few times that Beecher caught him off guard. This man was unlike Myra; Beecher could hardly believe that William was her father. William Wellington's grandfather had been a buccaneer on the high seas of finance and business, back in the days of unrestricted free enterprise. William sailed those same seas more circumspectly, but he was no less at home than his ancestor in the world of high finance and large mergers.

It was obvious to Beecher that William doted on his only daughter and didn't want to see her wasted on an aspiring painter from the Midwest.

The conversation would have faltered after a discussion of the weather if it hadn't been for Harriet. Beecher's knowledge of business and his interest in golf were limited, and William considered art too far removed from the "real world" to be a serious concern.

Beecher and Harriet seemed to find plenty to talk about. As they were finishing coffee, Harriet announced with her unique combination of belligerance and charm that Beecher was to call her "Harry", a privilege reserved for family and very close friends. Even though Beecher was sure that Harry liked him, William was an enigma.

The Wellingtons excused themselves early and went upstairs to their large sitting-bedroom. The evening was unseasonably chilly and Fred had a fire going in the stone fireplace. When Harriet came out of the dressing room in her robe, she found a gloomy William staring into the flames.

"I like him, William, really I do. I have a feeling he is right for Myra."

"Can't understand why. He's a hayseed. She's had too many advantages to waste her life on a farm in Indiana, the middle of nowhere." William slammed the magazine he was reading down on the coffee table and walked over to the window.

"William, if you would just leave your prejudices on

Wall Street, we might be able to discuss this in a rational manner."

"She could have Beenie Randolph or Andrew Warren at the snap cf her fingers," grumbled William.

"She doesn't want Beenie or Andy. They're both boring and inane. I wouldn't want them either. This man is not a hayseed. He's very attractive. It's obvious they are in love with each other. Myra says he's extremely talented, which I'm willing to take her word for, and if I 'm any judge of character, he has plenty of that, along with integrity. I don't need to remind you that Myra needs someone with strength."

William turned from the window. "You know I care about her happiness, Harry, just as much as you do."

Harry poured William a small brandy and walked over to the window. She handed it to him and stood beside him looking down at the lawn which sloped gently to the woods, where Myra and Beecher walked arm and arm down by the lake.

"I know you love her as much as I do, William," Harry resumed. "But if you remember, before she met Beecher she was determined to go to Paris this fall to paint, just strike out on her own, live in the proverbial garret, overlooking the quaint little rooftops of Paris, surviving heroically on sprouts and crusts of French bread. That's her idea of the artist's life, wearing a black beret and sitting around evenings in a Montmartre café, over a bottle of wine, with Toulouse Lautrec and Company, discussing art with a capital A. William, that's reality to Myra. Are you prepared to take a chance on what might happen? Remember Lavinia."

In 1893, Lavinia Hartley had gone on a grand tour and while in Venice, had fallen in love with Alessandro Rosetti, who claimed to be able to trace his ancestors back to a court painter in the palace of Lorenzo the Magnificent. When the Hartleys got wind of the affair, they sent an emissary to try to stop the wedding. Unable to accomplish this, Matthew Williston Hartley III, a master of Yankee ingenuity, switched to his alternate plan. If he could not break up the romance and stop the wedding, he would lure the young couple back to the United States, where Alessandro would be assimilated into the Williston-Hartley clan, becoming eventually, if not a first-class, at least a second-class Hartley, which was still greatly superior to anyone else Matthew could think of.

The Willistons and Hartleys had succeeded better than even they had hoped. They had actually assimilated Alessandro to death. He was given an office job in one of the family's shipyards. He was dressed by Matthew's tailor and the young couple moved into a home purchased and furnished with Lavinia's money.

Alessandro, who had always worshipped beauty, found himself in the midst of this inbred Yankee clan that worshipped money and old New England family background.

The Hartleys were not at all impressed by the court painter of the Medici, in fact, they weren't even impressed by Lorenzo the Magnificent, who was after all, only another foreigner.

Alessandro's longing for Venice became almost a sickness: the Piazza San Marco, the Grand Canal with its lazy gondolas, the Doges' Palace. His life in Venice had been ordered to the beautiful pealing of the bells from a dozen campaniles.

Lavinia interupted her round of social activities and charity balls long enough to bear him two beautiful daughters, Marianna and Claudia. Both were blond, blue eyed Hartleys. Even in this, Matthew Williston thought smugly, God had proved to be on the right side. The brutal Connecticut winters, along with the assimilation process, were too much for poor Alessandro, and in February of his eighth year in America he caught influenza and died. Life went on as usual for the Willistons and Hartleys, and it was almost as though Alessandro had never existed at all.

At least, not until three generations later, when Myra was born. Myra had to be a direct throwback to the

Rosettis. Her dark beauty had an almost Byzantine quality. Myra was a lush exotic poppy in a field of Williston, Hartley and Wellington daisies. Myra possessed the Mediterranean temperament, as well as artistic talent, a talent the Hartleys and Willistons were proud of not having, as they felt it usually accompanied a rather sloppy temperament.

Harriet Wellington was a maverick in this staid introverted family. She campaigned for women's rights and was considered a political radical, as she admitted openly that she had once voted for a Democrat. Harry encouraged her daughter to pursue an art career, just as she now recognized in Beecher, not a hayseed, but a true aristocrat of the mind and spirit.

By September, Myra had overcome both Beecher's and her father's misgivings, and she and Beecher were married quietly in the historic Congregational Church that had witnessed Wellington family weddings for the past two centuries.

Beecher's mother, Sara, attended the wedding. She had made a special trip to Meridian Springs, the small midwestern city some thirty miles from Sparta to find something special for her son's wedding. The slate blue, silk shantung jacket dress that she and her friend Ellie had selected after much deliberation had seemed just right for the occasion, but now Sara realized, as she looked around the church, that styles in New York were light years ahead of Meridian Springs.

But Beecher was proud of his mother, standing straight in her new dress. Her white hair was worn in the neat bun he remembered so well, and she was wearing the string of pearls that Grandmother Hornbeck had given her on her wedding day. Beecher thought Sara had more class than anyone there, with the exception of Harry Wellington who had discovered her own unique style years before and refused to follow the ever changing dictates of fashion.

After the young couple honeymooned at the Plaza Hotel in New York—a wedding present from William and Harry—Beecher took his bride back to the farm.

Sara and Myra hit it off right away, but the village definitely reserved judgment. Myra's arty way of dressing caused some consternation among the locals, who were not used to Peruvian ponchos, black leotards, dirndl skirts and peasant blouses, worn off the shoulder.

Cora Dietrick had gone to call and returned with the report that Myra had on a loud, strange garb, "just like Jane Russell had worn in that *Outlaw* movie, that was banned."

"Shocking", said Ellie Witherspoon, shaking her head, "I told Sara that she was making a big mistake, when she sent Beecher to that art school, drawing nudes and such. What can you expect?"

Myra's next mistake was taking Quiche Lorraine to the fellowship dinner at church. It was eyed with suspicion, and eaten only by the Hornbecks and a few intrepid souls who decided to chance it. Ellie remarked to her husband, Herman, after they got home, "Who ever heard of the like? Pie crust is for fruit and eggs and bacon is for breakfast."

At the next Wednesday's quilting session, when all the ladies were gathered, bent over their quilting frames, outlining with thimbled fingers in tiny stitches, pastel Dresden plates and colorful grandmother's fan patterns, the subject of Beecher Hornbeck's new bride came up again.

Maude Kratcher spoke with the authority of a matriach. "We haven't been very Christian, it seems to me. She's a strange one, that's for sure, but let's give her a chance to get used to our ways." It never occurred to any one of them that possibly it should be the other way around and that they should try to understand and accept Myra's "ways".

"That's right, Maude. We should wait and give her a chance to prove herself. There's no point in being hasty," answered Ellie. Not too many years ago, canning and preserving had been the status symbol in Sparta and one's fruit cellar and pantry were as important as one's "parlor".

Beecher has aware of the discussion in the village over Myra's "ways"—news travels fast in rural areas—but Myra went blissfully on her way, never dreaming that she would be put to the test; that her value as a woman and wife would be judged by her domestic skills.

Myra told Beecher about her plans for the winter. "I want to paint the children. I've seen so many interesting subjects in the village, those two Witherspoon children, Herman and little Lydia, with her red hair and translucent skin. And I'd love to paint Sally Dietrick. Her face has such an elfin quality."

Myra worked on drawings and portraits of the children all winter. She gave many of them to the parents, on condition that she might borrow them for exhibits. By the time spring came and Herman Jr. and little Lydia were framed in gold leaf, looking down from the wall over the piano in Ellie Witherspoon's parlor, Myra's place in her neighbor's affections was firmly established. She had painted her way into their hearts. Herman Sr. declared Quiche Lorraine to be his favorite food, and Myra's dubious domestic skills were not mentioned again. The villagers were delighted with Beecher's new wife, their own version of Auntie Mame.

5.

Beecher and Myra had been planning their trip to Europe for several years and were now actually getting ready to leave. It was to be a painting expedition, three whole months in the British Isles and on the Continent. They were packed. Their paints, supplies and portable easels had been shipped on to London a month earlier.

After spending time in London, Beecher planned to rent a car and drive through England, Scotland and Wales. They would go wherever the spirit led, stopping to paint the scenes that captured their imaginations, spending as long in each locale as they liked. They would sketch and paint in Paris and tour France and Switzerland and wind up their trip in Italy. Myra wanted to save at least four weeks for Italy, so they would have ample time to take in Rome, Florence, Venice, Naples and Capri.

"I want to look up the Rosettis in Venice. There must be some relatives of Alessandro's still around," she said. "Just think, an artist whose patrons were the Medici. Isn't that exciting, Beecher? That's roots to be proud of."

Their plane tickets had arrived from British Airways, and most of the last-minute details had been taken care of. Hollis Franke's boy Walter was going to look after the farm.

Myra left that morning with a list of errands, chatting happily about the trip. "Darling, I can hardly wait. We've planned so long for this. I guess I never thought it would really happen, that we'd be able to leave the farm for three whole months."

He had never seen her so bubbly and excited.

Myra waited in line at the First National Bank in Meridian Springs, having stopped for travelers' checks for their trip to Europe.

She had just stepped up to the cashier's window at First National when two men in ski masks burst into the bank and held up the cashier. They already had the money when another teller pressed the alarm button.

The thieves opened fire with a shotgun, killing the teller, Myra, and a young man who had knocked her to the floor too late to save her.

6.

Every day Beecher discovered a dozen ways that he missed Myra. He found that he even missed the things about her that had annoyed him when she was alive. She had talked a lot more than Beecher, even when they were both working in the studio. This had irritated him. He had tried to hide it; he hoped now that she hadn't known it.

Myra was not too tidy. Probably came from growing up in a household with servants, Beecher often thought. But now, he found that under the stern rule of Mrs. Daily, his home was neat and cold and celibate. He hated it. He would have given all that he possessed to walk in and see Myra's lacy satin nightgown casually tossed across the arm of the chair in the living room or have a can of mixed nuts roll out from under his bed. "Only saving them for a midnight snack, darling. Here, have some."

He missed seeing her paint-encrusted palette sitting beside the kitchen sink, instead of where it belonged, in the studio.

He missed the vases of wildflowers in their bedroom. Mrs. Daily had stuck silly little crocheted doilies on every table and dresser in the house. They were as stiff and starched as Mrs. Daily, and he detested them. Countless times he reminded himself to tell her they must go, but he never did.

In those terrible days after Myra's death, Beecher was often filled with self-doubt and recriminations. Maybe Myra hadn't been as happy as he thought. What about her sudden mood changes? Was it possible that he was too immersed in his painting to recognize the signs of unhappiness? Had she been secretly bored with rural life? He had always felt a little guilty about depriving her of the life she had before their marriage. He knew she had missed the excitement of attending concerts and opening nights on Broadway. They had made occasional trips to Chicago, to the Art Institute or an exhibit in Cincinnati, but it wasn't the same as Connecticut's accessibility to New York, the Metropolitan Museum, the Guggenheim....Now his depression fed on these doubts and fears.

Beecher's boyhood friend, Conner Hannigan, helped him get through this bad time. Beecher, not being a Catholic, could never understand why Conner hadn't even been allowed to carry his own name over into that monastic world that he had chosen to enter. Conner was now Father Pythias, but he would always be Conner Hannigan to Beecher, even though the years had turned his freckled, redhaired boyhood friend into a cherubic, florid-faced cleric. Beecher decided to discuss his problem with Conner.

Conner's parish was in Meridian Springs, but he had been stopping by the farm frequently since Myra's death. He knew that Beecher would need his friendship more now than ever.

The two men sat in front of the fire in the den with mugs of coffee. Cassie lay close to Conner's chair and looked up at him with soulful eyes.

"Conner, you know you're the only person that dog has

ever taken up with beside me," Beecher said as he reached for his pipe.

"She knows I like her, don't you girl?" Conner said as he bent down to pet Cassie. "I think that kind of devotion deserves a cookie, don't you Beecher?" Conner chuckled. He broke off half a cookie and fed it to Cassie.

Conner led Beecher gently into a discussion of Myra's death.

"Take it from me, Beecher, I've counseled more people than you can imagine. What you are going through now is a stage I refer to as the hindsight of bereavement. It's wonderously acute, in a morbid sort of way, but has very little foundation in reality. Was Myra a good wife to you?"

"That's a jackass question, Conner. You, of all people, know how wonderful she was."

"But do you realize that if she were left and you had been the one who shuffled off this mortal coil, she would probably be here talking to me now, blaming herself for all the ways that she had imagined she had failed you, dredging up incident after incident—everything from burning the biscuits and serving you sandwiches for dinner when she was involved in her painting, to something as serious as not being able to give you children.

"Did you know that Myra came to me six months before she died and wept and confided in me that she felt she had ruined your life because she couldn't have them?

"I asked her why she was so sure it was her fault and not yours, and she gave me a strange answer. She said she was sure because it was a punishment on her from God. I tried to find out why she felt that way, but couldn't get any more out of her. I told her that didn't sound like the God I knew."

"Why didn't you tell me, Conner?"

"Confidences are confidential. Whether they are shared in the confessional, or my office or on the street; it makes no difference. I'm only telling you because it might help you to know, and it can't hurt her now."

"Conner, Myra made me happier than any other woman

could have, children or not." Beecher's voice was hoarse with emotion.

"That's exactly what I told her. But do you get the point? Whoever has the misfortune of being left, after the loved one has departed, plays this little guilt game with himself. Face up to your humanity, Beecher. You're just like the rest of us. Sure, you weren't perfect, but neither was Myra. Join the human race, pal, and quit crying over spilt milk."

"I do like your homey touch, Conner. That's what makes you the `Dear Abby' of the archdiocese, I suppose. Your grey hair is distinguished, and your cassock is dignified and impressive, but what would your bishop think if he knew his Father Pythias had planned the panty raid on the Presbyterian girl's camp?"

"Oh, the sins of me youth. I was thirteen and you were nine, a very willing accomplice, I might add. Do you remember the Exlax-laced cookies we smuggled into the D.A.R.'s Christmas tea? That one was not very original, somewhat beneath us, I feel, looking at it in retrospect. But as wild oats go, ours were pretty mild.

"The things I hear these days in the confessional booth make me feel old and sad: lifelong grudges, hatred within families, selfishness, greed, gross infidelity. Some of these men, who are so called pillars of the community—flaunting the Lord's injunctions.

"You should thank God, Beecher, that you and Myra had such a rich, happy life together. The Lord is not pleased with this type of introspection and self-recrimination."

"How do you know?"

"He told me so. I always remind these middle-aged Lotharios what the book of Proverbs has to say about playing around on the side when they've got a good wife waiting for them at home." Conner proceeded to quote Scripture. "For the lips of the strange woman drop as an honeycomb and her mouth is smoother than oil, but her end is more bitter than wormwood and sharp as a two-edged sword."

"Do they listen, these middle-aged so and so's, whatever you called them?" asked Beecher.

"Lotharios. Sometimes. Once in a while one even returns to thank me for keeping him from falling into the abyss, like the grateful leper, leaping for joy. More often they have plastic surgery done on the bags under their eyes, join a health club to firm up their paunches and flesh out their spindly legs, buy themselves a new wardrobe and some vitamin E and leap into bed with the floozy of the week."

"I've never heard you sound so apocolyptic, Conner."

"I've become apocolyptic of late. The world of child abusers and wife beaters had finally done it to me. I'm fed up with cruelty and hypocrisy. I'm tired of hearing confessions. I need a retreat. Better yet, we both need to go out in search of the wild turkey and the March hare, like we used to do, before you got so involved in your painting and I became Dear Abby.

"A priest is not without problems," Conner said. "What do you think it cost me to become, as you so quaintly put it, the Dear Abby of the archdiocese? The accuser comes to me in the middle of the night and tells me that my service to God is flawed; that I have offered God my second best, the part of me that was left after Nell died, and that God is never pleased with second best. The devil cites the example of Cain, whose offering was not acceptable to God. The devil is good at quoting Scripture. If he dared to quote Scripture to Jesus, how can we expect to be spared? He reminds me about Nell, how if Nell had lived, I would have married her and been a middle-aged farmer, now, surrounded by my loving brood. He reminds me that serving God was my second choice.

"Always remember, Beecher, there's some element of truth in the devil's accusations. Otherwise, we could refute them at once. He is perfidious, the master of the lie. The most damaging lies always contain a hint of the truth."

"And what do you answer him, Conner?"

"I don't fight him anymore, or bother to answer. I tell

the Lord that I offer him all that I have left to give, flawed and second-rate though it may be. There's peace in that.

"That's what you must do, Beecher. Offer up all that bitterness you're carrying around, all that self-doubt and recrimination. It's excess baggage. Part with it now before it's too late."

Beecher knew that his friend was right. They would go on their hunting trip—later. But first Beecher had unfinished business with the police.

7.

Beecher did try to blot out of his mind forever that brief glimpse of Myra's body in the morgue. The whole incident had taken on the surrealistic quality of a nightmare: doors clanging shut, echoes reverberating down deserted corridors, the icy coldness of the room. Strange that he could see in his mind the shaking hand of the police detective as he lit a cigarette, as he handed Beecher a bag containing Myra's purse and clothes. The mind has its own ways of healing and protecting itself, and now Beecher could remember the color of the detective's tie; he could see the spot of mud on the brown wing-tipped shoe, but he could no longer remember his wife's disfigured face. Thank God, at least he had been able to spare Harry and William that. Myra's body had been cremated. It was her wish.

After the funeral, Harry decided to stay on with Beecher for awhile, and William returned to Westport. William aged ten years in a week. Beecher went through the motions of caring for the cattle like a robot. The rest of the time he just sat in the den or his studio, staring into space. Poor little

Cassie couldn't understand why he never talked to her anymore or gave her sweets. Harry cooked and served the meals, and Beecher ate them without comment. Once a day, he shaved, showered and went to visit the police.

Trees were beginning to bud. The countryside was growing greener and more lush every day. For the first time in his life, this beauty gave Beecher no joy, but seemed alien and unreal, almost a mockery, for deep inside he carried the glacial, barren landscape of grief.

The scandal that broke over City Hall two days after the bank robbery had cast its shadow on the police department, as well. The indictments, and charges of bribery and corruption, seemed to be absorbing all their time and attention. Every day the media dredged up more slime. Beecher was growing more cyncial with each visit to the police. The detective who had taken him to the morgue to identify Myra's body had been indicted.

The last thing the police wanted was the help of an amateur, and an artist, at that, but Beecher got tired of waiting around for justice to be done. As the days passed, his grief began to turn into a cold fury that seeped into his very bones. The police appeared to have shelved the case.

The role of amateur detective that gained him international fame had been forced upon him. He had learned his skills in the school of anguish and desperation.

When Beecher first conceived the idea of tracking down Myra's killers himself, Harry humored him, thinking that this was just his way of holding on to his sanity. Then, as he talked to her about his idea, she realized he just might have a chance.

"I'm going to offer a reward, Harry, for information leading to the capture of the killers. I'll use the $20,000 we saved for our trip abroad. It's the last gift I'll ever be able to give her. Maybe it's a slim chance, but there's someone out there who knows who the killers are, and for $20,000 they may be willing to come out of the woodwork."

Beecher ran the ad in the *Meridian Springs Herald* and made it just ambigious enough to discourage cranks who had no knowledge of the crime. He gave only the number of a post office box in the city. On the third day after the ad appeared, he found two replies in the box.

The first demanded that he leave the reward in a defunct phone booth two miles out of town and then return at the same hour the next day and pick up a letter containing the identity of the killers and their whereabouts. He tore it up and threw it in the fire.

The second letter was more difficult to read. The handwriting and the spelling were almost illegible. The sender had information she refused to divulge unless Beecher promised not to go to the police until she was safely out of town. If he agreed to these terms, he was to run an ad in the classified section, advertising a dark green Lawson style sofa and matching chair, like new, and give a phone number where he could be reached.

Beecher placed the ad, and the phone call came two hours after the evening edition came off the presses.

From her voice, Beecher made a number of deductions about the woman on the other end of the line: middle-aged, white, definitely uneducated but by no means stupid, probably from some remote southern area, perhaps Tennessee or Alabama. It took some fast talking to convince her that he had no intention of going to the police, but planned to conduct this search himself. She was still suspicious, but when he told her about the seeming indifference of the police, he knew he had struck a chord.

"That's the way it was when I tried to tell 'em little Lainie didn't fall down those steps herself. She might have been slow-witted, but she was like a cat on her feet. There was whiskey spilt on her dress, and I told 'em Lainie only drank grape Nehi, but they wouldn't listen, and didn't want to bother. Those two pushed her down the stairs because she heard 'em talkin' about the job they was goin' to pull. At first I paid her no heed because Lainie had always been right fanciful. I told her to stay away from them two, because I could tell they was mean, just to look at 'em. They took the room down the hall two weeks before the bank robbery.

"I had to go to work. I couldn't watch Lainie every minute, and Russ and Lilly was at school. The little spidery one hung around her. My Lainie was pretty and sweet, and she was a good girl. The night Lainie was killed, she went out to the corner fer an ice cream cone and never came back. When I started out about ten o'clock to look for her, I found the poor little thing at the bottom of the stairs, all crumpled up in a heap. Police said her neck was broke. That weren't no accident. Those two was already gone, skipped out.

"The First National was helt up the next day and all those innocent folks shot down. When I saw it on the news, I knew Lainie wasn't crazy or bein' fanciful and that was what she'd been tryin' to tell me about. They was careless about talkin' around her cause they thought she was a half-wit and then decided they wouldn't take no chances."

Beecher arranged to meet his informant near the monkey house at the zoo in Meridian Springs, and she would give him the rest of the information.

During the thirty-mile drive to Meridian Springs, Beecher wondered if the woman would be waiting for him. He remembered the fear in her voice. What right did he have to expect her to trust him?

He parked his Ford Bronco in the zoo parking lot, showed his pass at the gate and headed toward the monkey house.

Visitors to Meridian Springs were always impressed that a city of three hundred thousand could boast of having a zoo. An impressive endowment from Millard Jarvis, a wealthy industralist and native son, had made this possible.

Myra and Beecher had come here often to sketch animals and were friends of the Freemans, the eccentric husband and wife team who ran the complex. Dining with Joe and Linda Freeman could be quite an experience, if one enjoyed having a yak looking over one's shoulder.

The land was gently rolling with lots of trees and a

stream—a perfect natural setting for the animals. Children loved to ride the small train that threaded its way among the attractions.

The monkey house was surrounded by the usual crowd of children. Several adults, probably teachers, were trying to maintain order. The woman was sitting alone on a bench under a large oak. There was a tension in the straight back and clenched hands. She had come here to meet him in spite of her fears.

Florie Fowler was amazingly like the picture he had formed in his mind. Her once sandy, graying hair was pulled back in a tight little bun. Piercing light blue eyes under colorless lashes studied his face warily as he sat down beside her and introduced himself.

She still wonders whether to trust me completely, he thought. Beecher told her about Myra, that, right now, catching the killers was his only interest in life. Florie was clutching her worn black leather purse with large capable hands. They were red and chapped and looked older that the rest of her. Beecher had seen hands like those lots of times. Hands that were busy scrubbing floors, waxing furniture, milking cows, making apple butter, soothing children, sewing fine handwork. This woman, thought Beecher, is a little like a primitive, uneducated version of Sara, fiercely loyal and protective of her own.

Florie Fowler was a mountain woman, and after talking to her five minutes, Beecher knew she was incapable of subterfuge. She wanted to see the killers caught and punished as much as he did. She asked for only enough of the reward money to get herself and her two remaining children, Russ and Lilly, out of town, to start fresh somewhere else—someplace with no bad memories. If the information she gave him enabled him to catch the killers, he could send her the rest of the reward.

After she heard about the robbery on the news, she had started remembering all that Lainie had told her; at different times the men had mentioned Raleigh.

"That's where the North Carolina state prison is at," said

Florie. "Lainie kept talkin' about hikin' in the mountains and Ebenezer's Rest. That's wild country. I know cause Mama's people came from close to there. You got to hike up there from Little Ivy; might take two days. There's plenty of mountain streams fer drinkin' water, but you'll have to pack your food.

"They used to be two old cabins, when the moonshiners was up there in the thirties, but they long since burnt down. Those two are hidin' at Ebenezer's Rest until they think it's safe to come out. They could hole up there forever. The tourists never go near them parts 'cause the bears kilt two hikers a couple of years ago."

Florie trusted Beecher, and she had tears in her eyes when she took the envelope containing a thousand dollars. "I'm not doin' this fer money. It's fer Lainie. I want you to know that. I'm takin' the money cause I want to make sure nothing like this ever happens to Russ or Lilly."

"I understand, Florie," Beecher answered, "We're both doing this for Lainie and Myra and the others. I'll catch them and the law will punish them. You'll have the rest of the reward when I return from Ebenezer's Rest."

Lainie had called the men Larry and Hal. Florie gave Beecher a description of both of them, as they sat on the bench near the monkey house. Beecher sketched the two men, making the changes Florie dictated.

"Larry's eyes was a little closer together, a little squintier. That's right. Hal's nose was more flat, looked like it had been broken." Florie was amazed when Beecher ended up with drawings that so closely resembled the two men.

That night was unusually cool for April and Beecher and Harry sat in front of the fireplace as he told her about his meeting with Florie Fowler and his plans for reaching Ebenezer's Rest.

Harry made few comments while Beecher told her of the meeting with the mountain woman. Now she went to the kitchen and brought back the coffee pot, refilling both their cups. She pushed the sugar bowl toward Beecher and put a log on the fire, before she sat back down in Myra's flowered chintz wingbacked chair facing Beecher.

"Harry, I don't know what I would have done without you these last few weeks. I've been so consumed with my own grief that I've virtually ignored you, but your presence has meant more to me than you realize."

"I'm aware of that, Beecher. You don't have to say it. We've always had an understanding, you and I."

He smiled for the first time since Myra's death. "Yes, ever since that first night, all those years ago, when Myra brought me home with her. William was so full of disapproval and then you asked me to call you Harry. And I'll never forget the time Myra became so depressed because she couldn't get pregnant. Lost interest in her painting and got the crazy idea it was some kind of judgement on her.

"I could usually talk her out of her moods, but this time everything I said seemed to make her worse. Then you flew down from Westport, talked her into coming out of her room and took her away for the weekend. When she got back, she was the same old Myra. You're a wonder worker, Harry.

"You never really explained to me at the time what was wrong with her. I was so relieved that she was back to normal, I guess I just put it out of my mind. But you'll have to admit, Harry, there was something strange about that whole incident. Never did make sense to me. I had the feeling she wanted to tell me something that was on her mind, but just couldn't."

Harry looked uncomfortable, "Oh, I wouldn't start imagining things, Beecher." She extended the plate, offering him another cookie. "You know how emotional Myra was. Sometime her moods were simply not explainable."

Harry was saying no more. Maybe she really didn't know any more, thought Beecher.

"Now you can go back to William knowing you helped me out again. Better get your plane ticket tomorrow, Harry. I'll talk to Walter Franke in the morning about staying here at the place, and I'll start making my plans to leave for North Carolina. There's some equipment I'll need first."

Harry looked at Beecher over the top of her coffee cup. She nodded but didn't reply.

Beecher knew Harry well enough, after all these years, to realize that when she was this quiet it meant something. He had a feeling she was planning something on her own.

8.

The next morning after their talk, Harry found Beecher in his studio. "You must let me help you, Beecher. I want to go with you to Ebenezer's Rest."

"Harry, I've always been one of your most ardent admirers, but I'm sorry. This is not a march for women's rights. These men are ruthless killers and they're hiding in some of the roughest territory in Appalachia. My scheme may be harebrained. At this point, I don't know. I only know I must do something. But I'm certainly not going to risk your life."

"You seem to have forgotten, Beecher, Myra was mine before she was yours," Harry added with a trace of belligerence. "Have you thought of that? I have some ideas of my own. And another thing, don't ever underestimate me. It makes me angry. By the way, is there, by any chance, a second-hand clothing store in the village?"

"There's a little hole-in-the-wall place next to the feed store. You have to go around in back of the ice house. It's called the Next to New Shoppe, with an 'e' on the end, but if you're looking for vintage L. L. Bean or Anne Klein, I'm afraid you're out of luck. Was there by any chance a stock market crash that I missed out on?"

"Very funny, Beecher. I'm glad to see that your sense of humor is returning. I'll see you later. I have several errands to run in the village. Will you need the Bronco for the next few hours?"

"No, go right ahead and take it. The keys are in the ignition." Beecher walked to the door of the studio and called after Harry, "You better see about a plane reservation. It's spring break and it may be hard to get one."

Harry didn't answer him. She just kept walking toward the Bronco. She got in and drove off.

Two hours later, Beecher looked out of the studio window in time to see Harry drive up. She hurried into the house, carrying several parcels.

Beecher was getting the studio ready to leave. He didn't know when he would paint again. He didn't really care. Cold fury was the driving force behind everything he did. He could think of nothing but his plans to pursue Myra's killers. The thought that he might not live to return to his studio and his painting didn't really bother him much. He had been overcome with sadness when he came across a portrait Myra had painted the second winter they were married. It was with some early paintings he was storing away.

Later that same afternoon, Beecher left the studio, locking the door behind him and walked to the house. He was in the kitchen putting on the coffee pot when he heard a noise behind him and turned. It was at least thirty seconds before he realized that the bent, shabby little figure standing in the doorway to the hall was Harry. She had always taken care to keep her birdlike legs encased in designer slacks or long skirts.

This figure in the old faded 1940s vintage print house dress was pathetically thin and bent with age. On her feet, she wore once-white socks with the kind of sandals hippies wore in the 1960s. Her hair was all gray now, not just streaked, and pulled back into a tight little bun which accentuated her high cheek bones and made her neck look scrawny.

Beecher's trained eye even noticed the dirt under her broken fingernails. The final touch was a real stroke of genius. Harry had removed her partial plate. This had turned her into a chinless, toothless mountain woman.

"Just what do you think you're doing?"

"I'm old Evie, who hunts ginsing, or 'sang', as they call it in the mountains. I can get closer to them than you ever could, Beecher. I can observe their movements, their habits. Can't you see now that I'll be indispensable? You could never get as close to them as old Evie can."

Beecher had long suspected that Harry was a direct descendant of that particular New Englander who had traded the Indians a few strings of shiny beads and a hand mirror for Manhattan Island. Only Harry could have talked them into throwing in Connecticut. She was a master at making him propositions that he couldn't refuse, but this time she had really outdone herself. Beecher realized that when a woman cares enough about something to take her teeth out to get it, she's got you licked. By now, he was scraping the bottom of the barrel for an argument.

"What will William say if I expose you to this kind of danger?"

"William got used to my political 'agitating', as he calls it, and he will get used to this. He has Wall Street, and I do my own thing. You should know that by now." Harry could tell by the expression on Beecher's face that she had won.

Beecher put Harry in charge of buying the hiking clothes and supplies. He was an excellent shot. He took a Ruger 220 Swift that he used on the farm as a varmint gun, and he had a .38 Smith and Wesson that he bought right after Myra was killed.

They left in two days. The highway going south was crowded with traffic, kids on spring break and retired people with Air Streams and motor homes, heading for Gatlinburg, Palm Beach and the Caribbean. As Harry and Beecher drove along, they discussed all their options. They finally decided it would be better to play it by ear when they got there.

Beecher solved the problem of the Bronco by leaving it at the local Ford dealer's for service, telling the service manager that he was going backpacking and he might even be gone a week.

Beecher and Harry proceeded with caution, covering their tracks carefully. Both wore warm clothes and heavy hiking boots and carried back packs. Harry had carefully packed her Evie outfit, her passport on the manhunt. In Beecher's attic, she had found an old motheaten cardigan sweater of Sara's. This completed her wardrobe.

Everything that Florie Fowler told him was true. The terrain was rougher even than Beecher had expected, but Harry never complained. Beecher admired his tough little mother-in-law.

They passed rusted, broken down stills, long since covered by vines and tree roots, as well as the remains of both the cabins that Florie had mentioned—now only charred foundations and broken chimneys. The forest was alive with wild life—deer, rabbits, possums.

The first night, they took turns watching, and Beecher had heard the eerie cry of a large cat while Harry slept.

Their destination was a day and a half's hike from the town of Little Ivy. On the second day's march, the forest became grim and forbidding. They were now climbing at a higher altitude and vegetation was sparser, trees gnarled.

They had no trouble finding the cabin at Ebenezer's Rest that Florie had described, and they camped above it and a safe distance away. Harry had been gathering ginsing root along the way and by the time they made it to Ebenezer's Rest, she had her knapsack half full.

"How can you be sure you've got ginsing root there, Harry, or is it the latest thing in Westport these days?"

"Beecher, I bet you've never even been in the health

food store in the village, being as you are basically a steak and potato man. `Back to Eden' it's called, and if there's anything those kids know about, it's berries and roots."

Harry pulled out a root and offered it to Beecher. "Here, have a chew. It's supposed to be good for what ails you, everything from gout to impotence."

"No thanks, Harry, not today. I've been a meat and potato man too long to change now. I wish it were that simple; that we could all get back to Eden by eating roots and berries."

"Well, the kids that run Back to Eden are real nice, if a trifle undernourished looking, and everyone has to have something to believe in, even if it's just vitamins and berries. You ought to go in and meet them sometime."

They settled down to watch the cabin. Florie said the state had built it some years before when they planned to annex the area into the adjoining state forest. It never happened because of some political dispute and the cabin was never used by the forest rangers.

Smoke rose from the chimney and Beecher, who was watching the cabin with binoculars, saw Hal come out and empty some garbage and beer cans in the woods next to the cabin.

"That's him all right. Florie's description was pretty accurate. He's just a little taller than she remembered." He looked at Harry and she could see the strain and tenseness in his expression. "Now we're committed. There's no turning back. These two have killed four people, including Lainie, and they know it won't go any harder on them if they make it six."

"We can train ourselves to think like criminals, Beecher. We must." And so they had.

They observed the cabin for two days and dared not light a fire. They ate chocolate bars, nuts, cheese and canned beans. Hal went down to the spring, morning and evening, to fill two large buckets with water.

Sounds of drunken laughter and loud arguing often came from the cabin. "They get drunk at night. They must feel pretty safe," said Beecher.

At first they considered the possibility of moving on the cabin while the two men slept. Beecher was only able to wait and keep his anger under control because he was responsible for Harry's life.

"Drunk or not, you can be sure they sleep with their guns next to them," Beecher said. "We don't know the layout of the cabin, and I doubt that we could get them both without a shootout. Even if we got one of them and the other got away, he could just hide out in the woods and pick us off. I want to hand them both over to the law without firing a shot, if possible. We'll just have to think of some other way."

Late that night, they came up with another plan. Old Evie would show up at the spring the next morning when Hal came for water. Beecher didn't want her to take the risk, but Harry insisted she would be safe because Beecher would be armed and hiding close by. Hal would accept her for what she pretended to be, an old mountain woman who hated the Feds because they had destroyed her husband's still and burnt down their cabin years before.

"Beecher," she said, "you seem to forget I'm smarter than Hal. I want him to get used to seeing me, so I can get him at gunpoint tomorrow night at the spring while you surprise Larry alone in the cabin, hopefully drunk."

The next morning, at the spring, Hal grabbed Evie's knapsack and rummaged through it, spilling her ginsing on the ground. Old Evie got down on her hands and knees and frantically started gathering it up. "You don't have no call to do that a way!" she whined. "I just seed you was up here and hoped you had a still and would trade me a jug for some sang. I been fancyin a drink of good, old-time white lightnin."

"Where you live, old woman?"

"Oh, I camp down in the holler, in the spring, gatherin sang. It brings real good money. The rest of the year, I weave rush baskets to sell to the tourists. You goin to build a still?"

"Yeah, old woman, but if you tell anybody, you're dead, understand?"

Evie spit tobacco juice and gave him a toothless grin. "Who would I tell? I hate the Feds for what they done to us. After they busted up the still and burnt our cabin to the ground, Ned just lost heart. He give up. He got the consumption the next spring and died. I buried him myself, up at Craggy Point. Ned, he just loved the high places."

That night when Hal brought his buckets to the spring, old Evie was waiting.

"Did you bring me any whiskey?"

"Shut up, you old hag. I told you, I don't have no still." He snarled a few threats, but didn't bother to search her knapsack. She had counted on this. He had been drinking. She could tell. When he bent over to fill the buckets, she pulled the revolver out of her knapsack.

"All right Hal, put up your hands and if you make a sound I'll kill you."

Hal looked stunned, but he put up his hands. "You old creep. What do you think you're doing? My friend will come down here in a minute to find me and he'll take care of you."

Beecher moved out from behind the trees. He quickly gagged and tied Hal. "You two won't be taking care of anybody. You may live long enough to go to the electric chair, if you're lucky, but don't tempt me. I've a better idea. How would you like me to give you the same sporting chance you gave those people in the bank? Then there's little Lainie." Beecher saw the terror in Hal's eyes.

He turned to Harry. "You stay here with him and don't take your eyes off him for a minute. Don't hesitate to shoot him if you have to."

"Please be careful, Beecher," Harry pleaded.

Beecher moved stealthily through the trees. Soon Harry heard Larry's drunken singing stop. Then he yelled, "Hal, that you, Hal?" The next noise was a thud.

Time stood still, for Harry, when the dark figure

appeared in the doorway of the cabin. Suddenly, the madness of the plan that she and Beecher were attempting to carry out was revealed to her with a sickening clarity— why now, she groaned inwardly, when it was too late?

At that moment, the rising moon cleared the tops of the pines and shone down on the cabin and the lean familiar figure of Beecher standing in the doorway with his unfired rifle in his hand. "Thank God," she whispered. To Hal, Harry's words sounded only like a weary sigh. Beecher's reappearance had destroyed his last hope of escape.

After Beecher had tied them up, Harry guarded the prisoners in the cabin while Beecher slept for a few hours. Then Beecher took over at midnight while Harry slept till dawn, when she could begin her trip back down the mountain for the sheriff.

Before daylight, Harry was ready to go. She had bathed in the icy mountain spring, dressed in her hiking clothes and put in her teeth. "What a relief!" said the elegant L.L. Bean model. Old Evie was gone forever.

Harry returned to Ebenezer's Rest two days later in the police helicopter. FBI agents, landing in a second helicopter, commented among themselves that in 1990, criminals were *not* tracked down and captured by amateurs—that this whole affair was too much like the scenario of an Indiana Jones movie to be real.

Most of the bank money was found in the cabin. Caught with the evidence on them, Hal and Larry signed confessions to the bank robbery and murders and the murder of Lainie Fowler, as well.

"There'll be no plea bargaining on this one," the FBI agent announced with satisfaction. "With the evidence we've got on these two, they'll get the chair or life."

Beecher and Harry made front page headlines and thoughtful features all over the world:

MURDER VICTIM'S HUSBAND SCOOPS POLICE, CRACKS MERIDIAN SPRINGS BANK ROBBERY!

MIDWEST ARTIST AND SOCIETY
MOTHER-IN-LAW TRACK KILLERS

BEECHER HORNBECK RESTORES
AMERICA'S FAITH IN COMMON MAN

Articles ran on the front pages of all the leading newspapers, giving an account of both the crime and Beecher and Harry's adventure, with pictures of Beecher, Harry and Myra.

The press wanted personal interviews, but Beecher's answer to the media was a firm "No". No to Phil Donahue. No to the Today Show and the hordes of reporters and photographers that beseiged him when he returned to the farm. He received calls requesting that he endorse breakfast foods, security systems, burgler alarms— that his picture be used on T-shirts. He finally had his phone number changed to an unlisted one—something he said he would never do.

Beecher was giving no statements, but his picture and the account of how he and Harry had tracked the killers to Ebenezer's Rest was seen and read all over the world. He had captured the imagination of a public that was tired of being victimized by hoodlums, hijackers, terrorists and con artists. Beecher was a folk hero, whether he liked it or not.

And he was on his way to becoming an internationaly renowned artist in the process.

9.

Beecher had been working day and night in the studio for the past two weeks. The deadline was rapidly approaching when he must ship his paintings to Rome, but in recent days he had grown stale—the spark was simply not there. He knew enough not to try to force creativity.

That morning the weather had warmed up dramatically. It was now mid-April and spring was in the air. There was a duality in Beecher's nature that he was only too aware of. He was a farmer as well as an artist and he always would be. "Bred in the bone," Silas Hornbeck had often said to the young child, "Son, a love of the land is bred in the bone." Beecher was a painter's painter. He enjoyed the companionship of serious artists, but the arty small talk of the gallery reception and cocktail party bored him beyond words. Beecher was not a social animal, in spite of Myra's efforts to broaden his horizons.

That morning, he stepped out on the porch with a cup of coffee, looked around him, breathed deeply and decided he needed a change. Beecher had a craving to smell freshly plowed earth and feel the warmth of the sun. The painting would have to wait. He could still have them ready for Brazzano by May. Today he would farm. But first he had to drive to Sparta and pick up some seed corn.

As Beecher drove into the town square and parked the Bronco, he realized how little Sparta had changed in the past forty years.

The local citizens were most proud...and justly so... of the small beautiful courthouse designed by Gideon Shryock. Sparta had been a county seat in the 1800s but had failed to grow, while neighboring Meridian Springs had become a boom town.

Kentucky could boast of many buildings designed by this well known nineteenth century architect, but Sparta possessed the only one in Indiana. Beecher never failed to admire the perfection of its simple Greek Revival lines. The sight of Stan's pool hall and video game room directly across the square once again grated on his asthetic sensibilities.

He waved at Mrs. Daily who was coming out of the general store with some bags...no doubt callico for aprons and more crochet yarn, or whatever she used to whip up those hideous creations with which she adorned his furniture. She gave him a cheery greeting and called to him that she would be over that afternoon to do his ironing...Mrs. Daily had her own key. She trudged on to the lending library. Mrs. D. was addicted to "spicy" reading. She never failed to denounce it as "sleazy" but was always going back for more. Beecher smiled to himself. She was a dear soul, he thought, in spite of lace doilies and bad taste in literature.

He bought his seed corn and tried to chat with Calvin Moore over the sound of the blaring radio–some country music song about love, deceit, revenge and sudden death. After he picked up milk and oranges at the grocery, he headed back to the farm.

He had plowed all day and was returning on the tractor with his orange flag on the back, when a Volvo flew past him, narrowly missing the tractor and covering him with a cloud of dust. "Damn fools," he muttered under his breath.

The car stopped a short distance ahead and waited for him to catch up. The driver rolled down her window and eyed with thinly veiled contempt the dusty figure in faded jeans and Redwing boots. Beecher was wearing his favorite old green DeKalb Seed Corn cap and chewing on his unlit pipe. He knew he had "clod" written all over him when he saw the expression on the chic young woman's face. There was no apology for nearly running him off the road. "Do you live around here?"

"Yes, down a piece."

"Can you tell me where Beecher Hornbeck, the artist lives? We've been driving around this God-forsaken place for an hour." She pushed her sunglasses up on her head and turned to the man who sat beside her. Beecher could see camera equipment in the back seat. "Down a piece," she repeated to her companion.

Beecher couldn't resist. "I'll be glad to help ya. Just go down here to yer next corner. That there's Blue Lick Road." He took his DeKalb cap off and scratched his head, before continuing in slow drawl. "Jest go a quarter of a mile or so down Blue Lick. You'll see his mail box on the left. But, you know, them artist fellows is eccentric. I'd watch him if I was you."

"Got it," she said, and took off without another word. Beecher took his time, humming to himself. Let them cool their heels, he thought. Mrs. D. can give them the third degree. He wouldn't rob her of the pleasure for anything.

Beecher parked the tractor and walked into the house. Sure enough, Mrs. D. had served them lemonade, and the two of them sat there uncomfortably, probably eating their hearts out for a dry martini.

"Mr. Hornbeck, you have visitors. They're here to do a big publicity story on your Eye-talian exhibit for the Chicago newspaper. Isn't that nice?"

Part II - Rome

1.

Beecher knew he had arrived in Italy when he was greeted at the Rome airport by the shouts of striking baggage workers. The aircraft could not be unloaded, and Beecher stared back wistfully in the direction of his impounded luggage and ruefully envisioned himself in silk Italian suits and soft leather pointed-toed shoes. When he suggested that perhaps they should not leave the airport without the luggage, Pietro Reni dismissed this foolish concern with a condescending smile and a debonaire wave of his hand. The luggage strike would be over in a short time, only a matter of minutes, perhaps. Pietro Reni shrugged. All had been arranged. He had placed Giulio in charge of securing the luggage and it would no doubt be waiting for Beecher at the Excelsior when he arrived. Beecher had noticed an exchange of money between Pietro Reni and a shabby youth at the airport and had assumed that Reni was giving the boy a handout.

From the moment he was met at Leonardo da Vinci airport outside Rome by Guido Brazzano's young, knowledgable aide-de-camp, Pietro Reni, and ushered into his sleek Lancia sedan for the ride into Rome, Beecher realized his life had been temporarily taken over by a master showman. Pietro Reni was a rising star in the international art world, and had secured exhibits of the work of many of the world's most famous painters and sculptors for the Brazzano Gallery.

Reni drove at high speed along the Via del Mare with a precision and verve worthy of the Grand Prix. A blue haze of exhaust fumes rose from the pavement, and horns honked riotously as drivers zipped in and out of traffic. Beecher realized that this was a deadly contest; each driver was bent on proving something, probably his masculinity, or perhaps his creativity. Was this a Roman highway or the road to Armegeddon? Beecher hoped he survived. There were a few good paintings left in him still.

The Lancia flew through the shabby suburbs past endless blocks of apartment buildings, all alike, each with its own little balcony, a place to sit out and escape the summer heat. Many of the balconies were strung with lines of wash, some boasted potted, blooming plants or small orange trees, adding a little color and individuality in this grim expanse of concrete and graffiti. The newer buildings weren't too bad, thought Beecher, but most depressing were the ugly overscaled Fascist architecture of the thirties and forties, dilapidated but still standing, part of Mussolini's legacy. Beecher wondered if the trains still ran on time, if indeed they ever had.

Pietro Reni's running commentary was fascinating. He was full of both historical and political information and anecdotes about the country. He pointed out to Beecher that the Italians had very little trust of governments, in any form. In Italy, they changed with the seasons and were to be merely tolerated and often to be outwitted.

"There are many communists in our country, true," said Reni, in answer to a question of Beecher's, "but Italian Communism is different from Communism in any other country, a different animal. We are too individualistic to follow any system or leader like robots, just as Fascism, under Mussolini, never had the hold on this country that it did in Germany. At least half the population were partisans, fighting secretly or openly against the other half, the *Fascisti*. It was much like your Civil War, only not declared. No one could ever be sure who was who.

"The family is the strongest institution in Italy and will always remain so," Reni insisted. "The Italian's family is his ark of safety in a sea of troubles, and most of his loyalties are directed toward its strengthening and preservation, its survival. The Italian male might stray occasionally, but discreetly."

Reni turned to Beecher with a smile so full of ancient and cynical wisdom that it might have been Casanova's, two centuries before. That smile spoke volumes. It said, are we not men of the world, you and I? Isn't it only human, after all, to err a little, and would it not be almost a worse sin to be oblivious to all the beautiful women in the world, who are waiting, just waiting for Pietro and Beecher? A far worse sin, truly, to be surrounded by beauty and not to behold it.

"But," resumed Reni, "we do not desert the wife of our youth, the mother of our first-born son. Her position is secure." Beecher was learning a lot.

Reni chose, just at that moment, to pass a large tourist coach marked "Tivoli, Villa d'Este—Hadrian's Villa." Beecher caught a glimpse of round, red English faces, wearing horrified expressions, as the Lancia streaked by them, narrowly missing a head-on crash with a Vespa. The driver of the Vespa made an obscene gesture, which Reni pretended not to see.

Soon the road passed through an arch in the old Roman wall, surviving sections of which were to be seen, here and there, snaking in and out of the very heart of the city. When in Rome, it is not necessary to travel to get to the Rome of Caesar's, of the Renaissance or the Baroque. You are already there.

During his correspondence with Signor Brazzano about the exhibit, Beecher, true to his natural reticence and quiet tastes, had suggested that the signore might find him a comfortable, relatively inexpensive pensione with a quiet atmosphere.

But, alas, it was not to be. All had been arranged by his host, Signor Brazzano. A reservation had already been made for the American painter at the Hotel Excelsior, that grande dame of world class hotels who resided with pomp on the Via Veneto, one of the most famous boulevards in all of Europe.

Signor Brazzano, possessed of an urgency that could not be entrusted to the post, had called Beecher in Indiana.

"Signor Hornbeck, Maestro," pleaded the elderly Brazzano, "When in Rome, location is all. The civilized world travels the Via Veneto. It is there that you feel the very heartbeat, the pulse of Roma, surrounded, as you are, by her galleries, her shops, her fine restaurants. You are only a stone's throw, as you say in your country, from the antiquities, the Forum, Bernini's fountains, the Trevi, the Tritone."

Signor Brazzano waxed eloquent and his old voice gained strength, even though it had to travel across two continents and an ocean. His Roma was a great lady and in his opinion, was still mistress of the world. Where else, except in the bar at the Excelsior, could anyone hope to meet a prime minister, a Grand Prix winner, a famous British stage actress and Woody Allen, all on the same night? Almost as an afterthought, Signor Brazzano informed Beecher that his paintings had arrived safely and were being hung, even now, at the very moment, by the "brilliant and expert" Pietro Reni—"He is like my own son"—who could be counted on to see that each painting was displayed to advantage and lit properly.

Beecher had hoped to supervise the hanging of his exhibit himself, and had requested to do so in a previous letter. He now decided that his elderly Roman patron had only read the parts that he wanted to. Beecher knew when he was licked and acquiesced with grace, thanking his host for his thoughtfulness in taking his every need into consideration.

Reni apparently knew what he was talking about; ten minutes after he left Beecher at the Excelsior, the bags miraculously arrived.

The large old hotel room had a grace and elegance that was reminiscent of a bygone era, as were the sheer Austrian shades and ornate crystal chandeliers, the beautiful carved moldings and striped brocade furniture in the lobby and salons downstairs.

Beecher's room overlooked the Via Veneto. He walked over to the round table by the window. The casement windows were open, and a slight breeze stirred the sheer curtains. There was a large bowl of luscious fruit on the table. Each was perfect: peaches, pears, apples, grapes and apricots. Beside the bowl was a plate, and on it was a large, white, folded linen dinner napkin and silver fruit knife. A cold-beaded bottle of champagne rested in the silver ice bucket. What a subject for a still life, thought Beecher. He opened the attached card. "Welcome to Roma. Enjoy—Brazzano." The signore, as usual, had thought of everything.

Beecher stood by the window and looked down at the Via Veneto. He could see the trees a delicate shade of spring green, the Carabinieri directing traffic which was now moving at a snail's pace down the broad boulevard, the chic, high-fashion window displays in the shops across the street. A liveried doorman assisted a beautiful woman as she stepped out of her car and entered the hotel.

As Beecher looked down at the scene below him, the word "enjoy" seemed to float in his mind like a kite or ballon that had lost its moorings and drifts off out of sight, higher and higher.

Did he really enjoy life much anymore, since he lost Myra, or had he merely become accustomed to things as they are? He found joy in his work, that was true, and the artist in him would always rejoice in the beauty of nature. He loved the farm. But what of the small pleasures—the things he had enjoyed with Myra—a play, a picnic, a private joke. Had he become introverted and morose, an eccentric middle-aged nut who went around talking to his dog? His friend Conner had implied as much, trying to jolt him into getting out more.

He suddenly remembered the old adage: "When in Rome, do as the Romans do." He was not sure what it meant, but he was sure what it didn't mean. It didn't mean to stay in Rome, but pretend you were back in Indiana; to compare everything you ate with Mama's fried chicken and biscuits; to stay in the elegant old Excelsior and yearn for the sterile, cold, glass and tile of a Hyatt Regency.

Beecher resolved to give Rome his best shot, or as Guido Brazzano had suggested, to enjoy.

2.

The first night at the Excelsior, Beecher had trouble going to sleep, and at four A.M., Rome time, he took two aspirin. It would be only ten P.M. at home, and he and Cassie would be having milk and cookies and watching the news.

When in Rome, Beecher thought. He uncorked the bottle of champagne, drank two glasses, ate one perfect apricot and fell asleep at last.

The telephone woke him. Hollis Franke was pounding on his door, yelling that he wanted to buy hay. Beecher felt momentarily disoriented as he reached for the phone.

"Hello, Mr. Beecher Hornbeck?" said an unusual voice, quite cultivated, not at all like Hollis Franke's.

"Yes, this is he, speaking."

"This is Cristina Brazzano. I am calling for Signor Guido Brazzano. He hopes that your room is satisfactory and that you had a good night's rest after your long trip."

"Yes, fine, thank you. The room is more than satisfactory."

"Pietro Reni had to leave for Paris early this morning, on gallery business, and Signor Brazzano had a slight cold, but will be in later. He is most anxious to meet you. May I pick you up at the Excelsior later, at your convenience, of course, and bring you here to the gallery?"

Beecher couldn't place her speech. She spoke English almost too perfectly, with hardly a trace of an Italian accent, only a hint.

"We at the gallery are all anxious for you to see the arrangement of your paintings. Edoardo is driving Guido in from the Villa in time to meet us for lunch. He is an old man and has a heart condition. With even a small cold, he must be careful."

"I can be ready in an hour," said Beecher.

"Why don't we make it two?"

Tactful, he thought. She could probably tell that he had been asleep.

"I'll pick you up at eleven in front of the hotel. I'll be driving a red Lamborghini."

She must be Brazzano's daughter, or perhaps his granddaughter. Beecher was remembering his brief conversation with Cristina Brazzano as he buttered a roll and sipped his Italian coffee. His taste in coffee was definitely not midwestern. He loved French coffee and espresso.

The Excelsior dining room was elegant, with heavily starched table linen, sparkling crystal and a dewy fresh rose on each table. His elderly waiter stood off at a discreet distance with his hands folded in front of him and a guarded, patient look on his face that spoke of forty years of serving others.

Cristina Brazzano had referred to her employer several times as Signor Brazzano. But that wasn't significant, one way or the other, because she was talking to a stranger. Then, at last, she called him Guido. That didn't sound like a daughter. Could she be a very young second wife? A definite possibility, thought Beecher.

After breakfast, he took a brisk walk down the Via Veneto, stopped to buy an American newspaper and returned just in time to see the red Lamborghini pull up in front of the Excelsior.

The doorman, who had obviously been watching for

both Beecher and the Lamborghini, ushered him to the car and spoke to Cristina Brazzano. *"Buon giorno, Signora."* The car window was down, and she smiled and waved, *"Grazie,* Luigi."

"Mi permetta, Signor Hornbeck." Luigi hastened to open the car door before Beecher could. He eased himself into the low-profiled sports car.

Signora Cristina Brazzano was the biggest surprise of Beecher's trip, so far. This petite lady with the mane of golden brown hair was evidently old Brazzano's wife, after all.

She turned to him, sizing him up. "I've wanted to meet you ever since I saw your marvelous exhibit in London three years ago. I'm Cristina Brazzano."

He took the hand she extended. "I'm glad to meet you, and I'm excited about being in Rome."

The young woman at his side shifted gears and merged deftly into the traffic of the Via Veneto.

"The gallery is on the Via del Babuino. It's only a few blocks from your hotel, but I'm taking the long way around so I can drive you up to the Pincio and show you a view of Rome that you will never forget. The first time I saw it, it took my breath away and it still does. As you have probably guessed, Mr. Hornbeck, I'm not Italian, I'm English. But like those late religious converts who are the most zealous, I have become more Italian than the Italians, and my love affair with Roma has never grown cold. Guido, my father-in-law, pretends to find this amusing, but he is secretly pleased."

Ah, thought Beecher. All answers come to him who waits.

Beecher was not disappointed. The misleadingly named Villa Borghese, which is really a park, was lush and verdant, with the natural look that is typically Italian. He recognized the famous clock and the lake, with its small Greek temple, from photographs he had seen.

"You are right, the real thing is breathtaking." Rome was spread out at his feet, the dome of St. Peter's dominating the skyline, as it had for centuries.

"Can't you see why I fell in love with it?" she asked. "It gets in the blood. The Romans take all this for granted."

Cristina looked up at him. The top of her head barely came to his shoulder. In the sunlight her hair was more red than brown. He thought of liquid molten copper. It would be hard to capture in a portrait, elusive. There was something elusive about her expression too. How could a glance be both open and private, at the same time? She definitely had a Mona Lisa quality, this woman who was Italian, yet not Italian. Beecher could see now that she was not as young as he originally thought. She could possibly be thirty-five. Why did he suddenly remember that he was forty-six?

"Well, it's always so hard to leave this spot, but we must go on to the gallery. You will want to come back on your own. One can stroll for hours in the gardens, or take out a small boat on the lake. There are three museums here, the Borghese Gallery, the Galleria d'Arte Moderna and the Villa Giulia, which is not as important, but interesting if you like antiquities of the pre-Roman Etruscan period. There's also a famous restaurant here in the Pincio, Casa Valadier, named for the man who designed this park and gardens in the early 1800's, but I think Guido has planned a special luncheon there later, in your honor.

"My father-in-law is a wonderful man, as you will discover when you meet him. Guido is more like the art patrons of the Renaissance than anyone alive today in Italy. His private collection is something to see."

"You said that he is your father-in-law. Is your husband active in the gallery, also?"

"He was. Carlo is dead."

She turned away abruptly and headed back to the car. The conversation was over. On the drive back to the gallery, Cristina pointed out places of interest, but her earlier enthusiasm was gone.

When Beecher saw his paintings hanging in the Brazzano Gallery, he realized that Guido Brazzano had not been using superlatives, but was merely telling the truth about the talents of Pietro Reni. Reni had arranged the thirty paintings to stunning advantage. This would be his best showing, better even than London. The depth and scope of his recent works was a revelation to him. Art knows no boundaries of country or race, and Beecher found in the old Italian art dealer a kindred spirit.

Marble floors and creamy fabric-covered walls lent an air of elegance to the Gallery. Although Beecher was no authority on furniture, he was certain that some of the pieces in the art dealer's office were priceless antiques. The old man's desk–a Florentine masterpiece with beautiful inlays–dwarfed the small elderly Italian sitting behind it.

Faces had always fascinated Beecher and Guido Brazzano's was exceptional. In repose Guido's expression was brooding, even sad, but when the old man smiled the change was startling. His whole countenance was transformed. Guido's smile seemed to travel from the inside outward like a simple melody that is gradually taken up by the entire orchestra—spreading from the thin mobile mouth upward to the kindly dark eyes and shaggy brows and then engulfing his entire being.

He stretched both arms out to Beecher in an all-embracing gesture an then motioned for him to be seated in the elegant chair opposite the desk and welcomed him to Rome.

The old man looked more like Cristina's grandfather than her father-in-law, and his attitude toward her was protective and paternal. She gave Beecher her shy smile when he told her how pleased he was with the exhibit catalogue. One of his sketches had been reproduced on the cover.

Cristina excused herself, saying she had work to do, and disappeared into her office.

Brazzano showed Beecher many of his treasures. "You must come to the Villa. My real beauties are there, the Caravaggios and my little Rubens, a jewel. Cristina will plan a small intimate dinner, when Pietro returns from

Paris. Cristina acts as hostess at my dinner parties, just as she did when Carlo was alive. My Maria has been gone for fifteen years." He sighed. Just where did Pietro fit in, Beecher wondered.

"But enough about me. We must talk of your exhibit. Pietro has been *direttore* and has invited everyone who is anyone, as you say, to the opening. The critics will be there from *Il Messaggero* and *Corriere della Sera*. Antonio Sarpi is the one to watch. A bitter man. He tries to hide it behind a *paravento*," the old man paused, groping for the correct word in English, "a facade. Sarpi is a failed painter. No one knows. It was long ago, but I remember. He and I were art students together, in Florence. It was a different world then. Antonio and I were both pupils of the famous teacher Guicciardini. He could see, after a time, that neither Antonio nor I had the seeds of greatness. Technical facility is not enough. But, I need not explain such things to you, Maestro.

"Since that time, our lives have moved in opposite directions, Antonio's and mine."

The old man sighed. He seemed immersed in his own thoughts for a moment and then continued.

"Years passed, and I became successful in business. Later, I started the gallery. If I could not be a great painter, maybe I could help great painters. This was my dream. The Brazzano Gallery has flourished and now we have branches in London and Paris." As Guido spoke, his fingers lovingly caressed the small Etruscan statue on his desk.

"Signore, you have every right to be proud of what the name Brazzano stands for in the art world. I am honored that you invited me to have a one man show," Beecher interjected, but he could see that Brazzano was eager to continue his story.

"I became, in a modest way, of course, an art patron, and Antonio Sarpi became an art critic. He pretends he is on a crusade to uphold high standards, but he only takes delight in tearing down. His soul is eaten up with envy of that which he cannot produce and is dark and black inside, like a rose with a worm at its heart. He is a destroyer, and his weapons are satire and innuendo. But you need not worry about him, my friend, because he is afraid of me." Beecher was already beginning to love the old man, but when he looked into Guido's eyes, he realized he would not want to have him for an enemy.

Cristina would not be joining them for lunch. There was some work she must take care of. Beecher wondered what pressing business could have come up in the past hour. She had mentioned earlier that the three of them would be lunching together.

Edoardo, Brazzano's chauffeur, drove them to Alfredo's for lunch and infuriated Signor Brazzano by reminding him to take his medicine when he dropped them off at the restaurant.

"*Scellerto, scellerto,*" Brazzano hissed at Edoardo. "Villain" seemed to Beecher a pretty strong word to use on a faithful employee who was just doing his duty, but Edoardo didn't seem to be in the least disturbed and evidently considered it all in a day's work. Guido Brazzano ordered Edoardo to pick them up at three o'clock and, taking Beecher's arm, made his way into the *ristorante*.

"Ha! He thinks he must remind me of everything, always telling me to take pills, even counting the glasses of vino. He grows more arrogant each day, just because he had some small parts in the cinema, many years ago." Brazzano smirked with disgust. Beecher could believe that Edoardo had once been a movie actor. He was still a handsome man, and there were vestiges about him of a stage presence.

Lunch at Alfredo's was an event. No, Beecher decided, "production" would be a better work. The *originale* Alfredo— implying that Rome was full of frauds, and that fake Alfredos were lurking behind every tree, just waiting to deceive the unwary with inferior pasta—tossed the *fettuccine alla romana* at their table. Guido—they were now on a first name basis—ordered a chicken dish, *petto di pollo all' Cardinale* and after much deliberation with the wine waiter, a Soave Bertani 1979.

Photographs of famous personages lined the walls. A grinning youthful Alfredo tossed noodles for Gloria Swanson. A grinning older Alfredo was standing with his arm around Liz Taylor. In another photo, Leonard Bernstein was watching Alfredo do his thing. Jimmy Carter smiled broadly at Rosalyn over a plate of the famous fettuccine and seemed to have forgotten all about politics, peanuts and grits.

If Beecher had known what was in store for him, he might have planned his escape through the men's room window, but when Alfredo came bearing down on them, with the photographer in tow, it was already too late. The restaurateur was full of reasons why Beecher must join his ever growing gallery and would not accept no for an answer.

"Signor Hornbeck, you are not only famous as an *artista*, but we, in Italy, value even more that you took vengeance on your wife's killers. You are world famous."

"I think of it as justice, Signor Alfredo, not vengeance."

Alfredo looked a little disappointed, but still wanted a picture. Beecher would hang in a place of honor between Charles de Gaulle and Jane Fonda.

Edoardo picked them up at three o'clock and made the mistake of reminding Guido that he had missed his siesta. "Fool, siestas are for women and weaklings." Beecher could see Edoardo's face in the rear view mirror. The chauffeur remained unperturbed. On the drive back to the Excelsior, Guido fell asleep. Edoardo smiled to himself and muttered something about fools and siestas as Guido snored.

Guido Brazzano was still sound asleep when Edoardo pulled up at the Excelsior and let Beecher out. The chauffeur took out a lap robe and covered old Guido as tenderly as he would have a sleeping child. "The signore can take his siesta on the way back to the Villa," Edoardo whispered, as he winked and smiled at the American.

Beecher stopped at the desk and inquired about

messages, but there were none. While he was waiting for the elevator, he sensed that someone was watching him. He'd had the same feeling that morning when he left the dining room after breakfast, but he had dismissed it, telling himself that in Europe people-watching was a pastime. Hadn't Guido said that one could sit on the Via Veneto and watch the world go by?

But this was different. He knew someone was staring at his back. Beecher turned around casually, not too quickly, just in time to see the man raise his newspaper up in front of his face. Beecher recognized the rumpled gray suit. He had seen the same suit this morning in the lobby. The man had no face. This morning, too, his face had been covered by the newspaper. If Beecher saw him on the street, he would not recognize him.

Why would anyone in Rome be watching him? He could think of no possible reason, but from now on he would be on guard.

3.

He was being followed. There was absolutely no doubt
now. That morning while Beecher had been making a
pencil sketch of the bridge across the Tiber with the Castel
Sant' Angelo beyond, he had seen the man in the grey suit,
leaning over the bridge. This time he got a good look at
the man's face. Strange, thought Beecher, he's tailing me,
but he has a hunted look.

Once, the man had probably been handsome, but was
now seedy and paunchy: the chin weak, the eyes hollow
and darkly circled, deep creases at the side of the nose and
mouth suggested the kind of cynicism that corrodes the
spirit.

Beecher gave no sign that he recognized him. He had
enough experience to know that the stranger would show
his hand soon. Could Guido Brazzano be having him
watched? It didn't make sense, but Beecher suspected that
Guido was a complicated man, one could hardly begin to
understand him at first acquaintance. His vast business
holdings were scattered all over Italy: banking, vineyards,
exporting. There was probably not too much going on in
Rome that Guido didn't either know about or have ways of

finding out. Yes, Guido would no doubt be able to find out who was following him, but for the time being that could wait.

Beecher was discovering that the best way to see Rome is on foot. That day he had walked till he was too tired to go further, stopped at a sidewalk caffé to rest and then started out again. How could one people have produced so much art? Around every corner one found a statue, a beautiful Baroque fountain or an ancient crumbling wall on which an espaliered vine made an exquisite design.

He had left the Excelsior early that morning with his sketch pad under his arm and walked downhill on the Via Veneto past the old palace which housed the American Embassy. Marines stood on guard out front; flags flew. It was a touch of home right here on the Via Veneto. Somehow, a reassuring sight to the American citizen abroad.

Beecher rounded the corner at the bottom of the hill and entered the Piazza Barberini with Bernini's graceful Fontana del Tritone in the center.

That's how his day had started, with a sketch of the Triton, and now it was late afternoon, and he suddenly realized how exhausted he was when he sat down at a small table in the crowded Caffé Greco on the Via Condotti and ordered an espresso. Guido Brazzano had advised him, "The Caffé Greco is the place to observe young, beautiful, happy Romans. It is old. It has been a *Caffé* since before your American *Rivoluzione.* but the young love to go there and meet their friends, their lovers." The old building had a cozy atmosphere and was full of laughter, lively conversation and the hiss of the espresso and capuccino machines.

As he waited for his coffee, Beecher thumbed through his sketches: the Fontana del Tritone, Palazzo Farnese, a Renaissance palace, the Castel Sant'Angelo, a drawing of a little streetwise urchin selling "dirty" post cards outside the Colosseum—Beecher had paid the boy handsomely for posing—and a picturesque group engaged in an argument in the Piazza Navona. There was so much more he had missed. He hadn't even scratched the surface.

The opening night of his one man show had been a lavish, black tie, champagne and caviar affair orchestrated by Pietro Reni, who had returned from Paris. The guest list read like a Who's Who of the international art world. Beecher had met several well known Italian painters, as well as Vittorio Marconi, one of only two living sculptors who still carved his larger-than-life statues out of a solid block of marble. He selected his marble and supervised, and sometimes assisted with the quarrying at Carrarra, just as Michelangelo had done over three centuries before. The color and veining must be just right for his purposes. A flaw in the wrong spot could mar the whole thing.

Marconi invited Beecher to visit his studio in Florence. "If you think you have seen art in Rome..." He gave a depreciating shrug. Beecher was learning that body language, in Italy, often expresses much more than words. Raising one's shoulder an inch or lowering the eyelids a hair's breadth spoke volumes.

"You have seen nothing until you have been to Florence: the Uffizi; the Bargello, the Pitti, Michelangelo's David, Ghiberti's bronze doors at the Duomo, and I have hardly touched on the treasures to be seen. You must stay with me, my friend, and savor it all." Beecher made a mental note to extend his visit. This country was weaving its spell.

The opening night reception was attended by European art dealers, as well as some from the States. Art critics from the Rome newspapers were also present. The wasp-tongued Sarpi seemed to have had his stinger removed, at least temporarily, by Guido. His critique of the exhibit, while not as effusive as the ones in *Corriere della Sera* and *Il Messaggero,* had at least been fair.

Sarpi managed, however, to get in one barb, "Though no doubt a painter of some depth, with a mastery of his technique, we feel that Beecher Hornbeck's Midwestern subjects are a trifle boring and that his horizon is not broad enough."

"Ridiculous," snorted Guido, as he read the review to Beecher the next day. "All of the French Impressionists, with the exception of Gauguin, painted within a hundred-mile radius of their birthplace. The *serpente,* Sarpi, could not resist spreading his venom."

"Maybe he has a point, Guido. Even a venomous art critic can be right occasionally. I'm considering broadening my horizons by doing a series of Italian paintings."

"*Meraviglioso* ! I, Guido Brazzano, will be proud to handle them for you. Beecher, now I am happy to tell you that nearly half the paintings have been sold. Radley, from the Griffin-Toundsend Gallery in London and Ivor Swanstrom of Stockholm have not yet arrived. Swanstrom is a shark, but in the end, he will buy. He will not be able to resist the brooding, solitary splendor of your snow scenes. My friend, this is but the beginning of a long and profitable relationship between *Galleria Brazzano* and Beecher Hornbeck, greatest painter of the American scene." The old man threw his arms around Beecher and gave him the all-encompassing smile.

"You're too kind, Guido, but very good for an artist's ego."

Now, as Beecher sat in the Caffé Greco, sipping his espresso and studying his sketches, he decided that these would be the beginning of his Italian series. From the street urchin he would do a pen and ink, with watercolor washes. The sketch of the Fontana del Tritone would become an oil. He would make some more drawings tomorrow, perhaps some small watercolors, but now he must get back to the Excelsior. He glanced at his watch and realized he would be late for dinner with Cristina Brazzano if he didn't hurry.

Cristina had been rather aloof after their first meeting. It was almost as though she had offered her friendship that day in the Borghese Gardens and then decided to withdraw it. Since then, she had remained in the background. Her duties at the gallery, as Guido's Girl Friday, were extensive; she handled everything from ordering Guido's medicine from the *farmacía* and making hotel reservations for out-of-town clients, to cataloging paintings. Cristina was very knowledgeable about all periods of art, and Guido told Beecher that he had entrusted her with having two old masters that he was interested in buying authenticated. "That girl is like my own right arm. I don't know what I did before she came."

Of course, Cristina had been at the reception: mingling, greeting guests, checking the champagne, the food, making sure everything ran smoothly while Guido held court from his gilded antique Renaissance chair—his gout was worse—and Reni, vocal and officious, preened himself, giving the impression that he was the heir apparent.

Cristina was lovely in a long turquoise silk gown that accentuated her petite figure. The dress was intricately beaded on the shoulders, down the long sleeves and around the high neck. The perfect color for her, thought Beecher. Her thick hair, glinting with red highlights, was piled on top of her head, giving her neck a slender fragile look that was very appealing. Curling tendrils escaped the ivory combs, softly framing her face. Old fashioned yet chic, shy yet amazingly efficient in this fast-paced world of international art, Italian yet not Italian. Not ordinary, thought Beecher, no, not ordinary in any sense of the word. Pietro Reni couldn't seem to take his eyes off her. She avoided him.

During the past few days, whenever Beecher had been in the gallery Cristina had seemed to retreat to her office, always offering some excuse about schedules, long distance calls to be made, important work that couldn't wait. Was it his harmless question, that day in the Borghese Gardens, about her husband that had evoked this reaction? How could he have known? She had said that she was Guido's daughter-in-law. Anyone would have assumed that her husband was alive. Beecher had decided that for whatever reason, Cristina Brazzano did not want to talk to him about art, about Rome or about anything else.

So it came as quite a surprise when she approached him that night at the reception with two glasses of champagne and said, "I want to drink a toast to your extraordinary talent. This exhibit is one of the finest that *Galleria Brazzano* has ever known, a jewel in Guido's crown. He is eagerly awaiting Ivor Swanstrom's arrival next week, so he can gloat. Swanstrom has a first-rate gallery in Stockholm. They are old friends." Cristina sipped her champagne and then continued.

"I've been doing a lot of work behind the scenes, getting the exhibit ready. Pietro always seems to avoid the menial details, conveniently being called away to Paris or Antwerp, or wherever. Now that the pressure is off, I would like to make you a home-cooked Italian dinner. My specialty is *saltimbocca*. It is a Roman dish, one you should certainly try while you are here. And I hate to boast, but I have a way with artichokes."

"Sounds delightful. I don't even need to consult my social calendar. I'm available," Beecher announced with enthusiasm.

"Good. Let's make it tomorrow night then. I'll pick you up at the Excelsior at eight o'clock. You mentioned going out to sketch tomorrow. That should give you plenty of time. I have a small apartment here in Rome. I love Guido, but he makes so many demands on my time when I stay at the Villa."

Cristina was certainly unpredictable. Just as he had decided that she wasn't interested in giving him the time of day, as dear old Maude Kratcher would say, she had extended this invitation to dinner. He wondered if there would be other guests.

Well, soon he would find out. As he sketched the day away, he had thought of having dinner with Cristina expectantly, almost joyfully—but surely joyfully was not the right word. He hardly knew her.

Beecher had been lonely for a long time. Myra had not only been his wife but his best friend; she had understood his art, his struggles to express himself, his aspirations in a way that his friends and neighbors, even Conner Hannigan, never could.

Cristina would be picking him up in less than two hours. He paid the check, stepped out into the crowded, sunny Via Condotti and walked back to his hotel.

4.

"Federico is a charming fellow, but Ottavia insists on remaining mistress of her own destiny." Cristina stroked Ottavia, her Siamese cat, while the cat stared at Beecher with disdain.

"That cat knows I'm from the Middle West I'm positive, Cristina. I've seen that same look on the faces of Easterners when they hear that Beecher Hornbeck, painter, is content to vegetate in Sparta, Indiana. A case of, can anything good come out of Nazareth?"

"You must excuse Ottavia. She is something of a snob. Poor Federico, downstairs, is wasting away for love of her. He woos her with all the ardor of a feline Romeo, but her first husband belonged to a member of Parliament, and Federico is only a barbershop cat."

Beecher felt at home in Cristina's small apartment. There was nothing extravagant or faddish here. Not the Art Nouveau or Art Deco decor which was the rage in Soho, and all the little Sohos all over the United States. Beecher always felt a little out of place in the obviously arty milieu, where everything was studied, created for effect, from the decor to the conversation.

He looked around with interest. Handsome originals hung on the creamy eggshell walls, but Cristina Brazzano's taste seemed to run more to etchings and pen-and-ink drawings than to paintings. The living room had a high ceiling and contained a few Italian and French antiques, but the Chippendale sofa and the old flowered china tea set on the coffee table looked like they came straight out of a comfortable middle-class English home of the 1940s. A worn, jewel-toned Oriental carpet covered the shining wood floor. Bright cushions added satisfying bursts of color in an otherwise rather subdued color scheme, and the fire that glowed brightly in the Italian marble fireplace drew everything in the room into a circle of warmth, a delicate incorporation of elements that somehow added up to beauty. An individualist lives here, thought Beecher, one who loves beauty for its own sake.

A lovely arched window, framed in dark wood, looked down on the Viale Bruno Buozi, two stories below them. Cristina and Beecher stood at the window, and she pointed out a large building across the street. "Ingrid Bergman lived there with Roberto Rossellini in a ten-room apartment with lots of servants. That was in the early 1950s, after they filmed *Stromboli* together." Cristina's voice grew more animated as she spoke.

"The reporters used to camp out, trying to get pictures of Bergman when she left or returned with the new baby, Robertino. Rosselini broke cameras and punched reporters. He carried on a running battle with the press. Guido is full of these stories. So is Edoardo. You're lucky that you haven't fallen into his clutches yet.

"He has a heart of gold—he'd have to have, to put up with Guido's bullying—but is a little bit of a bore. Guido thinks he is doing everyone a favor to send Edoardo around with the car, to take clients on a guided tour of Rome. Edoardo is fine for St. Peter's, the Sistine Chapel and the Vatican Museum. He knows all the local color: about Michelangelo's demanding relatives, his love life and even how he mixed his pigments. He can tell you why the statues in the Vatican Museum all wear fig leaves and which Pope was responsible for putting them there. But from then on Edoardo will take you on his own sentimental journey, or maybe ego trip would be more accurate.

"He had some small parts in movies, years ago, so he'll take you to *Cinecittá,* that colossus of a movie studio outside Rome, and tell you about the time he played a Roman senator in *Quo Vadis.* The studio is still used today, but not as extensively as in the good old days of Italian movie making, in the '50s and '60s. You remember those monumental epics with casts of thousands!

"Edoardo still has access to the studio—I suspect Guido at work here. He is a man of tremendous influence. Edoardo is convinced that it is because of his own past 'illustrious' career–and will show you around, very much like touring the old MGM lot in Hollywood, I imagine. It is something to see, the most elaborate and colossal sets ever built. You might be interested."

"Are you warning me not to go?" Beecher asked. "It sounds fascinating."

They were still standing at the window. Cristina's perfume was intoxicating. Sparta and the farm seemed very far away.

"Unfortunately, the tour doesn't end here. Edoardo will insist on taking you north of Rome, to the Foro Italica, a complex built by Mussolini, which includes an Olympic Stadium. All of this was erected for the 1942 Fascism Fair which was never held because of the war. There's also a smaller stadium, encircled by huge statues, depicting all the ancient games, done in the classical Greek and Roman styles.

"You may well wonder why Edoardo feels that this attraction rivals the more famous sites: Villa d'Este at Tivoli, Hadrian's Villa, the Trevi Fountain. You will not have long to wonder. Edoardo will leap from the car, strike a dramatic pose beneath the statue of the discus thrower and explain that the Adonis-like body you are looking at was his at the age of nineteen. Here before you, is a youthful, twelve-foot, marble Edoardo, minus fig leaf. That old guy is so proud of that colossal marble statue of himself as a youth, stylized, of course—a young Roman god wearing a laurel wreath on his marble brow.

"Edoardo posed week after week in the sculptor's freezing studio, in the nude, holding up a ten pound discus—I'm sure the studio has become colder and the discus heavier with each passing year. He is convinced it made a man of him, that and swimming every morning in the Tiber. I'm sure that the Tiber is full of ten plagues, but Edoardo insists he survived by straining the microbes through his teeth. Very scientific, don't you think?" She laughed.

"Well it's colorful anyway," Beecher shrugged.

"Edoardo is eccentric, but I don't know what Guido would do without him. They've grown old together. Edoardo is more than just a chauffeur; he's Guido's bodyguard and nanny. Would you like a drink while I check on dinner?"

Beecher said he really didn't care for a drink. "If you're sure I can't help you in the kitchen, I'll just stay here and try to make friends with Ottavia. I'm really more of a dog man, but I like all animals," he said.

"Good luck," Cristina laughed as she hurried to the kitchen.

He glanced at his watch. It was after ten o'clock. He wondered if his stomach would ever grow accustomed to the European custom of late dining. He was touched when he saw that Cristina had gone to a great deal of trouble to make this dinner special. Flowers graced the small round dining table that was set at one end of the living room. Candlelight glanced off the faceted crystal wine and water goblets and illuminated the gold-rimmed plates.

Cristina poured from a chilled bottle of white wine and served the appetizer, artichoke hearts stuffed with crab meat.

"This is delicious, Cristina."

She was obviously pleased. "I'm glad you like it. It's my

own recipe, something I brought with me from London, along with my mother's china and Waterford crystal, my books and the Chippendale sofa. It was in my parent's home, and I'm sentimental about it." She sighed, and in the silence that followed Beecher could hear sounds from the street: the screech of a car's brakes, a man's voice raised in sudden anger. "There are things I miss about England," Cristina said, breaking the silence.

She returned from the kitchen with the *saltimbocca*. "I hope you like it. It's made with veal, ham and cheese. Guido's cook, Sophia, taught me how to make it." She served them both vegetables while Beecher poured more wine.

"Your paintings reveal a lot about you: strength, sublety, a certain austere quality, maybe loneliness. Am I correct?" As they chatted, her shyness seemed to evaporate.

"Possibly."

"But what of your life in Indiana?" she inquired.

"I farm, Cristina. Not very glamorous, but a good foil for my painting. The two complement each other. I love the land, nature. It's the inspiration for my work. I enjoy being alone. Creative work can't be done in the company of others, but I am lonely since my wife was killed five years ago." The horror returned momentarily, like a sudden blow to the stomach.

"It was in the London papers, all about you and your wife's mother catching the criminals. It must have been a terrible thing for you, losing her that way," she said softly— instantly sensitive to his mood.

"We were getting ready to leave for a painting trip abroad and intended to come to Italy. Myra planned to look up relatives in Venice. It's a long story." Beecher realized he had been rambling on in a way that was not typical at all. Maybe the wine had a little something to do with it, or was it something about the woman beside him?

"You have the advantage, Cristina. You say my work reveals a lot about me. Now you must tell me something about yourself. How did you happen to come to Italy?" he asked. He took another bite of his veal and marveled at Cristina's culinary expertise.

She tasted her wine and studied this man with the lean, interesting face and the deep-set light blue eyes. His hands were nice, but they looked more like a farmer's than a painter's. She didn't know why she found the idea exciting. She lowered her eyes.

She is trying to decide if she really wants to trust me, Beecher thought.

"Italian men have made me wary. Outrageous flirting is the norm, and pursuit is the game. They think it's expected of them. As children, they're spoiled and catered to by their mothers and sisters, indulged by their fathers. The myth of their uniqueness is perpetuated by their wives, and only too often by their mistresses."

"Pietro Reni gave me a little heart-to-heart talk on the way in from the airport, about discreet indiscretions," Beecher laughed.

"Pietro is a perfect example of the type of man I'm talking about. Even though he's married, his ego just won't let him believe I'm really not interested in him. It's the conquest that's important to Pietro, not the person. Sometimes, when he's making a pass at me, I can see his mind wander. He's playing a role. Everyone is this country is an actor; the only bad ones are on the stage and screen."

Beecher laughed again. "But you like it here?"

"I love it. The Italians are an exuberant, warmhearted people. The English treat their pets like people, but send their children off to boarding school at the age of seven. An Italian would never do that. His children are his very life's blood. He would never send them away. He thinks the English have no feelings; that they are cold. And they are.

"That's why I stayed here after my husband died. I love Guido, and he needs me, especially now that Carlo is gone. I love these wacky, warmhearted people and this fascinating old city, so I ignore the strikes and the Red Brigade, the horrendous traffic and the government red tape." She paused to spear an artichoke. "I'm something of an introvert, and these people are everything I'm not."

"Strange, you say you like the Italians because they're not like you. My wife often said that she was sure she would feel at home here because she was a direct throwback to an Italian ancestor. I sometimes think Myra believed in reincarnation. She came from a long line of New Englanders that could safely be described as cold, without fear of exaggeration. She was nothing like them." Suddenly Myra's beautiful face filled Beecher's mind.

"English writers and poets have migrated for centuries to Italy: Byron, Keats, the Brownings, more recently, James Joyce and Ezra Pound," said Cristina. "Even John Milton couldn't resist coming to Italy, to see what it was all about, but he felt he had to apologize for it, and his Puritan nature wouldn't let him relax and enjoy himself.

"Lord Byron took one look at this city and wrote, '0 Rome, my country! City of the soul!' and, 'I love the language, that soft bastard Latin, which melts like kisses from a female mouth.' Near the end of his life he said, 'Open my heart and you will see graved inside of it, Italy.' Keats' house is on the Piazza de Spagna. Have you seen it yet?"

"No," he said, "I haven't even thrown my coin in the Trevi Fountain. Something tells me I'm going to have to call Walter Franke, my neighbor who's looking after the farm, and make arrangements to stay longer. I told Guido I'm contemplating an Italian series, and I don't think he's going to let me forget about it. I'm pleased with the drawings I made today and I'm planning to go out again tomorrow. It's best to keep up the momentum. You understand, I'm sure." Beecher sipped his wine. "Do you think you could make my excuses to Edoardo, without hurting his feelings?" Beecher asked.

"Certainly. Besides, Edoardo is driving Guido to Milan for a few days, something to do with the exporting business."

"Cristina, no matter where this conversation starts, we always seem to end up talking about me. You were going to tell me how you happened to be in Rome."

"I'll get dessert and coffee. Let's sit in front of the fire, and I'll tell you the whole story, I promise."

Cristina went into the kitchen, and Beecher could hear the hiss of the espresso machine. There wasn't much left of the fire. He got it blazing again with newspaper and some small pieces of wood.

Cristina came in with a tray. "I made an English trifle for dessert. It's one of the things I miss about home. Italy is a sun-baked country of fierce bright blue skies, golden buildings and dry earth. I miss the lush greenness of the English countryside, the mist rising from the moors and even foggy old London. Sometimes I miss my job at the British Museum and the friends I left there." Her eyes grew misty.

After serving Beecher dessert, she took a cup of espresso, kicked off her shoes and curled up in the corner of the sofa, much as Ottavia would have done. The shadows cast on the wall by the flames reminded Beecher of a child's puppet show; a wistful Pierrot reaching out to touch a drooping Columbine. They sat in silence, except for the hissing and crackling of the fire.

"My parents are dead," Cristina said. "Mother died when I was a child, and my father raised me with the help of a part-time housekeeper. He fixed our breakfast and got me ready for school in the mornings, before he went to work. One of the few times I ever saw him show emotion was when he took me to the hairdresser to have my hair cut. It was almost down to my waist. Mother always braided it in the mornings, before school. I wasn't old enough to do it, and Dad couldn't. Having it cut made him terribly sad; looking back on it now, I realize that those braids must have symbolized, to him, everything he couldn't handle without her."

They gazed into the fire.

"My father was a civil servant, a man of small rituals and routines. You could hear a pin drop at our dinner table at night. He always asked me about my day, my school work... That duty done, he would resume his crossword puzzle. We dined to the sound of the ticking clock."

A vivid picture came to Beecher's mind, as Cristina spoke, of that London dinner table—the grieving man and the small, lonely girl who was too young to understand.

"My parents were quiet people too. I always knew they loved me but they had trouble verbalizing it. Myra was so different from anyone I had ever known...."

Cristina was silent for a moment. Then she said, "Can you wonder that I love dining at Guido's Villa: animated conversation, laughter, popping corks. Even the heated arguments! Dinner parties are wonderful. You'll see what I mean when you go there. If the souffle falls, the chef cries and has a nervous breakdown. Nervous breakdowns over here are like the strikes, of short duration.

"The dinner guests commiserate with the chef, more popping of corks. He is suddenly inspired and returns to the kitchen to whip up something better that the damnable souffle.

"Puccini arias drift from the kitchen. No one minds waiting; after all, dinner is more than food. In Rome it is a three-act play with a happy ending. The meal is a triumph. What's the matter, Beecher? You look a little doubtful."

"Sounds exhausting to me. I'm beginning to realize how humdrum and predictable dinner time is in Sparta, Indiana, where the longest speech is 'pass the potatoes'," he laughed as he lighted his pipe.

"I love it here. I'm tired to death of stiff upper lips."

Beecher laughed. "You're a one-woman Chamber of Commerce," he said.

"I warned you that day in the Borghese Gardens. I'm more Italian that the natives. Now I'm telling you why."

"How did Carlo come into the picture?" Beecher asked.

"Father died suddenly, of a heart attack, just after I started college. Archeology was my major at the University of London. After graduating, I got a job as assistant to the curator of Western Asiatic antiquities of the British Museum. The work was fascinating. The site of ancient Ninevah is in northern Iraq. The tension between Iran and Iraq had put an end to any archeological studies there, at least for a while.

"I met Carlo at a Museum reception. He was in London on Gallery business, and a mutual friend introduced us. Carlo held the position at the Brazzano Gallery that Pietro does now. I hate to admit it, but Pietro does a better job. I found out after we were married that Carlo was something of a playboy and more interested in sports cars and racing than he was in the Gallery. He raced his Ferrari in the *Targa Floria* in Italy and was always taking off for Le Mans and Nurburging. Guido knew, of course, but he was willing to overlook a lot in Carlo. Guido has other sons, much older than Carlo, all successful businessmen with large families. None of them have much time for the old man. Carlo was Guido's favorite, the son of his second wife, his beloved Maria.

"I know I behaved strangely that day in the Borghese Gardens but the waves of sadness still come over me at times—often when I least expect it."

Beecher took her hand for minute. "There's no need to explain. I, of all people, can understand what you're going through."

"Carlo had more charm and charisma than any man I had ever met, and he swept me off my feet. It still happens you know, to romantics like me, I guess. He wouldn't leave London until I promised to marry him. Guido kept calling everyday from Rome. Why hadn't Carlo returned? What was going on? Well, if he was really in love, why didn't he bring the girl back to Rome and marry her? Guido's persistence is awe-inspiring. He didn't get where he is today by accident." She laughed.

"Don't forget, Cristina, I've experienced something of Guido's persistence already myself—and his charm." Beecher spoke through an aromatic haze of tobacco smoke. "At first I had several doubts about exhibiting in Rome but Guido disposed of each of them with the finesse of Machiavelli. He left me without a leg to stand on, as they say back home." Beecher smiled, remembering the numerous phone calls from Rome. Martha Sue, the local operator had been in a tizzy, and word spread through Sparta that Beecher was selling the farm and moving abroad.

"Go on Cristina, I'm anxious to hear. Did Guido win out? Did you return to Rome with Carlo?"

"We flew to Rome and were married in the church of Santa Maria Maddalena. It's a Baroque view of Heaven, with angels in the choir and over the altar and door. The walls are pink marble, with statues in blue niches, and a white dove hovers in the cupola. Carlo and I were encircled by a vast crowd of beaming Brazzanos, a little like the heavenly host.

"Then I took off the wedding gown and the jeweled tiara and veil that Carlo's mother had worn—when Guido saw that I was the same size that Maria had been, he became obsessed with the idea of my wearing her wedding gown—and began my married life as a young Roman matron.

"We lived at Guido's villa. Carlo left for the gallery every morning, and the brothers' wives introduced me into Roman society. They were quite happy with their lives: lunch with friends, card parties, teas or the cinema in the afternoons, shopping, talk of their children and the latest fashions, volunteer work for the *Amici dei Musee di Roma.*"

"Sounds like quite a change after your job at the British Museum," Beecher commented.

"I must be boring you to death—telling you my life's story. It's getting late. Are you tired? I can drive you back to your hotel any time," she said.

"Unless you're ready to get rid of me, Cristina, I'd love to stay and hear the rest. I've never been less bored in my life, but I will take another cup of espresso."

She flushed with pleasure as she filled first his cup, then her own, and continued.

"Carlo and I were in love and were happy when we

were together, but I was bored to death with this kind of life. Guido could see what was happening and rescued me. He suggested I start going in to the gallery with him. Carlo left early. Guido and I rode in later with Edoardo. He got the idea that I should start cataloging his own private collection when he heard about my job at the British Museum. There were storerooms full of antiquities and paintings that he had acquired through the years. Some really valuable pieces were buried with mediocre stuff. I know quite a lot about restoration.

"Gradually, I took over some duties in the gallery: our ads in European art publications, taking out of town clients to lunch or their wives sightseeing.

"Carlo and I were only married four years. He was killed in that crash of an Alitalia air liner during take off at Orly Airport three years ago. Perhaps you remember?"

Beecher nodded, remembering the horrible accident.

"When Guido heard the news, he had a heart attack and nearly died. It was a bad time. I assured the old man that I would stay on at the villa and help him at the gallery, that I would not return to England. It was no sacrifice. I loved Guido and my job at the gallery. Rome is my home now, mine and Ottavia's." The cat, who was asleep in Cristina's lap, looked up when she heard her name.

In the silence that followed Beecher became aware that the sounds of the street had become muted. He knew he should look at his watch but deliberatly chose not to. He was only too aware that Cristina didn't want the evening to end any more than he did.

He had a momentary desire to take her in his arms, but the presence in the room of Myra and Carlo was so strong—"But you're living here in Rome now?"

"I did live at the villa, all the time until six months ago, and I still act as hostess at Guido's dinner parties and arrange gallery receptions, but I explained to him that I need a little place of my own. He was becoming increasingly dependent on me. We agreed to compromise. He took it quite well, actually. He said he wanted me always to feel that the villa was my home, insisted on buying me a whole new wardrobe, so I could leave my clothes and everything intact in my suite at the villa. I usually stay there on weekends and often for a week or two at a time, but when Guido is in Milan or Turin on business, I always stay here at the apartment... Do you live alone, Beecher, out there on your farm in Indiana?"

"I live with Cassie, my boon companion."

"Oh?"

"She's a little Cairn terrier. I've had more philosophical discussions with that dog than I've had with most people. Then there's Mrs. Daily, my part-time housekeeper, who comes in two days a week to wash and iron, clean the house and check on my spiritual condition. She sees herself as the keeper of the flame, a protector of 'Miss Myra's things'. She declared war on my pipe; she's a crusader, making weekly forays to recapture Jerusalem from the infidels, Cassie and me. That woman has covered every flat surface in my house with stiff crocheted doilies. It's part of her reclamation campaign."

"Why don't you simply remove them?"

"I'm afraid it might destroy her."

"Something tells me you're just an old softie," Cristina smiled.

"Well, I've warned her that my studio is off limits."

Beecher really didn't know how he got started, but he was telling Cristina all about Myra, their life together, how they had met. He hadn't been able to discuss these things with anyone since Myra's death.

This is totally unlike me, he thought. It was as though he stood outside his body listening to his other self confiding in this woman he hardly knew. He felt more relaxed and at ease than he had for a long time.

"Myra's death left a terrible void in my life, but I've no desire to rush out and fill it with another relationship. I guess I'm afraid," he admitted to himself as well as Cristina.

"The creative person often channels his emotions, even his sexual desires into his work. I can understand how this seemed a better solution to you than risking disappointment by trying to fill the emptiness with a relationship that might not be satisfying," she answered with empathy.

"You can understand that? I didn't reason it out, but I think that's what I did."

"Of course I can understand. I did the same thing with my work. Guido needed me even more after Carlo's death. That filled a place in my life. I have made friendships here in Rome. I decided these things would have to be enough until I met the right person. Later, I faced the possibility that they might always *have* to be enough. The world is full of Pietro Reni's but I'm not interested." Cristina shrugged off the thought of Reni's suggestive leer.

"Does he bother you?" Beecher asked.

"Not really. He knows that I would only have to say a few words to Guido, and he would be gone from the Brazzano Gallery. Pietro just lets me know from time to time that he's still available in case I've changed my mind. He can't help himself. That's the way he's been programmed." She smiled ruefully.

Beecher looked at his watch and was amazed to see the time. "It's late—. You're not driving me back to the hotel. I'm getting a cab."

"It's later than late; it's four o'clock in the morning. I'm going to cook some breakfast, and then I'll drive you back."

"I apologize. I'm on vacation, but you have to go to work."

"No, I'll call in. There's nothing important going on this morning. I can sleep till noon and go in to the gallery after lunch."

Cristina fed Ottavia, who was demanding her breakfast in a loud Siamese voice. Then she made a Florentine omelet which she and Beecher breakfasted on, along with croissants and coffee, while Ottavia sat in the corner washing herself and glaring at Beecher, as though he were guilty of some terrible impropriety.

5.

Old shopkeepers, sweeping the sidewalks in front of their small businesses, stopped to look as the red Lamborghini passed by. It was just getting light and Rome's coming alive was accompanied by myriad smells and sounds. Flower vendors and newsboys were setting up on street corners and in the piazzas. Butchers hung out dressed chickens, rabbits and quail for the housewives, who still shopped every morning for food. Romans walked briskly down the street with long, thin loaves of freshly baked bread and morning papers tucked under their arms, and a few of the elderly, dressed in black, entered churches to pray.

There were no tourists about. Perhaps this is the only time these people have their city to themselves, thought Beecher, in the first morning hours before hotel doors open to disgorge hoards of tourists, and the tour buses start arriving from Fiumicino Airport.

In front of an open air fruit market, a young man was painstakingly arranging an elaborate display: a pyramid of apples, pears, apricots and oranges that was a work of art. More varieties of grapes than Beecher had ever seen were arranged in a glistening array of color, like an abstract painting. It pleased him to see such pride taken in a small thing. The streets had been washed down during the night, and now a fine mist rose to meet the sun, giving everything a hazy intangible look.

Cristina spoke for the first time since they left the apartment It was almost as though she had read Beecher's mind. "Isn't it fascinating to watch the city come alive like this?" she said. "You see before you the age-old *Commedia dell' Arte*; Rome refurbishes her costume with a touch of lace here, a jewel there. She applies fresh makeup, and one no longer sees the fine wrinkles, the sagging skin. She studies one last time the lines she already knows by heart. She is tired, but she gives the performance that is expected of her. But now, she can be herself in these private backstage moments before the curtain rises on the next act, when strangers aren't watching, before tourists arrive and cameras start clicking."

"You said that very beautifully."

"I love the old girl, warts and all," she said. "Sorry to be sounding like the Chamber of Commerce again."

Cristina pulled up in front of the Excelsior and let Beecher out. It was so early that even Luigi wasn't around.

"I'm a little embarrassed. I don't usually come to dinner and stay all night. I hope you really can get some rest before you go to the gallery," he apologized.

"I'm fine. Do you always have to do what you usually do? Why does it matter?" she asked jauntily.

When in Rome, Beecher decided, maybe nothing turns out as it usually does. "It was a wonderful dinner, Cristina—and evening. Thanks for everything." He reached into the car and gave the small hand on the steering wheel a squeeze.

"When you need a break from the sketching, call me. I won't call you while you're busy," she hesitated and then added, "I can take you some places that aren't on Edoardo's agenda, not the usual tourist stuff. Until then, *ciao*." She shifted gears and glanced in the rear view mirror.

"Goodby Cristina, and thanks again." He watched until the red car turned the corner and disappeared from sight.

As Beecher entered the hotel, the desk clerk looked up.

For a second his expression showed surprise and interest. Beecher was sure he was about to smile, then a bland guarded look, like a veil, came down over his features. "Good morning Sir," he nodded, almost too politely. False assumptions, thought Beecher. How many times had he, himself, been guilty of making a false assumption?

Beecher glanced around as he walked to the elevator. He didn't really expect to see the man in the rumpled suit at this hour. He would be recognized too easily in the almost deserted lobby. However, the fellow wasn't too astute or he wouldn't have allowed himself to be seen twice already. If Beecher had thought about it, he might have mentioned him to Cristina that evening, but lots of things seemed to have left his mind, temporarily.

As he lay in the darkened hotel room, listening to the muffled daytime sounds of the city, sleep eluded him. He felt uncomfortable, vaguely guilty, as though he had too good a time with Cristina Brazzano, had been somehow disloyal to Myra. "That's ridiculous," he told himself, "she's been gone five years."

The problem lay in the fact that Myra's death still had some degree of unreality for Beecher. There had been no illness with which to get used to the idea that he would lose her. His mind had blotted out the image of her body in the morgue. There was not even a grave to visit. Placing flowers on her grave was a small ritual that might have given her death the reality of remembrance at the changing of the seasons and on holidays and special days. Flowers placed on the grave are meaningless to the dead, but provide a small comforting act of atonement for the living.

Myra's ashes were in an urn, stored away somewhere in Connecticut, among the conclave of deceased Hartleys and Wellingtons. He sighed, for he couldn't bear to think of his beautiful, vivacious Myra among all those ancestors who had been slightly dead, even when they were alive.

Why do I still have to keep reminding myself after five years that she's really gone? Beecher thought. Why do I sometimes get the eerie feeling that she's going to finish that portrait in the studio?

Maybe Conner's right after all. Have I really turned into a middle-aged nut who goes around having conversations with his dog?

Conner had insisted on driving Beecher to the airport and had pulled a Dr. Jekyll and Mr. Hyde en route, turning himself, without benefit of a magic elixir, into Father Pythias, the Dear Abby of the Archdiocese.

"Beecher", Conner had said, "I want you to really enjoy this trip. Since Myra died, you've practically become a hermit. You seldom go out anymore."

"Conner, what makes you think it's possible to produce art without dedication? Dedication isn't limited to the clergy, you know. I can't fritter away my time and still produce the work I'm striving for." Beecher sounded edgy.

"Another thing I'd like to mention, I'm something of an animal lover, myself, but you need someone to talk to beside your dog and that old curmudgeon of a house-keeper. Maybe you'll meet interesting people on this trip, someone special that you'd like to get to know better. Don't withdraw into a shell if you do," Conner advised in a tone of voice that Beecher thought of as "priestly".

"Conner, for a priest, you're awfully interested in the carnal side of life. Only last year you tried to fix me up with your cousin from Cincinnati. My life isn't as dull as you seem to think. I went to Chicago for the Toulouse-Lautrec exhibit and to St. Louis for the Monet."

"I'm not talking about art exhibits. I'm talking about romance, if you still remember what that is."

"Don't patronize me, Conner."

"Myra has been gone for five years. You're only forty-six years old. Do you think I would urge you to be promiscuous? I'm suggesting that you might find someone to share your life with. Promise me you won't close your mind and heart to the idea." There was real concern in Conner's voice.

"I haven't closed my mind to anything, but it just hasn't happened. Drop the subject, Conner."

When they had said goodbye at the airport, Conner had raised his hand in a gesture that looked to Beecher like a combination pontifical blessing and old boy salute and said, "Don't forget, I'll be praying for you." Conner believed in prayer; so did Beecher.

He lay in the dark and remembered Cristina: just relaxing in her apartment with its civilized feminine touches, being served a delicious meal by a beautiful woman, her intelligence, the all but forgotten pleasures of female companionship.

Conner, you jerk, thought Beecher, you're just sitting back there in Sparta, under your fig tree on your sanctified rear end, beseeching the Almighty to shake up my life. You're still a troublemaker, just like you were when we were kids, only now you think you have God on your side.

He decided that trying to get to sleep was a losing battle. He would order coffee from room service, take a cold shower, dress and go out to make some more studies for future paintings. He hadn't been to the Forum yet or the Trevi Fountain or the Spanish Steps. To hell with lying here psychoanalyzing himself. That would get him nowhere. He dialed room service.

Beecher walked through the streets of Rome for hours, stopping frequently to make drawings and atmospheric watercolor sketches. Romans were used to artists, so no one annoyed him with questions or special attention. The afternoon had been fruitful, if exhausting, and his sketch book was half filled. Some of the drawings were detailed studies for paintings with extensive color notations; others were just jottings: a haunting expression on the face of a disenchanted youth, a bent old lady feeding the pigeons, a run-down enclosed courtyard with a crumbling statue.

And now, as he stood in the Piazza di Spagna, lighting his pipe and studying the play of light and shadow on the Spanish Steps, Beecher saw Myra.

6.

Twisters often strike the Midwest in spring, and once when he was a child, Beecher stood on a hill and watched in terror as a funnel cloud appeared in the distance and advanced with the shriek of a freight train on the town of Sparta, which lay below him in the valley. The tornado flattened houses and barns, while other buildings stood close by untouched. To the child it was an apocalyptic vision of the Scriptures he had heard Parson Wyckliff intone only the Sunday before. "Two shall be planting. One shall be taken, and one shall be left." He saw a horse tossed casually into a tree, as though it were a child's ball. The boy thought he was witnessing the end of the world.

Now Beecher had been drawn into the vortex of such a storm. He sat in the darkened Church of Trinitá dei Monti, in the quiet eye of the whirlwind, while unanswered questions raged around him like shrieking, destructive winds.

Was he losing his mind? Had Beecher's desire called Myra forth from the tomb, resurrecting her from the winding sheets of his dreams, or had he actually seen her on the Spanish Steps? The long conversation with Cristina

Brazzano the night before had brought back vivid memories of Myra, something he hadn't allowed himself to
indulge in for several years. Could it be the power of
suggestion, combined with loss of sleep, that had set the
scene for his imagination to run riot? Hadn't he lain in his
darkened hotel room, only that morning, and felt vaguely
guilty because he had enjoyed the company of a beautiful
woman so much, that he had betrayed Myra in some way?
True, he had rejected that guilt as ridiculous, but perhaps
what the mind rejects on a conscious level is only stored
beneath the surface, to come forth later in another guise—
the same actor, playing many parts.

Surely it was significant that he had seen Myra, who had
looked so Mediterranean, here in Rome. Probably only a
striking resemblance to an Italian woman, an understand-
able thing. It could easily happen.

"Why am I doing this to myself?" Beecher was shocked
when he heard his voice echo in the empty cathedral.

It had grown dark outside. He had no idea how long
he had been sitting there. Why am I trying to convince
myself that I didn't see her, that I only conjured her into
being for an instant? The answers to that question was so
frightening that he could hardly bring himself to face it, for
it opened a Pandora's box, full of old doubts and new fears.

If Myra were alive, it could only mean that she had
deliberately allowed him to believe that she was dead for
five years and was herself party to some terrible, dark
deception.

Beecher had finally come to grips with Myra's death and
had obtained a measure of peace, even though he was now
only part of the person he had been before. It was a simple
problem in math. If two become one, and then half leaves,
what remains is only part of the whole. Beecher was
functioning well and producing his best work—the finest
things he had done, so far. The part of his nature that was
gone was that more elusive part that had to do with joy and
spontaneity. What he had experienced the night before,
while dining and talking with Cristina, was a little like a

rebirth of those feelings.

He had made peace with Myra's death, but could he ever make peace with a living Myra who had betrayed him, had rejected his love and their entire life together? Satan had invaded the sanctuary, and dark demons of doubt and suspicion lurked in the shadowed corners of the church. A terrible oppression settled on him, and the cloying odor of incense became a breath from the tomb. The tomb—he remembered seeing Myra's body in the morgue. But that was the problem, he really couldn't remember. It had been far more like a dream than reality. What he had thus far considered a blessing now became a fresh source of anxiety. If he couldn't remember what he had seen, how could he be sure now that the body he had identified had been hers? He had been sure at the time. Not any more. Not now that he had seen her again.

He had been in a state of shock when he went to the morgue. Naturally he had seen what he was told he would see, what he expected to see. His wife had been blasted at close range with a shotgun. That horror pushed everything else out of his mind.

He had been warned by the police detective that it would be a shock. The man had been sympathetic, had ushered him in and out in a hurry. The detective's hand shook when he reached out to give Beecher the parcel containing Myra's purse and clothes. Strange he had never wondered about that before. Now that fact took on fresh significance, sinister meaning. Could the detective have been part of a plan to deceive him into believing that Myra was dead? There had been something vaguely unsettling about him at the time—bad vibes. Then, Beecher found out later that the detective had been taking bribes, that he had been involved in the city hall scandal.

He hadn't thought about the missing money for a long time. That had never been explained, another loose end left dangling. The six thousand dollars Myra had taken with her to the bank to purchase the traveler's checks for their three-month trip abroad had never turned up. It had not been in her purse. It was difficult to believe she would have taken such a sum from her purse before stepping up to the window. Hal and Larry's haul had been exactly the amount that the teller had handed over to them. The police told him that the purse, which contained her wallet, watch and rings as well as all the other paraphernalia women carry about with them, had been locked in a safe in the police station. Beecher had come to the conclusion that the money must have fallen on the floor and been pocketed by someone in the bank. Any number of people would have had an opportunity in the ensuing carnage and confusion. Or it could have been removed from her purse later. He didn't press the matter; it was the least of his worries at the time. What were a few thousand dollars to a man who had just lost everything he valued? Had she used the money to escape?

The shadows were blacker now. They were no longer in the corners of the cathedral, but were moving in upon him. Unseen demons of suspicion moaned and wailed and plucked at him with leprous fingers, trying to draw him down into the nether regions of madness. The oppression was like a tangible weight that had settled, not only on his mind, but his body as well. It took all his strength to rise and stagger out of the church.

The cool air of the Via Sistina revived him. He felt just like he had when his appendix had been removed and he was coming out from under the anesthetic. The sights and sounds of the real world were sane and reassuring. The shops were closed, but many people were walking or standing around looking in boutique windows. Couples strolled arm in arm, laughing, chattering in Italian, alive.

Beecher decided not to hail a cab. He needed to walk, even though he was exhausted. He took deep breaths as he walked down the hill from the church. He was a short distance from the Via Ludovisa when he saw a familiar figure duck into the entrance of the Eden Hotel, on the corner. The street light had shone, for an instant, on the sallow dissolute face. His gray rumpled suit had been exchanged for an equally shabby brown one, but there was no mistaking the man.

Suddenly, Beecher was terribly angry. He was tired of playing it cool and no longer cared if Guido was the one who was having him watched. He would get some answers. People turned to stare as he dashed into the small, luxurious lobby of the Eden. It was certainly not the type of place where the rumpled man would be staying. He was nowhere in sight.

Beecher approached the desk clerk. "Did you see a short man in a brown suit come into the lobby only a minute ago?"

"Sir, I have been checking reservations for the past few minutes." He eyed Beecher curiously. "Perhaps if you give me his name, I can check our guest list."

"I don't know his name, but I saw him duck in here. He's been following me for days." Why am I telling him this, Beecher thought, as the desk clerk looked at him with thinly veiled contempt.

"I'm afraid, in that case, that I can't be of help. You look ill. May I call a doctor?"

Beecher abruptly turned away, without answering, and headed for the bar. The same old music seemed to drift from bars all over the world. He stood in the entrance and looked around the darkened, cozy room. Couples lingered over drinks, and several men sat at the bar while a tired-looking trio played American show tunes. No point in checking the men's room or the restaurant. The man had surely slipped out another door.

The anger drained out of Beecher, leaving only an unbelievable exhaustion and a sense of desolation that he couldn't fight any longer. How would he ever find Myra in this city? Meanwhile, all he could think of, now, was making it back to his room.

7.

Beecher was still asleep with his clothes on when the phone rang. This time there were no dreams, only the drugged stupor of shock and exhaustion. Even the sunlight streaming in the windows had failed to waken him. He hadn't thought to close the drapes the night before, but had collapsed on the bed that had been turned down by the maid while he was out. His last thought before falling asleep was that he never wanted to wake up and face the questions that had torn his life apart in a few short hours.

The phone rang insistently, and Beecher's mind made a desperate effort to resurface from sleep and think of some answer for Guido or Cristina, some reason for not meeting them for lunch or going sightseeing. He was ill. That's what he would tell whoever was calling. He couldn't tell either Cristina or Guido the truth.

"I saw my wife Myra, who was shot down in Indiana five years ago, on the Spanish Steps yesterday." Or the other side of the coin: "I fear I'm losing my mind."

It was ten-thirty. He picked up the phone and said "Hello."

There was silence, but he could hear breathing and

sense the presence on the other end. It was the rumpled man. Beecher knew it even before he spoke. "Signor Hornbeck, is it he?" The man's voice was hoarse.

"This is Beecher Hornbeck, speaking. Who are you?"

"I desire to have *conversazione* with you—to speak." His English was not the best.

"Then speak. I'm listening. But first, tell me who you are and why you have been following me. If you're so anxious to talk, why did you run from me last night? I saw you sneak into the Eden Hotel."

"I follow you because I can not approach at once. There was danger last night. In detective work, there is danger, as you well know yourself, Signor Hornbeck. You are known in Rome, even before you arrive."

"Get to the point. You haven't told me why you are following me or what you want to talk about."

"I was in the Piazza di Spagna yesterday. I, too, saw what you saw."

"You were following me before yesterday. I saw you on the Bridge of Angels, the day before, and in the lobby of the Excelsior three days ago. You say you are a detective. Who has hired you to follow me? Is it Guido Brazzano?"

"I do not know Guido Brazzano and am hired by no other to follow you. I have *informazione* no one else knows, now that Aldo is dead—information about your wife."

"What do you know about my wife?"

"I need money. There are reasons that make me leave Rome quickly. Only yesterday I know it must be soon or it will be too late for me. If you give me a million lire, not a large sum surely, for you. Do you not want to know what I have to tell you about your wife?" The man gave a rasping cough.

The morbid doubts and fears of the night before were gone. Beecher knew now that Myra was alive. Nothing else mattered but finding her. There had to be an explanation. Myra would never leave him of her own free will. How could he have doubted her? He could never forget all the years of love and mutual trust. No matter how things appeared, he trusted Myra. That's what he had to remember.

"Yes, I want to know about my wife, and you better really have information, or you don't yet know what danger is. It will take me about an hour to dress and go get travelers checks and American money changed into lire. I just don't happen to have a million lire on me at the moment. Where do you want me to meet you?"

"I will come to your hotel room in two hours, but if there is danger, if someone follows, then it will not be possible for me. If I do not appear by twelve-thirty, it will be thus. You must go to Hadrian's Villa at three. It is only a short ride outside Rome by bus or taxi. Buy a ticket and enter. Do not take a tour. The ruins are *enorme*–how you say, spread out. Walk about in all areas. I will find you. Signor Hornbeck, you will have the money in two hours and you will wait in your room?"

"Yes, I'll have the money. But remember I have warned you not to try to deceive me."

"I will knock one, then two. If not, then Hadrian's Villa at three." His oily, confidential tone of voice sickened Beecher. "You haven't told me your name."

"You do not need my name. I will make contact with you." "

My room number is 321."

"I already know," he answered smugly.

After Beecher hung up, he remembered he hadn't eaten in nearly twenty-four hours, but there was no time for the dining room. He called room service from the phone in the enormous marble bath as he undressed to shower. "Can you bring it pronto, please? I must leave soon."

"We assure you, Signor Hornbeck, *subito*." The Italians are so quick to promise what is demanded of them, and they do it, all the while, with tongue in cheek.

The shower revived him and as he stood in front of the mirror and shaved, he thought of Myra. She was so beautiful and had changed so little. She was wearing her hair slightly different now, a little longer. One could be mistaken perhaps by a close facial resemblance, but everything about her was the same; her figure, the slant of her shoulders, the gesture as she turned, all so familiar. There was a dull ache in his chest. After these long years, he was to have her back again in his life?

Would she think he had changed? He studied himself in the mirror, something he seldom had time or inclination for. There were fine lines at the corners of his eyes and mouth that weren't there five years ago. His hair was a little darker than straw and still thick, hardly touched with gray, and he didn't have a paunch to be ashamed of. Myra had often teased him about having a farmer's tan. He had no patience for lying around in the sun, "like some damn gigolo," so his arms and face were always darker than the rest of him.

"Why do you have to get so belligerent, darling? I love you the way you are. You have always reminded me of the gamekeeper in *Lady Chatterly's Lover*."

"That's quaint Myra—real cute. So you married a farmer. Don't rub it in." At the time of the discussion, they had been married a year. It couldn't even be called a quarrel, but they never missed a chance to make up. He left his painting a lot in those days.

After one such interruption he had asked Myra, "Do you know what Deuteronomy 24:5 says?"

"No, you tell me. But I hope you're not going to hit me with Conner's favorite, about the honeycomb and the lips of the bad woman being sharp as a two-edged sword."

"I think you've got two texts mixed up there, Honey. Deuteronomy 24:5 says, 'When a man hath taken a new wife, he shall not go to war, neither shall he be charged with any business, but he shall be free at home one year and shall cheer up his wife whom he hath taken!'

"You do a good job of that, cheering up the wife whom you hath taken. That's another thing I love about you. You're such a Bible scholar."

"I should know some Scripture. Sara took me to church whenever the bell rang."

"Why don't you write the senator from Indiana, Beecher, about a one year exemption for bridegrooms? I think it's a wonderful idea."

"Myra, I hardly think it would work. Ancient Israel was a theocracy. The Lord set up the rules. Unfortunately things have changed a little since then."

"Well, then you'll just have to keep cheering me up, as the Bible says, with or without the exemption." He remembered how Myra had laughed and reached up and pulled him down beside her on the couch.

So incredibly long ago, it all seemed now.

There was someone at the door. That would be room service, he hoped, and grabbed the large white terry robe furnished by the hotel. "*Un momento,*" he called, as he hastily wrapped it around him and hurried to answer the door.

The waiter trundled in the cart with silver domes covering the steak and eggs he had ordered, along with panettone and a large pot of coffee. When Beecher was really hungry, he reverted back to being a steak-and-potato man. The service had been fast, and he tipped the waiter handsomely.

He was famished and in a hurry to get dressed and go out to the bank, but he made an effort not to bolt the food. Changing a large sum of money might cause attention in the hotel, so he preferred to go to the bank on the Via Veneto, and reminded himself that he would need to take his passport in order to make the transaction. He must not forget that or the traveler's checks.

He dressed in a dark suit, instead of the casual clothes he had been wearing while sketching in Rome: bulky knit pull-over sweaters and corduroy slacks. It looked more natural for an American business man in a suit to be exchanging a thousand dollars for lire. It was important that he not attract attention. He didn't want to do anything to hinder the visit of the man he now thought of as "the seedy detective", if indeed he were a detective. Beecher didn't really care who he was, as long as he could tell him about Myra.

The visit to the bank proved to be as uneventful as he had hoped. No surprise shown, no questions asked. After all, Hornbeck, he told himself, What did you expect? You're in Rome, an international city, not Lake Woebegone, where the bank will only cash your forty-five dollar check if you agree to spend the money wisely.

He was back in his room by eleven forty-five. Nothing to do now but wait. He stood by the window and watched the crowd outside in the street growing larger. When he had gone out to exchange the money, there was a small gathering in front of the hotel. They were mostly young people. Some carried signs written in Italian. Beecher's Italian consisted largely of phrases like, "Where is the bathroom?" and "When does the train leave?"—though he was beginning to do quite well with menus—so he asked Luigi what was going on.

"They have nothing better to do than strike, *pigri!* These are kitchen workers from other hotels and are calling on our people to go out on strike with them. When I was their age, I went out in the middle of the night and gathered sticks to burn so my Mother and sisters would not freeze to death. It was the war. The Germans took all the food and Rome starved. So they have good jobs and they strike."

The age-old generation gap, thought Beecher, seems to vary little from country to country. Luigi continued, "Don't be concerned, Signore; they will quit soon and go to the beach." He shrugged and gave Beecher a cynical smile, "Strikes in Roma never last long when the weather is nice."

Now Beecher watched from his window with real concern. The crowd had grown much larger and was being exhorted by two young men who were standing on the hood of a car. There was shouting and shaking of fists. A bottle was hurled by someone in the crowd. Police were arriving.

This might keep the man from contacting him at the hotel, as planned. Of all times, thought Beecher, why did this have to happen now? On the other hand, the detective might consider the strike a perfect cover for getting in and out of the hotel unnoticed. The man had sounded genuinely afraid on the phone.

All I can do is wait, thought Beecher, and pray he shows up here, so I don't have to go to Hadrian's Villa and wander around the excavations for hours, maybe, until he decides it's safe to come out. I was nuts not to suggest someplace closer. The guy had probably seen too many American spy movies and wants to impress me with his expertise, real cloak and dagger stuff, Agent 007 creeping around the ruins. I just didn't think fast enough, wasn't half awake when he called.

The minutes dragged by, and Beecher had time to think. The fears and doubts of the night before lurked at the edges of his mind, as the imagined demons had lurked in the shadows of Trinitá dei Monti. He must exorcise them once again. The thought came to him that there was something about Myra's death that had eluded him. Was it a fact he had known at the time, but considered to be of no consequence?

It was past twelve-thirty and he was beginning to lose hope. He walked to the window again. Riot police were arriving. The street was blocked off, and the crowd looked ugly. Luigi had been wrong this time. The strikers had no intention of going to the beach.

Just as he decided that he must brace himself for another long wait and the trip to Hadrian's Villa, he heard a knock— one, a pause, then two.

The shot rang out immediately. At first Beecher thought it came from the street, then a feeling of despair came over him as he realized what had happened. The nightmare was closing in again.

8.

The rumpled suit was covered with blood, and the man who looked up at Beecher with glazed eyes was dying and he knew it. Beecher had thought at first that he was already dead. The bullet had caused a massive chest wound and had probably gone through the lung. The red stain had spread over his entire chest, and there was no pulse. Then Beecher caught a few faint erratic beats.

No one was in the corridor. He could pursue the killer, who had undoubtedly escaped through the exit at the end of the hall. It was only three flights down and by this time, he was sure to be mingling in the crowd outside the hotel, which afforded a perfect opportunity to escape. Or Beecher could try to find out what the detective knew about Myra, before it was too late. The decision only took a second to make.

The man's eyes were glazed, but Beecher was sure he could hear him. "Tell me about my wife."

"Your wife," he whispered. It was a bubbling, raspy sound, and blood appeared at the corner of his mouth. His eyes closed again, and there was no pulse.

"Oh God, please try to tell me. Where is she?"

His eyes fluttered again, and Beecher put his ear to the man's mouth. His voice was so faint, Beecher could hardly hear, "The truth—see Dino Romano," then another bubbly rattle and a final word that sounded like "Rose—". He was gone.

At that moment three *guardie* and two hotel employees came rushing up. The desk clerk reacted to the sight of the body with all the exaggerated horror of an actor in an old silent movie. One of the policemen pushed Beecher aside in his haste to examine the body, while a second entered Beecher's room and made an excited phone call, and a third asked Beecher's name and searched him for the weapon.

The policeman on the phone kept gesturing and glancing at Beecher all the while he was talking. There was blood on Beecher's suit and his hands, which he was allowed to wash . He was asked to show his passport and driver's license and was told to remain in his room until Superintendent Zinelli arrived.

The special squad arrived so soon, one would have thought that they were already in the hotel. Beecher had heard of these crack Italian police units. He never dreamed he would have the dubious pleasure of watching one in action. Most of the procedures were similar to those used by the Sparta police. One man dusted the outside of the door and the adjoining walls for fingerprints and then started on Beecher's room, while another examined the dead man and drew diagrams on the carpet in the corridor before he motioned for the medics with the stretcher to remove the body.

After the body was gone, Superintendent Ricardo Zinelli ushered Beecher back into the hotel room, put away his notes and introduced himself; he asked to see Beecher's passport. He sat down on the side of the bed, lit a cigarette, offered Beecher one and handed him back his passport, without comment.

"Please sit down, Mr. Hornbeck," Zinelli said, motioning to a chair, "I am acquainted with you, by reputation. I pride myself on keeping up with important cases abroad. You distinguished yourself when you tracked your wife's killers to the wild west."

"Not the wild west, actually." Beecher was careful not to show his amusement. Zinelli didn't know that the "Wild West" had become the Los Angeles freeway. "I tracked them to a remote mountain area in North Carolina, one of our southern states. I'm flattered that you would remember my name after five years."

"All in all, you have a distinguished reputation, I would say." His mouth smiled, but his expression remained hard.

"And you, Superintendent Zinelli, made the international news in the far more serious matter of the Red Brigade, in 1984. Our newspapers print stories of world interest too, especially those involving terrorism," answered Beecher.

"I understand you are also a painter, Mr. Hornbeck. Are you in Rome on business or pleasure?" Zinelli's cold eyes scanned the room for something he might have missed.

"Both, I have an exhibit at the Brazzano Gallery and am also on vacation."

"There are some questions I must ask you, but first of all, I am curious to know how an American, and a man of your reputation, could have become involved so soon after your arrival in Rome with a man like Luca Caserta?"

"He told me he was a private investigator," Beecher answered, trying not to sound like he was on trial.

"And you had need of his services?" Zinelli raised his eyebrows.

Touché, thought Beecher. This man was certainly no bumbler. Beecher tried to keep his hand steady as he lit his pipe.

"I have nothing to hide. I'll tell you the whole story of how and why I became involved with the man you call Luca Caserta, but first Superintendent, do you have any idea who might have killed him? He was afraid, and told me he was being followed. He sounded overly dramatic. I must confess, I really didn't believe he was in this kind of danger."

"Luca Caserta was a private investigator, of sorts, but he operated on the outer fringes of the underworld. He was involved with mobsters and known criminals and had collected blackmail from an important political figure. He played a dangerous game. Caserta had many enemies. As for who killed him, the possibilities are almost limitless. He had made a trip to Palermo recently, which I find highly significant. I'm afraid Luca Caserta had gotten into deep waters. We don't even have the murder weapon, but maybe what you have to tell us will furnish some clues. I have a few ideas of my own. Now, please continue with your story." The detective lit another cigarette and blew smoke toward the ceiling.

Beecher started at the beginning and told Zinelli about being followed by Caserta.

"If I may interrupt here, Mr. Hornbeck, I'd like to ask why, after you discovered you were being followed, you did not come to us immediately?" Zinelli slammed his pack of cigarettes down on the bedside table.

How could Beecher say that he had suspected Guido of having him followed? He certainly did not want Zinelli to know that he thought the old man might be involved. It seemed incredible that such a thing had even occurred to him. Just an example of how one suspicion breeds another, like deadly bacteria in a culture. "Caserta was such a bungler, I didn't take him seriously, a man who lets himself be seen three times. Really, Superintendent, how could I have guessed it would come to anything like this?" Beecher hoped this sounded convincing to Zinelli.

"Continue, Mr. Hornbeck." The icy stare again.

Beecher told the whole story; about being followed, seeing Myra on the Spanish Steps and being contacted the next morning by Luca Caserta, who demanded money for the information about Myra.

"Foolish, very foolish, Mr. Hornbeck. He was a con artist. We could have told you that. It's doubtful that he had any real information at all." A policeman looked in the door and Zinelli motioned him away impatiently.

"I still believe he did. After he finally contacted me, there was no time. I had to do everything I could to find out about my wife. I only had two hours. If I had called the police, he would never have come around."

"I am not naive enough to believe, Mr. Hornbeck, that because you were an honest man five years ago, or even yesterday, that you are necessarily one today. No, I have seen too much of the world for that. But I do believe your story. It would be a difficult one to fashion out of thin air, even for an Italian." The irony of this statement was not lost on Beecher. "You spoke of seeing your wife on the Spanish Steps; how could this be possible? You say you identified her body yourself. Weren't you certain at the time?"

Beecher was beginning to resent Zinelli's attitude.

"At the time I made the identification, yes, I guess so, but I have considerable doubt now," Beecher admitted.

"Why don't you have your wife's body exhumed and put your mind at rest, once and for all? A forensic expert could tell you for sure, even after this length of time"

"Myra was cremated," Beecher answered.

"I see. Cremation is not common in Italy, a Catholic country, you know. Surely it has occurred to you that Caserta could have planted a woman who resembled your wife on the Spanish Steps, planning that you would see her at a safe distance. In the crowds there, it is easy for one to disappear. Take it from me. I have lost several suspects on the Spanish Steps."

"He couldn't have known that I would be in the Piazza di Spagna. I didn't even know that I would be there half an hour before, so that is not a possibility. I can understand your doubts, Superintendent Zinelli, because I've had them all myself. This was my wife. I saw her distinctly twice. At first, I told myself that I had seen a woman that resembled Myra, but it was not only her face, but her figure, height, gesture; everything was familiar. I believe she's alive, and I intend to find her. I have no idea how, at this point, but I can assure you that it will be on the right side of the law."

"Did Caserta tell you anything before he died?" asked Zinelli.

"Nothing about the killer. I don't even think he saw who shot him. He did leave me with a few words about my wife, 'The truth—see Dino Romano,' and then, a single word that sounded like 'Rose'. There is no doubt in my mind that he was trying his best to tell me something. He knew he was dying and he had nothing to gain by lying. Have you any idea who Dino Romano is, Superintendent?"

"You've never heard of Dino Romano, the movie director? But I don't see the connection here, because he was killed in an automobile accident last year," the detective explained. The street below had grown quiet as they spoke. The police had sent the strikers away.

Zinelli hesitated, as though he were having second thoughts, and then added, "I wish I could help you in your search for your wife. I must say that I'm afraid you will fail. You should face the fact that your wife is dead and resume your own life. I have seen these cases before. If you persist in this, it could destroy your reason." For the first time, Beecher sensed real compassion in Zinelli's voice.

"Just promise me Superintendent, that if, in your investigation of Caserta's murder, anything at all comes to light linking him to Myra, you will let me know." It was a plea.

"Of course, Mr. Hornbeck. By the way, it is understood that you will remain here at the Excelsior, for the time being, in case I need to question you again. If you remember anything else about Caserta that might be of value, contact me. I will leave orders that your call is to be put through.

Zinelli put out his cigarette, pocketed the pack and stood up. "Thank you for your cooperation, Mr. Hornbeck. I regret that your visit to Rome has been interrupted by this Caserta incident. We of the Italian police make every effort to protect our country's guests from this type of unpleasantness. I suggest once more that you take my advice about dropping the search for your wife."

The Superintendent's "advice" sounded more like a

threat, to Beecher. He hoped Zinelli wasn't expecting his compliance, because he wasn't giving it.

Zinelli shook hands with Beecher, turned abruptly and headed for the door as the persistent policeman looked in again. The interrogation was over.

9.

Beecher, who usually drank spring water or a coke, sat alone at a small corner table in the Excelsior bar and decided that he needed something stronger. Myra, the romantic, had loved wine with dinner; Beecher could take it or leave it. He felt that the fact that his parents had been teetotalers had left its imprint on his tastes and habits as surely as their genes had on his features, something residual, bred in the bone, like the "Protestant Work Ethic", whatever that meant, that Myra was always harping on. He had become quite tired of all these glib phrases, oversimplifications of more complicated truths; his own definition of these expressions was "instant smarts".

Beecher's mind had wandered as he studied the wine list and when he realized that his waiter was becoming impatient, he decided to order the same Italian champagne that Guido had sent to his room that first night in Rome.

Looking at his watch, he realized that at this hour yesterday he had been sitting in the Church of Trinitá dei Monti asking himself whether he had seen Myra or an apparition. It seemed like days ago. His whole life had changed since then.

Luca Caserta was now dead, taking with him to the grave whatever knowledge he had of Myra. His legacy to Beecher consisted of seven words that were so ambiguous that they could hardly even be called clues. This morning's phone conversation with Caserta hadn't seemed important then, when he was planning to meet the detective and get the information which was presumably worth one million lire. Now it was all he had, that and the seven words.

Maybe he had overlooked something. Beecher passed quickly over the discussion about being followed, the Eden Hotel, Caserta being in danger and needing money to leave Rome. He remembered saying, "Get to the point," and Caserta had answered, "I was in the Piazza di Spagna yesterday and saw what you saw." That could only mean that Caserta knew Myra by sight. Then he had said, "Do you want to know the truth about your wife?" And there was something else—a name, Aldo. Caserta had mentioned information only he had, now that Aldo was dead. This Aldo must have known Myra too, or at least been privy to the information about her. Was it possible that Aldo originally had the information and gave it to Caserta before he died? But Aldo is dead, thought Beecher, along with Caserta and Romano.

He had to evolve some plan. He just couldn't wander around Rome, hoping to see her again. There must be records of American citizens living in Rome. Was she still Myra Wellington Hornbeck or did she have a new identity?

The account of Caserta's murder would be in the morning papers, and undoubtedly Beecher's name would be mentioned. The detective had been carrying a dog-eared, five-year-old clipping, an article about the bank robbery, Myra's death and the capture of the killers by Beecher and Harry.

He must explain to Guido and Cristina before they saw the papers—tell them the whole story. He had no choice. Even if Caserta's enemies were legion, how could Zinelli be so sure that Caserta's murder didn't have anything to do with Myra? However, Beecher had been impressed with

Zinelli.

Beecher watched the bubbles rise to the top of the tall fluted glass. The champagne was beginning to ease the ache in his shoulders and the stress he had been under from the minute Caserta had called him that morning till Zinelli and his squad had vacated his room an hour ago.

He slowly sipped his champagne and glanced around the bar. Beecher didn't recognize any of Guido's promised celebrities in the Excelsior bar, but the old man was right about this being the gathering place of the beautiful people. Dior, Ungaro and Pucci were well represented, along with Cartier and Bulgari. These were the people who skied at Gstaad and gambled at Monte Carlo, who had breakfast in London and dinner in Rome.

Suddenly Beecher felt very far from home. He wondered how Walter was making out on the farm and if Cassie missed him much. Walter had just gotten married several months before, and he and his young bride, Judy, were living with Hollis. Beecher didn't envy them. He could understand why Walter Franke was pleased and excited at the prospect of him and Judy staying in Beecher's house while he was in Rome. Walter had insisted that Beecher stay as long as he liked.

I don't blame those kids for wanting to get off by themselves for a little while, he thought. Hollis means well, but he's an old goat; he sends Walter to Purdue to study agriculture and then is too stubborn to let the boy put his ideas into practice on the farm. Control was the name of the game as far as Hollis was concerned, and he would keep a tight grip on the reins as long as he could.

"Be sure and give Cassie plenty of attention," Beecher had told Judy Franke, as he and Conner loaded his bags in the Bronco, and Cassie looked up at him with sad and reproachful eyes. "Cassie is not Mrs. Daily's favorite person." Cassie looked down at the ground.

"Beecher, I've never seen anything like it," Conner chuckled, "that dog understands every word you say."

"Please don't refer to her as that dog, Conner. That's

what Mrs. Daily calls her, or worse, 'the beast', in a tone of voice that implies she's something out of the book of Revelation."

Judy reached down and petted Cassie. "Don't worry about a thing, Beecher. We'll take good care of Cassie and the place."

Beecher had been touched when Judy asked him to send her a picture postcard from Rome, saying she would like the stamp for her collection. He would buy Judy something really nice. That night at Cristina's apartment, Beecher had mentioned that he wanted to take presents back to all of them. Cristina had offered to go shopping with him and help him select gifts.

Mrs. D. would be the difficult one to buy for, as she had a figure he wouldn't dare try to fit, and she might eye with suspicion anything coming from Rome, which "a body knew" ran a close second to Paris as the ultimate sin capital of the world.

Well, Rome would surely have something, even for Mrs. D., perhaps a soft Italian leather tote bag to replace her threadbare carpet bag, relic of the hippie era. He would look in the leather goods shops on the Via Condotti for something really enormous, with many inside and outside pockets, zippers and secret compartments. Yes, that would delight Mrs. Daily; and he would buy her a nice cameo brooch. He could see her wearing it now on her ample bosom and proclaiming proudly that it had been hand-made by a real Eye-talian! He found that he was even lonely for Mrs. Daily; her cobblers were almost as good as Sara's had been.

Beecher sipped his champagne and wondered if Walter had planted the north sixty in soy beans yet. He probably had, unless there had been too much rain. I'll call tomorrow and see how everything is at the farm, explain to Walter I'll be here longer than I expected. He must remember to tell Walter to breed Duchess to Hondo.

The dogwood would be in full bloom now, and the woods ablaze with redbud and carpeted with violets and bluebells.

The sophisticated sounds of the Excelsior bar receded into the background, and Beecher could hear the sound of the stream, swollen with spring rains, rushing through the old crumbling spring house. He loved to walk in the evening and listen to the croaking of the tree frogs, the darkness lit up by a thousand fireflies, and wake to the call of the same mocking bird that came back every year and made her nest in the Norway spruce that he and Myra had planted together.

For a few minutes he had forgotten about searching for Myra, about the murdered detective, Superintendent Zinelli and a hotel room in a foreign city. What would he give to be able to put his feet under his own table, to watch the University of Indiana play basketball on TV, to sleep in his own bed tonight?

"Hornbeck, two glasses of champagne and you're getting maudlin. It's time to adjourn to the dining room and order some food."

The waiter, who had heard Beecher muttering under his breath inquired, "Sir, may I bring you something else?"

"No, just the check, please."

Beecher returned to his room after dinner and tried to phone Guido at the villa, only to be told that he had not yet returned from Milan. He looked at his watch. It was a few minutes past ten. He would call Cristina at her apartment.

"How is the sketching coming?" Cristina asked cheerfully. "I said I wouldn't bother you, but I have wondered how you are getting along with your work."

"Cristina, I have something important to tell you, but it's impossible to discuss over the phone. I wanted to talk to you before you saw the morning papers. A seedy private investigator was murdered here at the hotel this afternoon—actually it happened right outside the door of my room. I warn you this is going to sound strange. He had been following me for several days and had come to the hotel to contact me. He claimed to have information about Myra."

"I don't understand," Cristina sounded stunned. "How could someone like that know anything about your wife that would be of interest to you? Myra died five years ago, and you told me yourself that she had never been to Italy, that she was excited about looking up her relatives, the Rose—", Cristina coughed and resumed, "the Rosettis, in Venice."

That interruption and cough came as a sudden revelation. He could hear Caserta whisper "Rose," then a gurgle, and when he repeated the word, it had come out "Rosie" and drifted off into nothing. Could he have been trying to say Rosetti? Beecher was certain that he had; it made sense. Now he had a real clue.

"Beecher, what's the matter? Are you there? I don't understand any of this. Do the police think you are implicated in this man's death? Where are you now? Have you been arrested?"

"Don't get alarmed, Cristina. I'm here in my room at the Excelsior. I'm not involved in the murder, at least not directly. What I'm trying to say is, I'm not a suspect."

"Well, I certainly hope not. Why didn't you tell me you were being followed? This is bizarre. Why would this man follow you?"

"Cristina, trust me, I can't explain it all to you tonight. It's complicated. Other things have happened too. I'm not a suspect, but my name will probably be in the morning papers in connection with Caserta's death. I just wanted to warn you. What should I do about Guido?"

"I'll call Milan and handle it, Beecher, don't worry. But when are you going to tell me the whole story?" she pleaded.

"In the morning. Whenever you can make it," answered Beecher.

"I'll have to go to the gallery early to take care of some things. It will take me several hours. Can I pick you up around ten? We'll drive to an old monastery in the hills outside Rome, a short distance beyond Castel Gandolfo. It's a beautiful drive and a nice place for a picnic, very quiet and secluded, a good place to talk. If we stay at my apartment, I'm apt to get frantic calls from the gallery."

"That sounds fine. This tension is getting to me," he sighed with exhaustion.

"Oh, Beecher, have you thought, if your name is in the morning papers, you may be besieged by reporters." There was concern in Cristina's voice. "What ever you do, don't talk to them. Roman reporters are possessed. You may find them dangling outside your window or trying to sneak in dressed as waiters from room service or maids. Leave the hotel very early in the morning; breakfast someplace else. I'll pick you up at ten at the Piazza Barberini. It's down the hill from your hotel and around the curve."

"I've already been there and done a drawing of the Fontana del Tritone," Beecher explained.

"Oh, please bring your sketches along. I'd love to see what you've been doing. In the morning then, at the Piazza Barberini. Until then, *buona notte,* Beecher."

10.

Vineyards covered the hillside in the distance, and here and there a brown-robed Capuchin monk could be seen tending the vines. The vinedresser: cultivating, clipping and pruning, so the vines might bear more fruit. There was something ancient and Biblical about the sight. As Beecher looked away from Cristina and studied the hillside, he felt a stinging behind his eyes. If there was any more pruning done in his life, he wasn't sure he would survive it.

He cleared his throat, "Well, that's the whole story, more or less." Now Cristina knew everything about the afternoon at the Piazza di Spagna and his terrible night of the soul in Trinitá dei Monte, about Caserta and Zinelli.

She was silent for what seemed to Beecher a long time. "I don't really know what to say."

"You agree with Zinelli, don't you, that I'm crazy?" Beecher asked defensively.

"No," of course not," she protested as she reached out and touched his arm.

"Well, say something." His voice was sharp. "If you're trying to decide how to be tactful with a client, forget it. Tell me what you really think."

"I was just wondering what I would do if I were in your place. If I believed I had seen Carlo, and then someone showed up who claimed Carlo was alive. All I ever saw of him, after the plane crash, was his wristwatch, inscribed to him from me. His name was on the passenger list, and the remains of his luggage were found scattered a hundred feet from the charred wreckage. You could call all that circumstantial evidence, couldn't you? I would feel just as you do, Beecher. I would have to try to find out if he were dead or alive." Tears glistened on her thick lashes as she studied the vineyards on the hillside.

Beecher felt ashamed. Somehow, he cared a lot what this woman thought, and he was the one who had judged, and too quickly. "I'm sorry, Cristina, that I spoke harshly." He took her small hand in his. "I guess I'm getting paranoid. I didn't trust Caserta, and rightly so, but you can see that he couldn't have staged what I saw, planting a phony Myra on the Spanish Steps, as Zinelli had suggested. *I* didn't even know I would be there. I had no plans, was just drifting around, making sketches.

"Then there are those vague, inconclusive feelings I've had since her death. The recurring idea that she would come back and finish that portrait in the studio. That's the real reason I left her palette and brushes there, the picture on the easel, with her smock hanging beside it. I couldn't bear the finality of taking it down.

"Conner says the sudden, violent nature of her death has given me this sense of unreality, combined with the shock of identifying her body that day at the morgue. He urged me to store the portrait away with her easel and paints. He thinks that I'm entertaining ghosts, that keeping her painting paraphernalia about is a symbol of the fact that I won't accept her death. He's always telling me that I need to get on with my life, that I should—."

Beecher caught himself before he said, "meet another woman." He felt uncomfortable and strangely self-conscious about saying those words to Cristina, and he was angry with himself. Apparently Cristina didn't notice any of this. She was silent and absorbed in her own thoughts.

That morning, Cristina had picked him up at the Piazza Barberini, as planned. As he opened the door and climbed into the red Lamborghini, he noticed a bunch of flowers on the seat, every color in the rainbow: yellow lilies, pink and red carnations, rose and fuchsia and violet snapdragons and deep purple statice.

"You brought me flowers," he laughed. "That's very flattering."

"Not for you, for Brother Giaccomo," she said as she merged into the traffic amid the blaring of horns and shrieks of other drivers. Cristina smiled at him. "You're not wearing your dark glasses. Any trouble with reporters?"

"None. Apparently I underestimated Zinelli. He kept my name out of the papers. I got up very early, as you suggested, and crept down the stairs and out the back entrance of the hotel, made it to the nearest newstand and bought copies of three papers. I was congratulating myself on my craftiness in eluding the reporters, only to discover my name wasn't mentioned in any of the articles. I don't read Italian all that well, but 'Hornbeck' looks the same in any language." Beecher laughed as umbrella pines whizzed past the car window. Cristina was a fast driver.

"I can tell you, it was a great load off my mind, I went back to the hotel, which I entered by the front door; after breakfast I called Zinelli to thank him. He said he took care to keep my name out. It pays to give out as little information as possible, keeps the criminals guessing. He has some promising leads."

"I didn't have time to read the papers. I've been rushing like mad in order to pick you up on time, envisioning you being pursued by a mad horde. I knew you'd brief me. So—."

At that moment, Beecher saw disaster looming up ahead in the form of a flock of sheep, crossing the road. Cristina braked just in time, as Beecher braced himself to keep from hitting the windshield. The frightened sheep bleated as the old shepherd shook his stick at the red Lamborghini and shouted in Italian.

Cristina made an apologetic gesture which did not appease him in the least. She drove on and turned to Beecher, laughing. "I'd interpret, but you really wouldn't care to hear what he's saying about us."

"Cristina, if you don't mind, I'd rather wait until we get there," Beecher said, trying not to sound uneasy. "Driving through this traffic is bound to be a distraction. This is a bizarre story,as I told you before. Let's wait."

"Sure, I've waited all night. I can wait a little longer." The drive to the monastery was interesting for Beecher. They had driven through the quaint medieval village of Castel Gandolfo. Cristina pointed out the Baroque papal palace, a building that had been designed by the same architect as St. Peter's Basilica.

"In another month, this village will be crowded with tourists and pilgrims. Il Papa comes here in June and usually stays till September. During a mass audience, that courtyard is crammed with people, like sardines in a can. He steps out on the balcony, you can see it there," she pointed, "and blesses the people, repeating his message in French, German, Spanish and English."

Cristina showed Beecher the charming town square, with its sidewalk cafes and the beautiful little domed cathedral designed by Bernini. "Someday when we have more time, we'll come back and see the inside." The red Lamborghini crawled through the narrow hilly streets. They left Castel Gandolfo behind and continued on for several miles along a narrow, dusty road.

"These vineyards produce fine grapes. Some really good white wines are made in the area; that's one of the main industries at the monastery. It's Capuchin, a branch of the Franciscan order. I wanted to bring you here because it's such a special place. Tourists haven't discovered it. I hope they never do. The grounds are lovely, so peaceful and remote. I used to bring Guido here to see his old friend, Brother Giaccomo, who had been, of all things, a very successful art dealer in Florence. He just realized one day that he was bored and tired of it all and decided that he would rather store up treasure in Heaven. He sold the gallery, gave the money to the order, and entered as a lay brother. He died last year. He was a saintly old fellow, worked in the kitchen all those years, among the pots and pans." Cristina smiled as she reminisced about this old man whom she had obviously loved. They were driving now on an incredibly steep and winding road.

"Guido could never understand Brother Giaccomo's decision to enter the monastic life, but he valued his friendship and persisted in bringing his old friend Cuban cigars. Brother Giaccomo would accept only one, and they would sit and smoke and visit. I used to just walk around and feast on the beauty of the place or sit and read. The monastery grounds have always been one of my favorite places." Cristina said. "I can understand Brother Giaccomo's decision."

After they arrived, Cristina placed the flowers on Brother Giaccomo's grave in the little cemetery beside the old Gothic chapel. "He loved flowers so much. He worked in the gardens in his free time. It probably took the place of art in his life."

Now Cristina and Beecher sat in silence on an old stone bench in the grove of umbrella pines and acacia trees, a short distance from the monastery, which resembled a medieval castle.

The sky overhead was a brilliant blue and the sun was quite hot for the middle of May, but the grass was not as green as it would be at home by now, Beecher thought. The gently rolling hills, terraced and covered with vine-yards, enclosed the monastery grounds like two cupped hands holding the offering of these holy men up to God. There was a spirit of peace here, almost as if the rules of time and space had been suspended.

Beecher never dreamed that Cristina would relate what had happened to him to herself and Carlo. He had been too obsessed with his own problems to even consider her situation. "You really didn't expect me to understand, did you?" He could feel her withdrawing from him, just as she had done that day in the Borghese Gardens, but he couldn't lie to her.

"Can you forgive me? Grief is a terribly self-centered emotion." He reached for her hand. "Your believing I really saw Myra is a gift. Zinelli didn't believe me, and I was sure nobody else would. Please forgive me. I should have known you would understand."

She didn't withdraw her hand, nor did she answer right away, but sat beside him in silence, looking down.

"How do you plan to go about trying to find Myra? Have you faced the fact that if she is alive, she might not want to be found? Do you think you can handle that?"

"I've thought about that possibility. It was a terrible experience, like demons drawing me down into the pit, but I trust Myra. There has to be some explanation. I'll take my chances. If I didn't try to find her, the idea that she's alive would haunt me till my dying day."

"Yes, that's the way I'd feel. I'd have to know, one way or the other. Beecher, I want to help you if there's any way I can."

"You've helped me already, more than you'll ever know, just by believing me.

"There's one thing I haven't told you, Cristina; during our conversation on the phone last night, I realized that Caserta may have been trying to say 'Rosetti' instead of 'Rose'. It's a possibility; it involves going to Venice, but first there are some things I have to find out in Rome. Do you know anything about the film director, Dino Romano?"

"Only what everyone else knows. He was one of Italy's top directors, although not as well known abroad as some of the others: Fellini, De Sica, De Laurentiis. His heyday was in the sixties and seventies, but he made good movies until the time of his death in an automobile accident last year."

"If I could only find some connection between Romano and Caserta." Beecher said. "Then there's Aldo."

"Cristina, are there ways to check on aliens living in Italy. Work permits, that sort of thing?"

"Guido would know. He'll get started on it as soon as he hears what's happened, you can be sure of that. Nothing makes Guido happier than tracking someone or something down." Cristina chuckled as she reached down to brush an insect off her skirt.

"When Guido returns from Milan, I'll tell him everything you've told me. Guido is like an octopus with a thousand tentacles reaching all over Rome—and Italy for that matter. He loves intrigue.

"By the way," Cristina continued. "I didn't talk to Guido this morning, but to Edoardo, stressing the fact that you are not a suspect. Edoardo handled it well, I'm sure. Guido is due back late this afternoon. I'll see him at the Villa tonight. Do I have your permission to tell him the whole story?"

"I want you to," Beecher said.

"I'd insist you come to the Villa tonight and tell him yourself, but he'll be tired after his trip to Milan. Edoardo and I try to protect him from too much excitement. Sometimes it's very difficult. He'd stay up half the night talking to you."

"Have you forgotten our lunch?" Beecher pointed to the picnic basket sitting in the shade at their feet as he realized how hungry he was.

"I guess I did," Cristina exclaimed. "Who thinks of food when they're listening to a story like yours? Now that you mention it, I'm starved." She opened the basket. "I just grabbed what I had on hand: sausages, cheese, bread, some pears and a bottle of wine. Is that OK?"

"Wonderful. I hate to impose on you so much," Beecher said.

She had been putting sausages and cheese between thick slices of Italian bread, and she looked up at him with an expression both direct and secretive. Her face was flushed from the sun and her coppery hair escaping, as usual, from the ivory combs. "Beecher Hornbeck, you

really are a nice man. I can't see you imposing on anyone."
She laughed. "Don't look so miserable. What did I say
now?" She handed him a fat sandwich on a large linen
napkin.

"Nothing. I just never learned to accept a compliment
graciously, I guess. When I was growing up, there was no
lack of love, but Sara seldom gave compliments and Dad,
never. I'm not good at giving them, and pretty uncomfortable receiving them. I'm sure it's a flaw in my character,
along with the Protestant work ethic and a tendency
toward an austerity that's not too popular in these days of
conspicious consumption—all part of my legacy. Sara and
Silas Hornbeck resembled—just a little—the couple in
Grant Wood's painting, *American Gothic.*

Cristina smiled. "I'm familiar with the work."

"What I'm trying to say, Cristina, is that being made of
stern stuff has its drawbacks. It's sometimes hard for other
people to live with. I'm sure Myra found it so. She was a
person of extreme moods. Sometimes I wonder if life with
me just got too hard for her to take, and she pulled out.
There. It's out in the open," Beecher said. "I've said it out
loud." Beecher didn't know what it was about this woman
that invited confidences. Cristina certainly wasn't inquisitive
or pushy. Maybe that was it.

"You're being too hard on yourself," Cristina said.
"From what you told me about your relationship, I'll never
believe that Myra wanted to leave you."

"You said, yourself, Cristina, when you were telling me
why you loved Italy and the Italians, that you were sick to
death of stiff upper lips."

"But we're talking about individuals now, not stereo-
types. Besides, Beecher, on you the stiff upper lip looks
good."

He laughed. "I'm assuming that's a compliment. You
can't blame me for having doubts about Myra's death.
There are too many unanswered questions."

"Let's not think about it now. I'll talk to Guido tonight
and ask Edoardo what he knows about Dino Romano.

Edoardo prides himself in knowing all about the Italian movie industry—having been an extra and all—and he's the same vintage as Romano."

She handed him a glass of wine and held her glass up to his. "Now let's eat our lunch and drink to the beauty that's all around us and to today. That's really all we have."

Their glasses touched, "I'm sorry I—."

She interrupted him, "Just relax and eat your sandwich."

Cristina broke off small pieces of bread and tossed them to the ground squirrels, just as Myra had fed the gulls at their first picnic by the sea, all those years ago.

11.

Guido Brazzano went into immediate action on behalf of his American friend. Beecher witnessed at first hand, the Italian version of the old boy network in action.

Guido had turned nepotism into an art form; when operating in this area, he made Huey Long look like a rank amateur. Beecher thought it highly appropriate that the word had been derived from the Italian *nepotismo*.

But when the dust had settled, after "secret" files had been delved into by nephews of cousins, cousins of nephews and friends of friends, Beecher had to accept the fact that the Italian government had no record of Myra Wellington Hornbeck, and as far as official Italy was concerned, no one bearing that name or description had even landed on her shores. Guido was as disappointed as Beecher. He could not believe that his Machiavellian machinations had produced nothing.

Meanwhile, Beecher, investigating on his own, had discovered who Aldo was and had established a tenuous link between Aldo and Dino Romano. Inspector Zinelli gave Beecher the address of Luca Caserta's apartment and a talk with the building's concierge revealed that the detective had shared the shabby apartment with Aldo Gianotti until the time of Gianotti's death four years before. The woman was difficult to understand; she spoke broken English interspersed with Italian.   She did know that Gianotti had a sister, Anna, who managed a glove shop near the Trevi Fountain. She had come often to see him when he was ill; laden with food, taking home his dirty laundry and bringing it back freshly ironed, picking up his medicine at the *farmacía*. Aldo's last weeks had been spent in the hospital. He had died of lung cancer. The elderly woman grasped her chest and looked toward the heavens, as though she expected to see some sign of him there.

Beecher expressed his thanks tangibly, in lira, and wrote down the name of the sister, Anna Leone, and the address of the glove shop. He was glad to leave this ancient building; its walls oozed moisture and the dank hallway was permeated with the odor of stale olive oil and perspiration. The place depressed Beecher and reminded him vividly of Luca Caserta, that sad, rumpled little man.

The next day Beecher was on his way to see Aldo's sister at the shop on the Via del Tritone, when an excited crowd gathered around the Trevi Fountain attracted his attention. He stopped to watch and asked another passerby what the demonstration was about. The fashionably dressed young Italian wore a dark suit nipped in at the waist, a silk shirt with heavy gold cufflinks and a silk paisley tie and carried an expensive looking leather briefcase. He laughed, "No Signore. It is not a strike." He took hold of Beecher's sleeve and pointed through a gap in the crowd. A group of young men, all nude, were leaping and splashing in the fountain. At first glance, it appeared that the statues had come to life. The healthy young bodies were as virile and beautiful as Bernini's sculptures. "Our Roman soccer team has just won a great victory over the West Germans, Signore."

Two policemen stood at the edge of the crowd, laughing and chatting, making no attempt to break up the happy celebration.

Cristina was right. This city did have a way of getting under one's skin. For the past few days, Beecher had been blind to all of Rome's beauty and color. He had moved in a world of dull greys, where he could only remember Caserta's dead face and think of searching for Myra. Something tense inside of him started to relax a little as he watched the exuberant young athletes and the cheering Roman crowd, and he was reminded that there were still happy people in the world, and he was glad.

He turned away and walked down the Via del Tritone. He must find Aldo Gianotti's sister. Maybe she would be able to supply him with some important answers.

When Beecher entered the shop, he had no trouble recognizing Anna Leone from Signora Popolo's description. Aldo Gianotti's sister was probably in her early fifties. Her black hair was worn in a youthful pageboy with bangs and framed a face that had once been beautiful and was still arresting. She dressed with the simple Italian chic of women who knew how to display their assets and hide their liabilities. She wore a plain, smartly cut dark dress, fashionable jewelry and a bright silk scarf.

Beecher bought several pairs of leather gloves for friends back home—the woman tried them on for him, smoothing them down on her slim fingers and small delicate wrists to help him decide about sizes—and an umbrella for himself. Then he broached the subject that was on his mind.

Anna Leone was suspicious and fearful at first. After all, her brother's friend, Caserta, had been murdered. Beecher showed her his passport and urged her to call Guido Brazzano at the gallery. After the call, she became calmer, and Beecher told her only as much as he needed to about Caserta and seeing Myra on the Spanish Steps.

"Caserta told me the day he was murdered that he had information about my wife that only he knew, now that Aldo was dead. Those were his exact words, Signora Leone, so you can see how important it is that you tell me anything you know, anything your brother ever said to you about Myra."

"I'm sorry, but I can't help you. Aldo never mentioned anyone named Myra. He wasn't acquainted with any Americans." She was afraid, and there was another emotion underneath the fear that he couldn't quite put his finger on. He was sure she was lying.

"Did your brother know Dino Romano?"

Now she seemed to relax and was willing to talk, almost as if she were trying to make it up to him for something else. Beecher could see that Dino Romano was a safe topic for her. She told Beecher that her brother had once had a promising career as an actor. In the late 1960s the director, Dino Romano, had discovered him and given him his first part in the Italian version of *The Three Musketeers*. After that, Romano had used him regularly, in several films. He had played in *Intervallo* and *Il Castello Nero,* both fine films. "I don't suppose you would have heard of them. They were shown only in Italy. Romano gave my brother small parts," Aldo's sister continued, "but he kept promising Aldo romantic leads. Aldo trusted Romano and was grateful to him for giving him his start. He turned down work from other studios. The big role was always just around the corner. My brother was *un bel uomo* then." She produced a photo from her wallet. It was worn and faded, but the smiling young man in the eighteenth-century costume was indeed handsome. He looked very much like his sister. The picture had been taken on a film set. There were other costumed actors and a camera in the background.

"After about eight years, Romano suddenly quit using Aldo in films—just dropped him without any explanation. It was a terrible blow to my brother. His career seemed to be, as you say, jinxed, after that. He got some small insignificant parts in bad movies and then after a few years—nothing. He drank a lot and put on weight. Aldo couldn't accept the fact that his film career was over. I gave him money, from time to time, until my husband became angry. Aldo had made a great deal of money in those good years, but had spent it all on *la dolce vita*: women, cars, entertaining his friends, expensive clothes. Now he had nothing and was forced to take a job selling shoes in a cheap shop. You saw the disgusting place he shared with Luca Caserta.

"He never gave up hope that he would be able to break into films again, playing character parts. Romano wouldn't even receive his phone calls. I'll always believe that Romano was at least partly responsible for my brother's death. Aldo was only fifty-two when he died," Anna Leone said bitterly.

"I'm sorry Signora Leone," Beecher said. "I can see that you loved your brother very much. I too love my wife. Are you absolutely positive that you brother never mentioned the name of Myra?"

She looked away and started replacing gloves in the case. "I'm sorry, I've already told you, I've never heard of the person you are looking for." She turned abruptly. "*Mi scusa, Signore*, I have other business to take care of."

"If you remember anything you might wish to tell me, you can reach me at the Excelsior or through the Brazzano Gallery."

Beecher left the shop and hailed a taxi on the Via del Tritone. He was too tired and dispirited to walk back to his hotel. Tonight he was to dine with Guido at the Villa Brazzano. With luck, he would have time for a short rest when he got back to the hotel.

Well, it wasn't a complete dead end, he thought, as he looked out the window of the taxi. At least he had established a link between Aldo Gianotti and Dino Romano. He couldn't see that it was of much value, but one never knew.

12.

The sun was just setting when the ornate wrought iron gate of Villa Brazzano was opened by a young uniformed gateman, and Edoardo swung the Lancia into a drive that was guarded on both sides by rows of tall, stately black cypresses. The drive wound like a silver ribbon between the dark trees; their thin conical shapes lent a surrealistic quality to the landscape. Beecher felt as though he had entered a time tunnel and that when he emerged at the end of it, he would find himself in some other realm. After they had driven about a quarter of a mile, the trees opened and he could see the villa up ahead, resting like a jewel on a dark green velvet tray. The setting sun shone on its marble facade, tinging it with pink and turning the windows into mother of pearl.

The Villa Brazzano was a splendid example of Baroque architecture. There was a central portico with perfectly proportioned wings reaching out on each side. A wide terrace sloped down to the lawns, which were of formal design. Images of the tall cypress trees floated in the twin reflecting pools, and flower beds that had been laid out with geometric precision were ablaze with color. Marble statues viewed this stunning scene with the aloof, serene expression of the Roman classical period.

At dinner, Beecher remarked that he was surprised to see so many formal gardens in Italy. "This formality in design seems to be in such sharp contrast to the Italian temperament which is spontaneous and relaxed. Can you explain this to me, Guido?"

Guido and Beecher sat with Cristina and Pietro Reni in the gilded dining salon under a heavenly blue ceiling, painted with cavorting cupids and cherubs, pink feathery clouds and languid virgins. Venetian glass wall sconces illuminated Guido's treasures: a Rembrandt sketch, a small Goya and a Monet landscape.

The soup plates had been removed and the main course served. The food was prepared to perfection. Evidently there had been no crisis in the Brazzano kitchen tonight.

Guido sipped his wine slowly, with the deep appreciation of a man who knows that he is partaking of forbidden fruit. He leaned back in his chair and addressed himself to Beecher's question.

"We are a complicated people, and like most old civilizations, we have grown cynical and disillusioned. America is a young country, and you Americans are still idealistic enough to be shocked by your Watergates and your Contra scandals. We are not. It is not necessarily that Italians are more corrupt, but that we have learned to expect less of human nature. Italians appear lighthearted and gay to outsiders, always laughing and singing, eating and drinking. This impression is not insincere, but it is merely what is to be seen on the surface. Underneath, we know only too well that human beings are frail, and that life is full of disaster and troubles that man can do very little about." Guido shuddered as though a cold wind had blown through the elegant dining room.

"So we determine that during the little time we have on this earth, we will cherish beauty and make life good for ourselves and others in small ways: a good meal, a glass of wine, a beautiful aria—not profound, perhaps, but comforting. We are not too hard on ourself or others. We leave judgment to the gods." Guido's old face broke into a sad smile. "And out of the chaos of the universe, we fashion formal gardens, to fight back our fears that we are not really in control, and to make our little world more ordered and serene. Do you understand, my friend?"

Beecher nodded. This old man was always surprising him with his wisdom. "I understand, Guido. We all do the same thing in our own way."

While Cristina, Guido and Reni discussed gallery business, Beecher studied the Monet, which graced the opposite wall. One servant was serving a custard-filled puff pastry with chocolate sauce, called *profiterole*, while another poured champagne.

Cristina sat at the foot of the table. She wore a simple black dress with pearls that had an emerald clasp and emerald pendant earrings, her wedding gift from Guido. Everything she wore seemed to accentuate her beauty and the intense, vibrant color of her hair. Beecher felt disturbed, because he was so intensely aware of her beauty. Why should these feelings come to him unbidden, especially now that he believed Myra was alive? It didn't make any sense. He was angry with himself.

Guido's art collection was all that he had promised. Pietro Reni left immediately after dinner, and Guido took his American friend on a tour of the villa, leaning heavily on Beecher's arm and pointing out each of his "little jewels".

They returned to the library and Guido ordered espresso brought in. The two men talked until very late about painting. Cristina had fallen asleep, curled up in an oversized velvet chair with a haughty old cat named Fortunio in her lap. She looked like a child dressed for a party who had stayed up past her bedtime.

"All that you have seen tonight, the land, this villa, has been in my family for generations," said Guido, gesturing expansively, "ever since my ancestor, Cossimo Brazzano, the first Duke of Frascati, built it. But the fortune I have made with my own hands has restored it to its former magnificence. The Brazzano fortunes had been in a decline since the turn of the century. I will not go into all the reasons; some were political and historical, some personal, but in the 1930s—the great depression was worldwide, Beecher. You Americans think it only affected you—the villa was in a terrible state of disrepair. My family had to let many of their servants go. Plaster was falling from the walls, valuable furnishings had been sold, the della Robbia carvings in the grand salon had been replaced with cheap plaster copies. The family Brazzano occupied only a few rooms of this palace *enorme*, like 'squatters' on our own land. You see, my friend, I do know some of your American slang."

Guido chuckled. Beecher had noticed, but Guido's repertoire of American slang dated back about thirty years.

"During the German occupation of World War II," Guido held up his hand, "I know, my friend, you are about to say that we were their allies. This was true, technically, but not in reality. The German army overran my country, like a swarm of locusts. They ate well, while we starved; they looted our country. The Germans stole art treasures that had been in the Brazzano family for generations from this villa. My little Botticelli, I myself tracked to Berlin.

"During the war, my father burned many of the gilded chairs from the grand salon in the fireplace to keep from freezing to death. I was in the army. When I came home and saw what had happened to this place, I wept. 'What good are golden chairs, my son, to one who is dead?' my Father asked sadly. 'Your Mother was ill. What was I to do?' There are only three of those chairs left, the ones you saw tonight in the dining room.

"I've been a blessed man, Beecher. I have realized many of my dreams: to establish the Brazzano Gallery, then to open the branches in London and Paris, to set up the Maria Brazzano Art Scholarships all over Italy, to restore my family's home; I have seen them all come to pass. But often I still grieve for my dear Carlo. I will never see him take over the Brazzano Gallery, which was my fondest dream. None of my older sons are interested in art. But my Carlo left me this little one." His tired old eyes rested lovingly on the sleeping Cristina. "Five sons, and now God has given me, in my old age, this little daughter."

"Few people have had your gift for nurturing talent in others, Guido. You have used that gift to the full, in spite of personal tragedy that would have embittered lesser men," Beecher said.

"I have lived long, my son. These tired old eyes have seen much of life, of art, of love, of death—." Guido uttered a sigh that was filled with unspeakable pathos and melancholy, but when Beecher translated it from the Italian, he found it to be a sound of pure happiness.

Edoardo, who had been lurking about the hall for some time and had already made one foray into the room, made another attempt to escort the obviously weary Guido off to bed.

"Despoiler of my evenings, leave me in peace," Guido said with a frown. He dismissed Edoardo with a wave of his hand. "I'll summon you when I am ready."

Beecher had seldom seen a man so often thwarted in trying to do his duty as the long-suffering Edoardo. No wonder the chauffeur had a harried look and was constantly popping antacids into his mouth. They were like two crafty old chess players, that knew each other's moves by heart. The employer-employee relationship had long since taken a back seat to a friendship both of them were too stubborn to acknowledge.

Beecher hated the idea that he had deprived Edoardo of the pleasures of showing him his statue at the Olympic Stadium and of driving him out to Cinecittá, scene of his past glories. Maybe after he found Myra there would still be time.

Beecher put his foot down firmly when his elderly friend recommended the Hotel Danieli, next to the Doges' Palace, as being pure luxury as well as the setting of "all the action" in Venice, a phrase old Guido considered to be both youthful and American.

"Sorry, Guido, not this time. I took you advice about the Excelsior and Caserta was murdered on my doorstep. I think a low profile is in order and besides, I'm just a poor struggling artist from the Midwest. I can't afford to hang out forever in the haunts of the beautiful people." Beecher didn't choose to go into his other reasons for staying at the Hotel Bellini. They were too personal.

Ever since that long-ago summer in Connecticut when they met in Leland Randolph's painting class, Myra and Beecher had wanted to stay at the Hotel Bellini if they ever went to Venice. Randolph sang the praises of the small hotel that was named for the Venetian painter, Giovanni Bellini, many of whose major works are housed in the Galleria dell´ Accademia in Venice. Randolph found Venice to be the highlight of his own grand tour and returned there often, always to stay at the Bellini in the same suite that had once been occupied by Richard Wagner. Possibly he hoped to make contact with Wagner's own personal Muse.

Randolph's stories were colorful, and Beecher and Myra decided then and there that if they ever went to Venice, they would stay at the Hotel Bellini, which was also the scene of Randolph's hinted-at "friendship" with the famous Eleonora Duse. It was all too romantic for Myra too resist.

It was the only hotel reservation they had made for their proposed painting trip. Beecher had sent a telegram to cancel after Myra's death and had, to his great surprise, received a letter of condolence from one Raphael Matteotti, the hotel's manager. The black-edged, heavy vellum paper bearing the Bellini's gold crest spoke of grandeur left over from a former era. Yes, Beecher decided, there was something Wagnerian about the Hotel Bellini on the Grand Canal.

The old art dealer stopped abruptly in the middle of a sentence praising the larger, more luxurious Danieli when he noticed the vague faraway look in Beecher's eyes. Guido had spent his life dealing with artists, and was quite used to them drifting off into their own little world right in the middle of a conversation. He brought Beecher back gently from a far country with the words, "Maestro, you are much too modest for an American. Almost all the pictures in your exhibit have now sold. Swanstrom's purchases exceeded my fondest hopes. I told you he would not be able to resist, did I not? You are not a starving artist, my friend. Thanks to Guido Brazzano you can afford to stay in whatever hotel you choose."

Beecher had been guilty again of assuming that other people could read his mind. How could Guido be expected to know of the high regard in which he held him, of his gratitude for the chance to show his work to Europe's elite, to sell his paintings for the highest prices he had received to date.

"Guido, forgive me. I've become so obsessed by my search for Myra that I've neglected to tell you how much I appreciate what you have done for me here in Rome. You are a modern-day Lorenzo di Medici, my patron in the international art world, and have opened doors that were closed to me before. I am in your debt and will always treasure the friendship you extended to me freely, over and above our professional relationship." The old man was obviously touched by Beecher's declaration.

"Guido, I'm tired, even if you are not," Beecher said. "We both need sleep; so does Edoardo. My dear friend, I must tell you tonight that I am leaving for Venice tomorrow, as soon as I can make arrangements."

Beecher continued before the agitated Guido could give him an argument. "My search for Myra has come to a dead end here in Rome. As you already know, Anna Leone claims that her brother never mentioned Myra to her. She may be telling the truth. The woman is so frightened because of Luca Caserta's murder, it's really hard to tell. I've established the relationship between Aldo and Romano, but it's not clear where that piece fits into the puzzle. I feel sure that when Caserta whispered the word 'Rose', as he died, he was trying to tell me to see the Rosettis, Myra's relatives in Venice. It's the best lead I have, but I've saved it till last, because I didn't want to miss anything here. You know how indebted I am to you for your help, in the matter of the official records, but unfortunately that led to another dead end. So now you can understand my sense of urgency in leaving for Venice."

"You must do what you must do, Beecher, but don't you think it's possible that you always come to dead ends because your wife is dead, that you saw an Italian woman who resembled your Myra? I understand what you have gone through. I too lost my beloved Maria."

"Possibly you are right, Guido. I think I'll know, one way or the other, when I get to Venice. Now call Edoardo. We all need to sleep and I must get an early start in the morning."

"Enough, my son." Guido patted Beecher on the arm as they stood in the doorway. "Godspeed. May you return soon to Rome."

13.

Dawn broke over the seven hills of Rome, much as it had since the days of Caesar. Beecher looked out the window of the speeding Lancia at umbrella pines, silhouetted against a sky that was changing from midnight blue to pearly grey, threaded with pink. Trees became giant mushrooms in a science fiction landscape, a glimpse of nature gone wild.

How blessed we are, he thought, that nature is most often predictable: summer follows spring and winter trails her hoary garments in the wake of autumn's exuberant fireworks, seed time and harvest always arriving in their proper order, the certainty that a peach tree will not bear apples or chicken eggs hatch out dragons. Beecher sometimes grew quite pessimistic about the ways that so called civilized man chose to use his intelligence and power. He prayed that the human race would draw back from the brink in time, before some cataclysm took place in the natural order. Future generations also had a right to see a pearly sunrise, a brilliant blue sky, a healthy forest.

Edoardo's running monologue on the cupidity of Dino Romano intruded itself on Beecher's errant thoughts about the problems of the universe.

"I called Ricardo Dante, an old actor friend. We worked together on the Romano film, *Il Disegno*, back in 1965. Ricardo remembered Aldo Gianotti, Signor Hornbeck. He said that Romano not only ruined Aldo's career, but that he took la bella Rosanna Perrone away from him. Aldo and Rosanna had a passionate affair before Romano lured her away with a starring role." The chauffeur's face, which Beecher could see in the rear view mirror, reflected ardent desire and then dark angry passion. Edoardo was no longer in the movies, but he would always be an actor.

"Romano cared for others only as long as he could use them. He sacrificed many careers to enrich his own. Aldo Gianotti's was one of them. Aldo was handsome then, Ricardo told me, loved by the ladies."

Beecher knew that something was eluding him. What if Aldo had not died of natural causes? Caserta had been murdered. Could they have both known too much about Myra? He was sure that Caserta was trying to tell him the truth, regardless of what Zinelli thought.

The high walls of the Vatican rose like a citadel on the right, and minutes later they were crossing the Tiber. Beecher stared with unseeing eyes at the panorama spread out before him—the old Roman wall and then the Borghese gardens. The Lancia started down the curving hill of the Via Veneto and Beecher could see the Excelsior ahead on the left—familiar and comforting. And now he must leave. If Rome couldn't give him the answers, he must seek them elsewhere.

After Edoardo left him, Beecher called the Hotel Bellini in Venice for a room reservation; next he phoned Alitalia and was lucky enough to get the last seat on a flight leaving da Vinci for the Marco Polo Airport in Venice at three o'clock that afternoon.

After a delay, the operator was able to put through his transatlantic call to Walter Franke at the farm. He hated to wake Walter at one A.M., even though Hollis had done it to him often enough. Walter assured Beecher in his cheery, energetic Indiana accent that all was well at home. Beecher could hear Judy's sleepy voice in the background, as she searched for a pencil and paper, so Walter could take down Beecher's address in Venice. "If you should loose that address, Walter, or call and I've checked out, you can always reach me through the Brazzano Gallery, here in Rome. They will know where to locate me in case of emergency."

"Don't worry about things back here. Cassie has taken up with Judy and follows her around like her shadow. The crops are in, and you have three new calves, two heifers and a little bull. Judy loves him. She named him Otto." A brief news report from that peaceful, bucolic world that seemed so far away.

"This is like a second honeymoon for Judy and me, Beecher— staying at your place. Judy says she's in the lap of luxury, with Mrs. Daily coming in to clean every week. We've even been having dinner by candlelight at seven in the evening. Dad always insists that Judy have the food on the table by five! I guess the old boy's pretty miserable over there eating TV dinners, but it won't hurt him for a little while longer," Walter chuckled. "He'll appreciate Judy more when we get back."

Beecher let Walter assume that sightseeing was his reason for staying on longer in Italy; he certainly wasn't going to mention Myra.

The course of future events frequently rests on a very slender thread: a chance encounter, a wrong decision in composing a resume, the happy choice of just the right picture sent to a prestigious exhibit, a plane missed by five minutes, a phone call considered, but not made.

Beecher lifted the receiver to make one last call and, changing his mind, put it down again. He had gone to the phone a dozen times during these past days since he had seen Myra and received those few rasping, dying words from Caserta, with the intention of calling Harry. He longed to tell her that he believed Myra was alive, and that he was searching for her. Now that he was going to Venice, he could use Harry's help.

After all, Harry was related to the Rosettis, just as Myra had been. They were both descendants of Alessandro. Beecher hoped the passing years had diluted the hatred and resentment that Myra claimed the Rosetti family had felt for the Wellingtons and Hartleys after Alessandro's death, almost to the point of swearing a vendetta. Remembering all this, Beecher decided maybe he would be received more cordially than Harry, a hated Hartley.

Myra had been optimistic about approaching the Rosettis, but then that was a different story. Myra not only had winning ways that made her hard to resist, but she was the image of the long departed Alessandro. Myra had shown Beecher the gold locket that had been Lavinia's. It had been Alessandro's wedding present to her, a piece that had been in the Rosetti family for many years. The smiling, dark-haired young man with the flashing eyes could have been Myra's twin. "I'm counting on that resemblence, Beecher, to get my foot in the door," Myra had said.

"Then, I can win the old girl over, I'm confident. I want so much to know my Italian relatives. They're as much a part of me as the Hartleys and Wellingtons—maybe more. It's time the rift was healed, and it's up to me to do it. Besides, I have another reason—a more important one."

Beecher had been curious, but Myra had remained mysterious, answering that some day he would know.

It was a week before they were to leave on their trip abroad when Myra had shown Beecher Lavinia's locket and the slip of paper with the name and address of the last descendent of Alessandro's, a Countess Teresa Bonciani Rosetti, who as far as the Hartleys knew, still lived in the family palazzo on one of the smaller canals, the Rio del Giglio, in Venice.

Beecher had planned to look up the Countess Rosetti because it had been one of Myra's last wishes. He looked in his wallet now, standing in his room in the Excelsior, to reassure himself that the paper was still there. The creases were almost worn through, but Myra's bold, slanting hand looked the same as the day she had written down the information five years before.

He never dreamed when he came to Rome that the slip of paper would become so important. Now it was a matter of life and death to him—Myra's life and maybe even his own. Five years ago Myra had calculated the Countess's age at between seventy-nine and eighty-two. He prayed that Teresa Rosetti was still alive. If she had died in the last five years, that left only one distant Rosetti cousin whose whereabouts was unknown.

Beecher was becoming superstitious about dead ends and dead witnesses: first Caserta, then Aldo, and finally Romano. All three had been much younger than the ancient Contessa Teresa.

Beecher took out his tobacco pouch and filled his pipe, tamping the tobacco down firmly. He lit it carefully with one of the small matches with wax coated paper stems that the hotel so grudgingly provided. In Italy, matches were very dear—his mother's word for any scarce item. Beecher took a deep puff. The aromatic smoke rose around him, wrapping him for a moment in the almost forgotten comfort of the familiar. The pipe was a reassuring little ritual, not only in moments of reflection, but in times of stress and loneliness as well. Beecher sighed deeply. He would simply have to go to Venice and hope for the best.

He decided he had no right to call Harry. It was a final decision and he would not entertain the idea again. It would be cruel to raise her hopes, and William's, before he actually found Myra. What if he were as mistaken as Zinelli and Guido thought, or that darker possibility, that Myra had evolved an elaborate plan to disappear? This would be as damning a rejection of Harry and William as it was of him. If he did find her and this were true, he would never tell them as long as he lived.

As he turned away from the phone and resumed his packing, Beecher had suddenly remembered Superintendent Zinelli's request—order—that he remain at the hotel, where he could be reached for further questioning.

"Damn, that's the first thing I should have done," Beecher muttered, angry with himself. He threw a handful of socks in the suitcase and started searching for Zinelli's number. Beecher wasn't accustomed to getting permission from the police before he left town.

Zinelli was quite reasonable and asked only for the name of his hotel in Venice in case he needed to reach him. The Superintendent was about to crack the Caserta case and make an arrest. He was certain the evidence he had would hold up in court. Zinelli implied that he had a secret witness up his sleeve; he wasn't free to go into details, but he was confident that Caserta was murdered by a hit-man from Palermo. He needed only one additional piece of evidence against the man who had hired the Sicilian before arresting them both.

"There is nothing connecting you, Mr. Hornbeck, with the murder, but I must add, that after a thorough investigation of Caserta's past, we found no hint that he knew your wife."

"Superintendent. that's why I'm going to Venice. I've come to a dead end here in Rome. I've established the relationship between Caserta and Aldo Gianotti and between Gianotti and Dino Romano, but I can't fit the pieces together. There's too much that's still missing. I hope to find the answers in Venice. Myra had a distant relative there, a Countess Teresa Rosetti who might know something. So you can see why I'm anxious to leave today."

"Good luck in your search. If you need me, don't hesitate to call, day or night."

"I may take you up on that, Superintendent. There's no way of knowing what I'll find in Venice."

Beecher resumed his packing in his own haphazard fashion. He found the job frustrating. Myra had always done his packing for him, just as she had coordinated his shirts, ties and socks. She had laughed one day at some combination he was wearing. It was early in their marriage. "Darling, with your artistic talent and eye for color, how can you wear that tie with a blue shirt and grey suit?"

He looked down at the tie as though he were surprised to see it hanging around his neck. "What's that got to do with it, Myra? I'm a painter, not a fop. Besides, I usually have other things on my mind when I'm dressing."

"So I see." She laughed again and mussed his hair as she helped him remove the offending tie. After that she started buying his ties and matching things up for him, to his great relief.

During these past days, memories of Myra had surfaced with increased regularity, encroaching on his consciousness until, at times, it seemed that he was living in two worlds. I must get ahold of myself, he thought, as he snapped the suitcase shut and checked the closet and bath one last time before calling the concierge to have his bags collected.

The red Lamborghini was caught in the mad exodus of midday traffic out of Rome, everyone retreating to the suburbs for a siesta while shops and businesses closed for three hours. Even with Cristina's considerable driving expertise, it was impossible to make any time in the bumper-to-bumper traffic.

No one seemed to think it was madness to go through this every day. Beecher, like most Americans, would never be able to understand the choas and inefficiency of such a system. These same people came roaring back into the city in a blue haze of exhaust fumes every afternoon at three or four o'clock, apparently refreshed. Not one, but two, round trips to work each day. Beecher shook his head. It was a great mystery to him why Romans seemed to enjoy this exercise in frustration.

"If you think that's frustration, Beecher, just consider the parking problem. There's no place to park all these cars. It's not uncommon to get six parking tickets in one day. Everyone ignores them. I don't know why the police keep passing them out. Some people hire boys to watch their cars and move them from one spot to another whenever the *guardia* approaches. The problem is brought up periodically in Parliament. There's always lots of screaming—insults and recriminations, but no solutions. Several years ago the government invested a huge sum in a public transit system with low fares and special inducements to ride, but hardly anyone would use it. Romans love tooting around in their cars too much, each man in control of his own destiny. They would rather gag on their own exhaust fumes, get six parking tickets a day and figure out how to outwit the police than to give up their personal freedoms. I could never seriously consider this country going communist. Anarchy is a more real possiblity, believe me." She laughed.

Cristina had eased the red Lamborghini through the traffic like a captain navigating stormy seas, shifting gears frequently and glancing nervously at her watch as she pushed a wisp of hair back from her flushed cheek. They made it to Fiumicino with minutes to spare, and she stood with Beecher at the gate as the well-modulated female voice announced his flight in Italian, French and English.

"You don't know how long you'll be in Venice, I guess?"

"It all depends on what I can find out from the Countess Rosetti. If Myra is alive and here in Italy, I have a hunch she has contacted the Countess. She's my best and last hope."

"Beecher, I pray that you will find out about Myra one way or the other. Anything would be preferable to this limbo you're in now."

When she looked up, he was surprised to see that her eyes were shining and tears glistened on her long lashes. Her manner suddenly became brusque and she quickly unzipped her large shoulder bag, pulled out a triple-folded map and thrust it toward him.

"Here, take this map with you, courtesy of Edoardo. It's the very best map available of Venice. The city's like a labyrinth, but this shows every canal and twisting narrow street and alley, or *rio* and *calle*, as they are called in

Venice, and remember that all *piazzi*, with the exception of the Piazza San Marco, its satellite Piazzetta San Marco and the Piazzale Roma, are called *campos*. Every place you see campo on the map, there's a square or piazza. The Rialto Bridge is in the heart of the market and shopping area. Oh, why am I telling you all this as though you are a child?" Beecher had never seen Cristina like this, flustered and nervous.

"What I really want to say, Beecher, is please be careful," she said. "Remember Caserta was mixed up in this, somehow, and you know what happened to him. There's darkness in Italy as well as beauty, and I just want you to promise me you'll be on guard. Guido wanted to send Edoardo with you. Maybe it wasn't a bad idea."

Now she sounds angry with me, Beecher decided. "I don't need Edoardo to hold my hand in Venice, and Guido does need him here, even if I did hear him call Edoardo a wimp last week when he suggested carrying a gun in the car as a deterrent to terrorist attack." Now they both laughed. He had succeeded in cheering her up.

Beecher took the small hand that rested on his arm almost as though she were trying to restrain him from leaving and carried it to his cheek and then to his lips. "You've been a special friend to me, Cristina, when I needed one badly." For a second he was sure she was going to put her arms around him, and then the last call was given for his flight. She stepped back abruptly, nearly tripping over a rucksack that a young man in lederhosen had set down a minute before. Beecher grabbed hold of her arm to steady her and she was in his arms before either of them realized what had happened. He held her close for an instant and kissed her gently on the cheek before he turned and headed toward the gate.

"Beecher, phone me from Venice. Let me know what's going on, promise?"

"I will", he called, as he hurried through the gate. He paused in the doorway of the Alitalia jet and looked back.

She stood at the gate waving, a small trim figure in a teal

blue suit with a bright halo of coppery hair. His throat felt tight and his voice was strangly hoarse as he replied to the stewardess' friendly, "*Buon giorno, Signore.*"

The stewardess was astoundingly beautiful and the smartly cut dark green Alitalia uniform molded her voluptuous figure like wax poured into a candle mold, but Beecher didn't even notice as he turned for one last look at the small retreating figure in blue and hurried into the crowded cabin of the DC-9 bound for Venice.

Part III - Venice

1.

"Fantasmagorical" was a word that Conner often used and Beecher took issue with. In fact, Beecher had doubted that the word existed, outside Conner's vocabulary, until he had tracked it down in Funk and Wagnalls. Even considering all its definitions and in turn the meanings of these, Conner was guilty of using it far too loosely.

"I don't give a damn. I like the sound of it. The word has pizzaz. I like the way it evokes images. You're being too literal-minded. You've got to guard against letting the German Hornbeck side of your nature gain the ascendancy. Myra was a great help in that area, always catching you off guard, keeping you on your toes with her zany ideas and impetuous schemes."

When Conner noticed the expression on Beecher's face, he stopped abruptly. "Sorry old man. Didn't mean to make you sad; I miss her too, you know. She was a breath of fresh air in this fusty old town. I only meant that now that she's gone, I guess it's my duty to remind you occasionally not to leave the fantasmagorical out of your life altogether."

Beecher bridled a little at the reference to the Hornbeck side of his family and the inference that his life was entirely lacking in fantasmagory. "My apologies, Conner. As a stodgy old German, I forgot that your Irish world is just one grand scene, inhabited by leprechauns and all manner of little people. When you uncover your next pot of gold, you can buy my dinner at Girioux's Place." Girioux's was the best that Meridian Springs had to offer.

"Touché, old friend. It's a deal," chuckled Conner.

Beecher's first sight of Venice, rising out of the sea like a phantom Baroque Atlantis immediately brought to mind Conner's word. Beecher had at last found a meaning for "fantasmagorical".

A forty-minute ride by motor launch from Venice's Marco Polo Airport on the mainland took him through the Adriatic and into the Grand Canal. The sea water of the canal and the marble and stone of the *palazzi* lining its banks became unfamiliar elements to Beecher. In the sunset, they had taken on strange hues that would have been difficult for him to duplicate on his palette or transfer to canvas.

Intricate ornamentation on ancient marble palaces was turned into fretwork of pure gold. Beecher stood by the rail, and the cool evening breeze off the water chilled him through his tweed jacket. He was happy to see some of the old pointed-prowed gondolas, graceful of shape and still regal in their black mourning for the lost *Serenissima*, the Serene Republic, when Venice had been the queen of the Adriatic, a sea power without equal in the fifteenth-century world.

With all the reports back home that Venice was sinking and stinking, Beecher hardly knew what to expect, but now he could see that this aging empress still had the power to dazzle, at least in the half light. In this witching hour just before dark, the Byzantine domes of San Marco were brazen gold against a rose and robin's-egg-blue sky. Dying bursts from the setting sun turned the cathedral momentarily into a sybaritic Xanadu of Kubla Khan and the ghostly silhouettes of black gondolas into Turkish slippers set adrift on a sea of glass. He would always remember

Venice as a dream-like city, devoid of the sound of automobiles and motorcycles, a city of mouldering pastel palaces and imperishable stone lace, a magic citadel guarded by bronze lions and golden tritons and water sprites in which the hours were struck by two huge Moors in the bell tower of San Marco.

That first evening at dusk, Beecher leaned over the rail of the barely moving launch and looked into the dark waters of the Grand Canal. He saw the apricot, moss and gold palaces reflected in rippling ribbons of color, like banners flying from a flagpole and knew that he was in a city of double images.

Beecher's reflections on the beauty and magical qualities of Venice came to an abrupt end when the launch deposited him at his hotel. The elegant but sedate Hotel Bellini, well situated on the Grand Canal, was a small palazzo hiding demurely in the shadow of larger and more pretentious neighbors.

Up half a flight of worn stone steps and across a narrow terrace flanked by marble urns of bright flowers and Beecher entered the lobby, where he could still hear the gentle lapping of waves made by the boats in the canal.

It's just as Leland Randolph described it, he thought. He suddenly had a vision of what it could have been like, entering the lobby of the Hotel Bellini with Myra: their bodies tanned from painting in the brilliant sun of Arles as Van Gogh and Gauguin had done, their portfolios bulging with drawings and water colors, their minds filled with excitement at all they had seen and done and felt. He had a fantasy that his staid Hornbeck nature would never allow him to mention—that other Beecher—the Beecher only she had known. Because it was impossibly wonderful, his vision was even more heart-wrenching than his memories had been.

He forced his mind back to the present and glanced around the lobby with its dark gleaming wood and ornately carved and painted ceiling. The crystal chandelier was lit in this hour before dusk and an enormous arrangement of fresh flowers sitting on the marble counter almost hid the desk clerk, a handsome young man whose head was bent over his writing.

How ironic, thought Beecher as he signed his name and offered his passport, that I should stay here now—that I should come to this city alone in search of a Myra that I have believed to be dead for five years. The waves from a passing boat splashed gently against the worn stone steps, and the clerk looked up and smiled.

"Signor Hornbeck, we hope that your stay with us will be most pleasant." With that, the handsome young Latin raised his hand and snapped his fingers with a self-assured, arrogant gesture in the direction of a bellman who looked old enough to be his grandfather. Beecher forced back the anger that rose like acid in his throat.

The old man arrived at a trot, smiling broadly, grabbed Beecher's bags and introduced himself as "Renzo".

"Here, Renzo, I'll carry the paint case." Beecher reached for the heaviest of the bags.

"Ah, Signore, you are an artist, I see. Venice, you will love."

Beecher and Renzo rode slowly to the third floor like two birds in a gilded cage. The ancient elevator was an ornate work of art and its brass grillwork was polished to a fair-thee-well, but Beecher wondered if they would make it. Renzo, who used the ride as an opportunity to acquaint the American with some of the glories he would be seeing in Venice, seemed unpreturbed by the elevator's groans, wheezes and occasional pause for breath between floors.

"Rosa will make it, Signore, never fear." He patted her lovingly and she, in turn, responded with a sudden upward surge that nearly caught Beecher off balance but propelled them abruptly to the third floor.

They traversed a dim corridor, lit by small wall sconces which illuminated the floral silk stripped wallpaper with rosy circles of light. Renzo stopped outside room 356, put down the bags and unlocked the door with a half-pound object that could have passed for the key to the city. The bellman crossed the large room and opened the slatted shutters onto the balcony through which ribbons of light had entered the darkened room, making ladder-like patterns on the carpet. A cool breeze fluttered the sheer draperies and blew into the shadowy room. Renzo turned on a lamp, removed a luggage rack from the closet, placed Beecher's suitcase on it and hung his suit bag in the closet.

"The dining room and terrace are open until ten o'clock, Signore, or there is room service for your commodita...your assurance...convenience!" Renzo smiled, pleased that he had finally latched on to the right English world. "Ring number five. Teresa will help you. You must be tired from your trip. Perhaps, here in your room a luscious melon with prosciutto, a tiny baked fish"— Renzo made a deprecating gesture, as though the fish might be too small to even mention—"with a sauce." At the happy thought of the sauce, Renzo's old voice grew more confident, and he went into a joyous recitation of the wine list for his triumphant finale.

Beecher had been known to say impatiently that food, after all, was just fuel, when Myra tried to pry him away from a half-finished canvas to come into the house for dinner, but now he decided that he loved the way the Italian waxed eloquent about the food. Renzo made "melon with prosciutto" sound like a line of poetry.

Beecher put a 10,000 lira note into the man's hand and thanked him for his helpfulness. Renzo backed toward the door bowing and smiling. "Anything you need, Signore, call Renzo Casello. I will hire you a gondola at the right rates from my nephew." He gave Beecher a wink.

Ah, nephews again, thought Beecher. They had followed him from Rome to Venice.

"I can direct you to the best jewelry stores, also hand-blown glass and leather goods, and if you are interested in real certified antiquities, I, Renzo know where they are to be found."

I'll bet you do, thought Beecher. Guido had warned him about "real certified antiquities" at bargain prices, but

Beecher liked Renzo and admired his enterprise. The old man was a fighter, still making his own way through a hard life, as he no doubt navigated the canals of Venice, using what strength he had left and his wits.

"Renzo, I"ll keep all that in mind, and I"ll be calling you about your nephew's gondola."

Beecher decided to pass on the "melon with prosciutto" and the "tiny fish" and instead enjoyed a light supper on the dining room terrace that overlooked the canal and then retired to his room to unpack.

He was tired after the long day but not sleepy, and he knew that if he went to bed early, he would lie awake thinking of Myra and the Countess Rosetti, Dino Romano and Caserta. Instead, he went out to the balcony to sit and smoke.

The breeze that blew across the balcony was cool and contained a mingling of odors that was hard to define. The comforting glow of his pipe repeated the larger glow in the night sky over Venice. Twinkling lights across the Grand Canal were reflected in the water, which at midnight was almost devoid of traffic. The vaporetto had stopped its regular runs some time before. Renzo had told Beecher about this Venetian version of rapid transit on their ride up to his room in "Rosa". Never had so much tourist information been revealed in such a short time.

An occasional motorboat passed and laughter and music drifted up to Beecher's balcony along with the myriad odors of Venice. What kept Beecher out here now, in spite of the night chill and his tiredness, was the sight of the gondolas, gliding silent as phantoms in the night, a gondolier balanced on the stern like a tightrope walker; the only sound was the swishing of his oar as it slid through the water, returning his passengers, most likely lovers, to their hotels.

There were plenty of wonderful things to be seen in Venice, especially for an artist, but Beecher's only desire at the moment was to contact the Countess Rosetti, if indeed she were still alive. All else would have to wait.

2.

Dreams he couldn't actually remember had haunted and disturbed his rest, and now the forgotten images stalked the edges of his consciousness like a pack of starving wolves waiting at the edge of a clearing.

Beecher was gliding down a narrow *rio* in a gondola manned by Renzo's nephew, Franco, when he was seized by an overpowering sense of dread. His disturbing dreams the night before had been of Myra, but he couldn't remember what had happened. Dreams don't mean a thing, he told himself, and feelings can be very unreliable. Hadn't Scrooge told Marley's ghost that he was only a bit of undigested meat? Maybe a forkful of pasta would be more appropriate here. Beecher decided it was time to rescind his motto "when in Rome" and rely instead on the Hornbeck stiff upper lip.

After some thought, he had decided against phoning the Countess Rosetti in advance for an appointment to visit. He had the address, why make it easy for her to refuse over the phone, he thought. Beecher became uncomfortable when he saw himself cast in the role of a salesman, trying to get his foot in the door, intruding where he very possibly wasn't wanted. There's too much at stake, he thought, to entertain such qualms now. He had told Zinelli that he would stay on the right side of the law, and he intended to do so, but short of that, he would do what he must to find Myra. Certain sensibilities would have to be put aside. He would surprise the old girl and see what he would find out.

Franco's gondola had traveled down the Rio dei Palazzi under curved bridges with delicate iron lace, past ancient buildings of rose brick with shuttered windows and flower-laden balconies. The brilliant blue sky was mirrored in the water; now the gondola glided for a moment into the darkness as it passed under a bridge from which gargoyles glared down at Beecher and Franco. Beecher had become confused by the frequent twists and turns of the canals; a narrow *rio* would open occasionally onto a square where children played and housewives gathered to chat. Brilliant red vines climbed crumbling walls. Rinds of oranges and lemons floated down the canal along with a gondola filled with priests in broad-brimmed black hats.

"*Un momento, Signore*, and we will be there. It is just beyond the next corner and down a short distance," Franco explained in his passable English. The lapping of the water against the buildings and the muted sounds of laughter and conversation coming from within shuttered walls border-ing both sides of the narrow waterway were suddenly drowned out by the roar of a motor boat, but none was to be seen. As Franco lowered his oar into the water on the other side of the gondola and deftly rounded the corner, Beecher could see the small launch, its motor idling now as a woman alighted at the door of a *palazzo* a short distance up ahead. She was wearing dark glasses and some sort of poncho or cape. The hood laid back around her shoulders revealing the thick black hair that Beecher remembered so well.

It was Myra.

"Row faster, Franco; I must catch that woman before she disappears!" Beecher shouted frantically.

Franco, startled, didn't waste time asking questions.

The gondola surged ahead just as Beecher saw Myra disappear into a doorway. The launch revved up its engine and took off rapidly, leaving Franco's gondola floundering in its wake.

Franco let out a rapid stream of irate Italian that Beecher couldn't understand. "I'll get you there, Signore, be assured. This is the address you seek. It is the same *palazzo* the beautiful lady, she enter. So you find her when you get there."

Franco looked pleased and studied Beecher with renewed respect and admiration. The American must be a fast worker. He arrives in Venice yesterday and is racing to meet with a beautiful woman today.

Franco jumped out and quickly secured the gondola to a post with a ring. Beecher's mind was racing; no point in sending Franco after the motor launch. He could never catch up with it in a gondola. "Just wait for me here, Franco, or at the square a few doors down."

Beecher stepped out onto the green slimy stone steps that led up to the doorway. He stood with pounding heart in front of the massive door and knocked twice with the heavy bronze dolphin door knocker. He could hear the sound reverberate inside the house, and after a minute approaching footsteps.

The door was opened by a small middle-aged woman in black. Her hair was pulled back severely, braided and wrapped around her head in a coronet effect. The pursed lips and small dark eyes under heavy brows all added up to an expression of suspicion and distrust. Definitely not the old Countess, thought Beecher, probably a companion or servant.

"*Cosa vuole, Signore?*" she asked curtly.

Beecher tried to take in as much of the first floor as he could without appearing to do so. It would be hard enough to get in here, impossible if he gave the impression that he was snooping around.

The small entrance hall where they stood—he had managed to get his foot in the door—led into a large salon or circular room with a flagstone floor. It was bare of furniture except for a few antique straight-backed chairs that looked as though they should be in a museum. The curved ceiling was painted with scenes too faded to recognize. The air was dank and chilly; the dampness from the canal was no doubt responsible for several dark crumbling spots in the plaster. No less than seven heavy ornate doors opened off the salon, like so many dark watching eyes. A graceful staircase led up to the second floor.

The salon was empty. Stupid, he reproached himself, did you think you would see Myra lurking in the shadows? Nor could she be a prisoner in this mouldering old palazzo. Hadn't he seen her enter alone, of her own free will? He had to remind himself that this was real life, not a Gothic novel, even though the setting was perfect.

Beecher had dressed with care that morning, desiring to look his respectable best when he called on the Countess Rosetti: dark suit—favored by all Italians—white shirt, old school tie, well-polished shoes. Then he had looked in the mirror and decided to wear his glasses which added to the total effect he desired to achieve, one of sincerity and trust. He felt like a wolf in sheep's clothing.

Her suspicious expression had faded a little, now that the woman had had a chance to look him over. "What is your business, Signore?"

Beecher never ceased to be amazed that these people spoke English. Better not to mention Myra right off the bat. Play your cards right, Hornbeck. One false move and you're out on your tail.

"Signora, I am an American artist. My name is Beecher Hornbeck, and I am here in Italy for an exhibit of my work at the Brazzano Gallery in Rome." Her expression softened somewhat. He had apparently struck the right note. "I wish to see the Countess Rosetti. I am (not was) the husband of Myra Wellington Hornbeck. My wife is a descendant of Alessandro Rosetti, who was, I understand, also a relative of the Countess."

"The Countess Teresa does not receive guests on Wednesday."

Thank God, thought Beecher, that at least she's still alive. "Please extend my apologies to the Countess. Perhaps I should have phoned before coming here."

"We have no phone. The Signora Teresa does not like the intrusion, the noise. She is very old."

"A moment ago, as my gondola rounded the corner of the rio, I saw a woman enter this palazzo." He could stand it no longer. He had to take the risk.

The suspicious look returned. She stared at him but did not answer. There was only silence in the vast salon. Best to drop it now and pursue the other matter.

"Would you extend my apologies to the Countess, for arriving unannounced, and ask if she will see me? Please explain to her what I have told you."

"The Countess is nearly ninety. She tires easily."

"Are you her companion?"

"Ah, yes." She smiled.

Beecher could see the suspicions taking a back seat now to her loquacious Italian nature. He must hasten to secure the few feet of ground he had taken in the campaign thus far. Trying to finesse his way into someone's good graces was hard for Beecher and alien to his nature. "I promise not to tire the Countess. I only want to speak to her for a few minutes. She is fortunate, Signora, to have you to look after her so well." He cringed inwardly at this bit of flattery, loathing himself. "Your name is—?"

"Beatrice." She smiled and tossed her head, "Beatrice Poldi." Suddenly Beecher got a glimpse of a much younger woman, the girl she must once have been. She stood straighter now and put her hand to her throat in a strangely touching gesture. Beecher always noticed hands; they were the hardest thing in the world to draw. Hers were delicate and beautiful. He could tell now that he had won her over.

"Signora Poldi," Beecher asked softly, "Would you please request that the Countess Teresa see me now?"

"Wait here, Signore. I will do my best. As I said before, she seldom receives guests and never strangers, only her old friends in these last few years, and then not on Wednesday." Beecher realized that he had stumbled into another world, like Alice behind the looking glass. What could Myra be doing here in this weird house? Was his mind playing tricks on him? Not this time. Franco had seen the woman enter the palazzo too.

Signora Poldi turned and started up the staircase. Beecher heard a door open and close at the top of the stairs, then muffled conversation—only a buzz actually, but loud enough to distinguish that there were only two voices, Signora Poldi's and a fainter one.

He glanced quickly around the dank, forbidding salon. Maybe it would be safe to try the nearest of the doors. This might be his only chance. The first to the left was a dining room. In an instant he could see that it was seldom used. The bowl of wax fruit in the center of the banquet-sized table reminded Beecher of something he had seen in his Grandmother Hornbeck's house when he was a small child.

The next room was some sort of small parlor. The furniture was covered with dust sheets, ghostly and sad. Did he dare another door? What if he encountered the cook lurking in the scullery and she screamed? He could be searching for the bathroom; that's it—the bath.

The next door led to a storage room cluttered with broken furniture and gilt birdcages. Dusty moss-green velvet drapes were thrown over a chair. He got a frightening glimpse of himself in a broken mirror. He quickly closed the door and hurried back to the entrance to the salon. The conversation was still going on in the room at the top of the stairs. Maybe there was time for the door to the right?

He decided not to press his luck. His instincts proved right, for at that moment the door opened, and he heard Signora Poldi start down the stairs.

A different woman came down to speak to him. What

had transpired in that room on the second floor, thought Beecher, as he saw the guarded, hostile look on Beatrice Poldi's face.

"The Countess is sorry, but she cannot see you today. She is not well." The voice was cold and formal. Twenty minutes before, the Countess had been merely old, now she was ill.

"The Countess asks where you are staying in Venice. Perhaps she will send word that she is well enough to see you another day." The small dark eyes were veiled now, evasive.

Beecher saw that he had two choices and very little time to make up his mind. He could remain the gentleman and leave politely, pretending to believe that she would contact him later, or he could push this small woman aside, climb the stairs and confront the Countess, demanding to see his wife.

Yet if Myra were in the house, what was hindering her from coming to him now? He was certain that if he did burst into the room at the top of the stairs, she would no longer be there, if she ever had been, and he would lose all hope of gaining the confidence of the old lady, who would be justified in bringing the police down on his head. An American, a total stranger, forces his way to the second floor of the home of two elderly women. Zinelli would not be pleased; neither would Guido, and news had a way of of traveling fast in Italy.

Suddenly Beecher remembered what it was that he should have heard but didn't, when Signora Poldi had come back downstairs to deliver the Countess's answer. She had not closed the door at the top of the stairs. There had been a sound of the door opening as she left the room and the sound of her footsteps as she descended the stairs, yet the door had been closed before she entered the room to talk to the Countess.

The old woman was obviously listening at the top of the stairs. He doubted that he would have remembered the unclosed door if he had not suddenly felt a third presence in the house. The vibes that reached him were malevolent and sly and they weren't coming from Signora Poldi. She seemed embarrassed and frightened, but not of him. That meant the old lady was at least a little interested in him. Maybe her rejection wasn't as final as he had feared a minute before. He decided to play his trump card now.

He spoke a little louder and more slowly. "I'm disappointed, but will expect to hear from the Countess soon. I am staying at the Hotel Bellini on the Grand Canal. I especially wanted to show Countess Rosetti this gold locket, which you can see contains a picture of Alessandro Rosetti." He removed Lavinia's locket from his inside breast pocket and opened it so that Beatrice Poldi could see that he spoke the truth.

"It was a gift from Alessandro to his wife Lavinia on their wedding day. I thought perhaps it should return to the Rosetti family after all these years." He had dropped the baited hook into the water. Now he must wait and count on the old lady's curiosity. "Please tell the Countess that I hope she will be feeling better tomorrow, and that I will be looking forward to returning to see her at her convenience." He felt that this courtly speech should be accompanied by a low bow from the waist, but restrained himself. This house had such an air of unreality, almost like a stage set.

The sound of a faint rasping cough came from upstairs. He had been right about her listening. Beatrice Poldi spoke quickly, as though to cover the sound of the cough, no doubt hoping he hadn't noticed. Beecher pretended he hadn't.

Signora Poldi opened the door and Beecher stepped out into the sunlight again, giving her his most winning smile. "Thank you Signora, for your kindness. I trust I will hear from the Countess soon." He could only hope she would put in a good word for him. Whether it would have any influence was a matter of speculation.

"*Adío*, Signor Hornbeck," said Signora Poldi with finality. The massive door closed behind him.

Beecher breathed deeply and looked around for Franco's gondola. He could see it tied up a short distance down the *rio*. There was a narrow sidewalk between the water and the buildings that led in that direction. Beecher wanted desperately to explore the narrow "assassin's lane" between Ca'Rosetti and the next *palazzo*, but he dared not. Several shutters on the second floor were open. He could swear they hadn't been when he entered the old mausoleum thirty minutes before. Both women were probably up there watching to see if he would leave or snoop around. Don't mess up now, Hornbeck. Play it safe to the end.

He turned and walked down the side of the *rio* to the small *campo* where Franco's gondola was tied up. The brightly polished brass triton on the prow made it easy to recognize, as did the red-fringed, black leather cushions and the red rug. Franco's traditional straw gondolier's hat, with the red band, lay on the seat of the empty gondola. Venetians took care to keep their city picturesque. There was money in it; that's the way the tourists liked it. They wanted to see a city that looked like Guardi had painted it in the eighteenth century, and the Venetians had seen to it that they did.

Franco was leaning against one of the brick buildings that surrounded the square, eating an orange and talking to a very pretty young girl. Water bubbled from the mouths of smiling dolphins that adorned the small fountain in the center of the campo. Children had gathered around a little girl with an antiquated wicker doll buggy while their mothers sat on the other side of the square in steamer chairs, knitting or sunning themselves. A teenaged boy swept the worn cobbled stone area in front of a fruit market.

Franco removed his arm from around the girl's waist when he saw Beecher and hurried over smiling. "Ah, Signor Hornbeck, I hope your visit was delightful." He leered.

"Not delightful, Franco. I can only hope that it will prove successful."

Franco looked a little confused by such subtlety; after

all, they were both men of the world. He shrugged, jumped into the gondola and began to untie the rope. Beecher climbed in after him and sat down in the overstuffed seat that made him feel like a floating potentate.

"Back to the hotel, Signore?"

"No Franco, take me to the Piazza San Marco."

"Very good, Signore." Franco put on his hat, dipped his oar in the water and deftly pushed out from the quay. He looked pleased to be taking Beecher to the most famous site in all Venice. He had never before been requested to take an American tourist to a mouldering palazzo on an obscure rio. It was all too mysterious. As they floated back toward the Grand Canal, Franco began his monologue on the history of Venice. "One must only behold San Marco's Basilica to see the strength of the Byzantine influence on medieval Venice ...."

Beecher didn't hear a word. His thoughts were on his own problems, which loomed large over his head like the tall crumbling palaces with their cracked tiles and blind eyes. The dark waters of the narrow *rio* lapped at the buildings and occasionally bubbled up, giving one the eerie feeling that its subterranean depths could be inhabited by loathsome creatures left over from another age. Beecher's earlier sense of dread returned like a prophecy of impending doom.

3.

Beecher sat at Florian's sidewalk caffé and watched the *passeggiata*, the endless promenade in the Piazza San Marco. This scene, which would under normal circumstances have been a delight to him, now only added to his sense of despair.

All this beauty and grandeur; the Baroque Cathedral with its giant bronze Greek horses, angels blowing golden trumpets, and glinting Byzantine domes topped with gold crosses looked less like a recognizable piece of architecture than a joyous exuberant exclamation reaching up to the heavens. Or maybe, Beecher mused darkly, this was simply an unnecessary excess, too much of a good thing— the "gilded lily" on a grand scale. The very lavishness of the spectacle spread out before him seemed an affront, increasing his sense of desolation and loneliness.

For Beecher, the scene lacked reality: the overwhelming size of the *piazza* bordered by Renaissance palaces, crowned by the cathedral itself, the "wedding cake". Over a thousand people—Italian families out for the air, scrubbed, brushed and groomed; preppy American tourists and Europeans, more casually dressed in wrinkled khaki shorts with hairy legs and Birkenstock scandals— strolled about or sat at outdoor caffé tables, as Beecher did, and watched the *passeggiata*.

Waiters hurried back and forth with trays of wine, espresso, *gelati* for the children, and for traveling Americans, the $3.50 Coke. Many of these Americans would greet the bill with understandable consternation, only to discover later that they had a story they could exploit to the fullest, warning their fellows, so easily recognized by the alligators and other creatures on their chests and the designer names emblazed on their rear ends, about the exorbitant price of Cokes in the Piazza San Marco.

An orchestra in the center of the piazza played the *Barcarolle* from *The Tales of Hoffman*. This is all staged, thought Beecher, with a cynicism that was quite unlike him. It's vintage C. B. De Mille or one of Dino Romano's epics with a huge budget and a cast of thousands, designed to bring in big bucks at the box office; and it had been, for hundreds of years, the longest playing show in the world. Henry James sat at this same sidewalk caffé in the 1850s collecting literary fodder and hatching plots in which unsophisticated Americans would be duped by wily Europeans.

Only weeks ago, back in Indiana, Beecher had looked forward with happy anticipation to sitting at Florian's and drinking an espresso or an aperitif. It was the perfect way to take in the spectacle of San Marco, just as so many other writers and artists had done through the years. Would he be able, he had wondered, to sense the presence of their ghosts: Gabriele d' Annunzio and his beloved Eleonora Duse, Wagner and Hemingway and Fitzgerald? But now he was here, and he didn't sense any presence except Myra's, and that not with joy, but with an ever-growing sense of despair.

Pandora's box was open wide, and there was no chance now of recapturing and imprisoning those dark things that had escaped. Myra had been in that mouldering old palazzo on the Rio del Giglio and yet had not come to him when she heard his voice. Both he and Franco had seen her enter the house alone, of her own free will. What hold could the old Countess possibly have on Myra that would keep her from him?

He suspected now that his decision to leave Ca'Rosetti in a gentlemanly manner had not been based as much on discretion and a desire not to alienate the Countess permanently and thus lose all hope of finding Myra, as on the fear that he *would* find her.

It had been so easy to believe in Myra when he was in Rome. She could not have deliberately eluded him that day on the Spanish Steps because she did not know that he was there. In Rome he could still thrust that terrible possibility from him that somehow she had tricked him into believing her dead five years ago and had made a new life for herself halfway across the world from everything he had believed she loved. Far away from him. Far away from him forever.

In Rome there had been other options. He had believed a few days ago that he would have Myra back. Guido, even though he thought that Myra was dead, had been supportive. Cristina had helped him convince himself that Myra would never have left him voluntarily. The answers lay ahead in Venice, logical answers, a happy outcome. He still longed to believe in Myra, but in the face of what had happened today, all thoughts of her returning seemed like pipe dreams. He didn't want to go on living if he could no longer trust his memories.

It seemed to him now, sitting among the happy throng in the piazza, that he should have taken the chance and forced his way up those stairs no matter what dreadful truths waited at the top. That would have ended it, at least. What had Cristina said to him at the airport? "I only hope you find out one way or the other. Anything would be preferable to the limbo you are in now." She was right, but he had not had the courage to risk everything, and so had only postponed the inevitable.

How could he have been foolish enough to think that Lavinia Hartley Rosetti's locket could persuade the old lady to see him, much less tell him the truth about Myra? When he had said so confidently to Beatrice Poldi, "I trust that I will hear from the Countess soon," it had only been a bluff, an attempt to turn a slim hope into a fact. How could he have believed for a moment that she would send for him? He had even entertained the idea that Myra had heard him mention the Hotel Bellini and that she would rush there to find him.

The espresso was strong, and the dregs were bitter in his mouth. The orchestra had just wound down *Torna Sorrento* and the musicians were putting their instruments in the cases and departing. The two huge Moors in the clock tower struck six. The chiming of bells in Venice reverberated strangely across the water, echoing through the labyrinth of canals and glancing off a hundred buildings before dying away with a sigh and sinking into the gently lapping waters. As the hour was struck, platoons of pigeons took to the air, darkening the sky momentarily, only to light again.

Italy would be the place Myra would chose to start a new life, Beecher realized with a sinking heart. This country was perfect for her. He had felt it in Rome, but in this magical city of islands floating in a hazy mist, of pink spires and marble seraphim blowing into conch shells, he sensed the very essence of Myra, like her haunting, familiar perfume. Venice was Myra's natural habitat.

How could I have ever convinced myself that she was completely happy in Sparta on the farm, he asked himself. I knew as soon as I met her that she was different, too exotic and lush to grow in Midwestern soil, Beecher thought. The irony was, that had made him want her all the more. They had both been young and there was the magic, the overwhelming attraction of opposites. He had ignored those nagging doubts about their compatability, the difference in their backgrounds, because he had loved her and wanted her so much; just as later, after they were married, he had ignored her moodiness. It's not important; it's simply her personality, he had decided.

He could see now that he had fled from seeing the causes, encasing himself in his natural reticence. But hadn't he loved her, even more as the years passed and not less?

Another voice, one that he could no longer ignore, spoke. You loved her on your own terms, always on *your* terms, in the context of what you believed *your* life should be, yours and hers. Had he made Myra's life a mere appendage to his own? She had told him often that she loved the farm. Perhaps she had rejected it, finally, irrevocably, in the only way she knew how.

Zinelli had been right. This could only lead to madness. When the unthinkable becomes possible, the normal no longer exists.

The crowd, the noise, the smells all became overpowering. He needed air. He rose, paid his check and walked out of the Piazza San Marco—all alone in the crowd.

Beecher wandered through the narrow streets and twisting alleys of the city, hoping to free himself of the doubt and despair that rested on him like a tangible burden. Where is the Hornbeck stiff upper lip now, he asked himself ruefully. He reminded himself that Myra had been dead to him for five years. After all, what had really changed?

"Jackass," he muttered under his breath. "Everything has changed and you're too old to start being dishonest with yourself now." He might lose his wife a second time, but he couldn't afford to lose his integrity too, to start lying to himself. He reminded himself that old Ephraim had survived and so would he. The Hornbecks had always been survivors.

Ephraim Hornbeck had been the first of the clan to brave the arduous journey from Virginia and settle in southern Indiana in 1786. He had lost one child to smallpox on the journey, and during the second winter, in what was then a wilderness and was now Beecher's farm, his wife and remaining child had been killed by the Indians while he was out hunting.

Old Ephraim was the family's prime example of the

Hornbeck stiff upper lip and was trotted out through the years to exemplify courage and determination. Beecher had learned all about Ephraim Hornbeck when he was still young enough to sit on Sara's lap. The intrepid ancestor had gathered up the pieces of his life and had gone on, like Job, to enjoy later-day blessings. He remarried—sending for a childhood sweetheart from his home in Virginia—and started another family. After he had finished clearing the land, he opened a law office in the town of Harmony, which later became Sparta. Ephraim ended up being the first judge in the territory.

"He could have just given up, you know, Son, and sat around drinking and feeling sorry for himself, or high-tailed it back East," Sara had said to a crying nine-year-old Beecher whose dog had just met death by a kick in the head from his father's bull. "We've just got to go on, Son, when we lose the people and the things we love, and someday the good Lord will show us the reasons why these things happen." She had hugged him to her in a rare gesture. Sara wasn't much for touching. He remembered Sara now and wondered what she would have thought of Venice. She wouldn't have believed that it was real.

And yet were people really that different? He thought of old Guido, how he had come back from the war and wept when he saw the condition of his family and his home, how he had struggled to restore the villa. Guido had not become bitter when he realized that he didn't possess real talent himself, but had helped other painters get established through his gallery. He had survived the deaths of his first wife, Maria, and finally, bitterest of all, the death of Carlo. That last night at the villa, Guido had pointed to the sleeping Cristina and said, "And in my old age, God has given me this little daughter."

If he could only be with Guido and Cristina tonight, or with Harry or Conner.

Beecher had no idea how long he had been walking. He pressed on across one more arched bridge, down yet another narrow walkway bordering a dark *rio*. Dusk was falling. Now there was only the sound of echoing footsteps and the incessant lapping of the water against the quays and buildings, greedy tongues licking away at the foundations of this floating city. He could hear muted conversations behind high walls and shuttered windows as he passed. Soft Latin accents and the tinkling of glasses drifted from a walled garden, completely hidden by a red flaming vine, lush and fragrant as Eden. Bruised anemones floated beside cantaloupe rinds. To Beecher, Venice was Eden after the fall, rank and decaying, but still retaining vestiges of the paradise it had once been, a morality play acted out in the piazzas and on the canals. The whole city was a vast ancient theater with magnificent stage sets.

Venetians were now gathered at the end of the day behind these high crumbling walls with their children, their aged parents, their aunts and uncles, observing the small rituals of domesticity that help civilize the human race: the communal evening meal, shared experiences of the day, the children's lessons, the game of chess eagerly anticipated by *Nonno*, the grandfather. Beecher had remembered the Italian word ever since he heard Cristina use it lovingly for Guido.

The lonely, narrow streets were empty of tourists. Only a few Italians were hurrying home with their briefcases or lunch pails. Then there were the others, the dispossessed, who lurked in the shadowed alcoves and dark alleys, people without a country who were the same in every country. Some had settled down for the night in empty gondolas or in a doorway, instead of in packing crates. An occasional gondola glided by, or the silence of the gathering dusk was broken by the obscene noise of a motor launch, churning up the dark waters of the *rio* and violating the peace like a fire engine at a wake.

During his wanderings, Beecher occasionally found himself in a lighted *campo*. The darkened city was punctuated with these squares like the commas in a winding, convoluted sentence. They were still filled with tourists and strolling Venetians and were bordered with shops, *ristoranti*, the more humble *trattorie,* and were crowned with the inevitable church. It was one of these small *trattorie* near the Rialto Bridge that Beecher chose. He realized that he hadn't eaten for nearly eight hours.

The small room was filled with bustling waiters and voluble Italians. The warmth felt good. He was chilled to the bone from walking for hours along the canals. He sipped a glass of Valpolicella as he waited for the ravioli that his amiable waiter had recommended, insisting that it was "the best in Venice, Signore." He had also ordered a plate of scampi. The wine warmed his insides.

Beecher forceably emptied his mind of all thoughts of Myra as he tried to do while he walked the streets of Venice, concentrating instead on the architecture of bridge and *palazzi*, the gestures and dress of the people he passed, an unexpectedly beautiful fountain in a run-down *campo*, the flower-filled gondola from which a tenor serenaded a bridal party as they came out of a small church. He had stopped for a moment to watch this unusual sight. The tiny flower girl had thrown her petals in the canal, and the fragile blossoms had drifted and fanned out, mingling the odor of crushed gardenias with the musky dark sea waters. Bread cast upon the waters, Beecher thought, life's inevitable mixture of beauty and darkness.

Survival is a strong instinct and Beecher realized as he sat in the small caffé that he must not think of Myra at all. Not now, not yet. Maybe tomorrow he would be able to decide what to do.

Not tonight. I can't decide these things tonight—maybe tomorrow. Tonight I must eat. I must walk back to my hotel and then I must sleep.

The waiter brought the food and he ate methodically, watching the other patrons of the *trattoria*, young couples, families, small groups of men. He tried to imagine what their lives were like, where they worked and lived. Anything to keep his mind off "the other", so that the wound could stop bleeding and begin to heal. The food was helping and the wine. He was getting sleepy. He decided to forget the coffee and get back to the hotel. He longed for sleep, the blessed oblivion of those who are at peace with themselves. He studied his map for the shortest route back to the Hotel Bellini, remembering for an instant Cristina's face at the airport as she had thrust the map at him: the unexpected tears glistening on her long lashes, the coppery hair framing her flushed face.

He finished his wine, paid the check and walked out into the night.

4.

His mind surfaced from drugged sleep, not an awakening so much as a returning from an unconscious state. Had he heard a noise or had he only dreamed? He heard it again outside his door—the sound of scuffling in the hall. There were two voices: one authoritarian, the other sounded distressed. Beecher threw on his robe and hurried to the door, trying not to think of Caserta.

He recognized one of the hotel's younger bellmen, Sergio, who was struggling with a strange-looking man. The scuffling stopped abruptly when Beecher opened the door. The bellman retained a firm hold on the other's arm and turned to Beecher.

"This *persona*, this fellow," he said, giving the sleeve a rough yank, "was lurking around the lobby, trying to get your room number. First he asked Ricardo, the desk clerk. Assuredly Ricardo would not give it to him. Later, when Ricardo came from his office, he saw this one," punctuating with a shove this time, "going into the elevator. He sent me up, Signore, to handle the situation."

Beecher could see why. Sergio was a large man, probably six feet three with a body scaled to his height, and certainly the man he held by the arm was no match for him, as he was not only small of stature but deformed, as well. The loose fitting black jacket over an equally loose white poet's shirt was obviously worn in a pathetic attempt to hide a hunched back that made the young man's neck thrust forward as though he were perpetually straining to hear a sound that eluded him. One arm appeared to be shorter than the other. All this was in startling contrast to his face, which was handsome in a dark Byronic way. The aqualine nose, full, perfectly sculptured lips and heavy jaw at first reminded Beecher of a Velzquez painting of Spanish courtiers, but as he studied the man's face again, he realized that an ironic twist of fate had placed the classic head of a Greek or Roman god on this poor deformed body. Only the eyes were different. The eyes of the gods had looked out with cold indifference from the heights of Olympus and the Roman Forum. This man's dark brooding eyes were filled with anguish and unfilled desires. Here was a figure from another century.

The man had not taken his eyes off Beecher's face and now spoke in a heavily accented voice that was curiously pitched, as much at odds with the rest of him as his head was different from his body.

"The Countess Rosetti sent me with a message for you, Signor Hornbeck. I am Marco, the Signora's servant. This *sciocca*, I try to tell him." He pulled free from Sergio's grip and glared at the tall bellman with contempt.

Sergio raised his fist. "Call me fool again, Romeo, just once more! Do it!"

"That's enough, Sergio," Beecher said harshly. The Romeo remark was cruel. Sergio did not impress Beecher as being brilliant, but he was astute enough to see that this man had a face that would attract women and a body that would repel them. "You can go now, Sergio. I know the Countess Teresa Rosetti, this man's employer. She would have to send a messenger as there is no telephone at the *palazzo*. He is no threat to me. You can tell Ricardo that he is to notify me immediately if anyone else asks to see me."

Sergio left reluctantly, muttering about unauthorized persons running loose in the Hotel Bellini. The long corridor was lined with shoes, carefully placed outside the doors the night before to be collected and polished. The elderly lady in the hairnet and flowered robe who had stuck her head out of the door across the hall earlier to witness the scuffle, had long since retreated to her room after delivering a long animated speech in Italian.

Beecher held the door open for the hunchback and said, "Come on in, Marco, and tell me why Signora Rosetti sent you here." Beecher pointed to a chair but Marco declined to sit down.

"The Countess said to tell you that she is feeling better today and that she can see you at three o'clock this afternoon. I pick you up at the *riva*—at the hotel front—in the Contessa's gondola one half-hour before."

Beecher was almost too stunned to answer. He had given up hope that the old lady would send for him. Marco looked at him curiously. "You wish to go, Signore?"

"Yes, Marco. I wish to go. Tell the Countess that I will be happy to call on her at three o'clock. I will be waiting for you in front of the hotel on the terrace."

Beecher was careful to hide all emotion. Go slowly, he told himself, and you may find out something. Keep Marco here for a few minutes. Get him to talk about the Countess. Catch him off guard.

Beecher was sitting on the side of the bed. He reached for his pipe and tobacco on the bedside table and started to fill the bowl. The pipe was a welcome distraction. It put Marco at ease and gave Beecher time to think. "Please sit down for a minute, Marco. I'm sorry you had trouble getting up here to see me. I'll leave word at the desk that if you ever come here again with a message for me, you are to be treated with respect. Will you accept my apologies for Sergio?"

Marco softened a little. He sat down in the chair opposite Beecher. "It is not your fault, Signore."

"The Countess must depend on you for many things."

This pleased Marco. He smiled. He's only a boy, Beecher thought, probably not over nineteen.

"I work for the Countess Teresa ever since I come from Umbria. It is four years. Marta was already here—my cousin. She cooks for the Signora."

"I can see that you like to work for the Countess, Marco." By now, Beecher was enveloped in a benign cloud of smoke and Marco leaned back and took a slightly crumpled pack of cigarettes from his pocket. Beecher lit the small Turkish cigarette for him.

"Ah, yes, Signore. I have my own room—a good room with a radio. I repair the gondola when I come from Umbria. Now I take the Signora to church, also to visit the graves with flowers and to see her friend, the Signora Zanobetti, at Christmas. The Contessa is very old, Signor Hornbeck. She does not go to call often."

"But she has many guests, Marco?"

"Not many, Signore. Only Dr. Piccini and the Countess Savini. Now Signora Zanobetti is too ill to come. Many that the Countess knew are in the grave, Signore. I polish the silver for Marta, but no one comes to dine."

"The lady with the black hair, that arrived just before I did yesterday, does she call on the Countess Teresa often?" Beecher asked casually. It was a shot in the dark, but what did he have to lose?

Beecher noticed an almost imperceptable change in Marco's expression. Was it a shadow of fear or anger that passed over the dark eyes for only an instant. Could it possibly be jealousy, Beecher wondered.

"You must have seen a visitor enter next door, Signore. The Countess never has beautiful signoras to call."

So you know who she is, Beecher thought, and you have been warned to say nothing. His Myra was beautiful, but Marco couldn't have known that if he hadn't seen her.

Marco stood up abruptly, put out his cigarette in Beecher's ashtray and glanced around the room. "I must leave now and stop at the Rialto as I return. Marta needs fruit and vegetables. The best will be gone. It already grows late."

Beecher glanced at his watch. It was eleven o'clock. "It does grow late, Marco."

The hunchback turned as he stepped into the hall. "Signor Hornbeck, the Countess Teresa wishes that you bring the locket."

"To be sure, Marco. I will see you then at two-thirty this afternoon."

What could have changed the old lady's mind, Beecher wondered as he stood on the balcony and looked out across the Grand Canal at the scene that still so nearly resembled a Guardi seascape. Dark clouds gathered over the Doges' Palace; the rising wind that rippled the waters of the canal already carried the scent of rain.

Beecher showered, shaved and dressed with care, once again conservatively in the dark blue suit that he thought of as his gallery reception suit. He had seen painters at their own reception in red bib overalls and combat boots or a faded plaid flannel shirt worn with a silk paisley tie and a velvet suit. The more picturesque the attire, the less talent, Beecher had decided a long time ago.

He closed and locked the door to the balcony and took his Burberry raincoat out of the large wardrobe. He had bought it in London three years before—one of his few extravagances. He gathered up his pipe and tobacco and remembered the Rosetti locket just as he locked his door with the huge key. Returning for the locket, he placed it in his breast pocket. This just leaves me enough time for lunch, Beecher thought, as he pressed the elevator button and heard the familiar snorting and wheezing as the reluctant Rosa began her ascent from the lower regions.

5.

The thought of Myra was uppermost in his mind, as he floated in the mist-shrouded gondola, but he must not let it cloud his reason or dull his perceptions. He must expect nothing and be prepared for anything. Without even realizing it, he had taken the locket from his pocket and was running the chain through nervous fingers, as though it were a string of Greek worry beads. He glanced out into the mist, but Marco hadn't noticed.

The bent figure threaded the way through the narrow *rio* with a grace and deftness that comes with much practice. Beecher sat in the back of the gondola, under a canopy, as the rain fell. The *rio* and the *palazzi* that lined its banks were veiled in mist, as was the figure of the gondolier. Marco had become a black, shadowy, Flying Dutchman propelling his craft through the dark, narrow waterways of a nether world, doomed to sail his ghost ship for eternity unless the love of a beautiful woman freed him from his curse. Beecher remembered the look on Marco's face when he had mentioned Myra to the hunchback. Was it possible that the man knew Myra well, maybe even loved her?

This isn't a scene from *Rigoletto*, Beecher reminded himself. Get hold of yourself. Your thinking has become increasingly weird ever since you arrived in this city.

He had longed to call Cristina last night just to touch down with saneness and reality, but he couldn't bear to tell her what had happened. Vocalizing his despair would somehow have finalized it.

Today everything had changed. The old lady had decided to see him.

Beatrice Poldi met him at the door and took his wet coat. She ushered him into the salon. There was a fire burning in the marble fireplace at the far end of the room, but even this was not enough to take away the damp chill. Marco had disappeared. Signora Poldi was more animated than she had been the day before. There were bright spots of color on her high cheekbones. She had taken care with her hair and wore a silk print dress with a short black jacket.

"The Countess will see you in her upstairs sitting room. It is more comfortable there," she said. "Down here, it is difficult to keep out the chill—the canals, you know. It is the price we Venetians pay. Everything has its price, you know, Signor Hornbeck." She threw him a glance, as though he should know what she meant.

He heard Marco enter the back of the house and speak with what must have been the cook. Beatrice Poldi led him up the curving staircase and into the room at the top of the stairs.

When Beecher saw the Countess Rosetti sitting in her salon, he realized that he had expected to find a withered old crone, waiting like a spider in a decaying room—an Italian version of Miss Haversham in *Great Expectations*. The reality was quite different, and the second floor of the *palazzo* was totally unlike the downstairs.

He could see why the family chose to live here. On a sunny day, this beautiful paneled room with the rose brocade ceiling and drapes would be light and cheerful. Now, lamps with fragile shades and dangling glass prisms reminiscent of the 1920s' were lit because of the darkness of the rainy afternoon. A fire burned brightly in the ornately carved fireplace and rococo cherubs adorned the mantle.

The Countess sat in a large, worn, rose velvet chair, which like herself, appeared to be of great and indeterminate age. She made no attempt to rise as they approached, and when Beatrice Poldi introduced Beecher, the old lady nodded but did not extend her hand. She motioned ever so slightly to a chair opposite her, and Beecher sat down.

Teresa Rosetti was very old, but vestiges of what must once have been a great beauty were apparent to Beecher in the shape of her face, her neck and her eyes. As a painter, he could see that the facial structure underneath the thin, transparent skin was flawless. Her eyes were large and were undoubtedly her best feature in her youth, but now the lids drooped slightly, as did the corners of her mouth. He looked into her eyes. They could almost be Myra's eyes, forty or fifty years hence. Myra really was a Rosetti, Beecher thought. It wasn't just a resemblence to the long dead Alessandro. This woman who had never left Venice could be Myra playing herself as an old lady. It gave him an eerie feeling that was hard to shake off.

Better to broach the subject of the common ancestor first, Beecher decided.

"My wife, Myra Wellington Hornbeck, as I'm sure you know, was a descendant of Alessandro Rosetti. We had planned a painting trip abroad, five years ago, and it was her desire to visit you, here in Venice. Myra was proud of her Italian ancestory and felt that she had inherited her artistic talent from the Rosettis. She told me of an ancestor in the fifteenth century who was a court painter to Lorenzo di Medici."

"This is true," the old woman said in halting English. "His name was Paolo Rosetti. He was not among the most famous painters of his time, but one of his works hangs in the *Accademia*, here in Venice. You may wish to see it."

"I am certainly interested. I have not yet had an opportunity to visit the *Accademia*. I only arrived in Venice two days ago and came directly here, yesterday, to visit you, as was my wife's wish."

"It is a pity that I could not have met your wife."

Did he only imagine that she avoided his eyes? "Yes a great pity. You see, she resembled you. I find it quite startling, in fact. As a painter, I notice these things more than the average person." No reaction to this, at all.

"Signor Hornbeck, I was sorry to hear of your wife's death, but I must wonder why you come here, after all these years, when you have no relationship to my family. The Rosettis have had no contact with the Hartleys since Alessandro's unfortunate and unnecessary death. I am the last descendant of Alessandro's older brother, Count Antonio Rosetti. The title passed down to me, and as I never married, will end with me. However, that is insignificant. Titles are of no importance in Italy since the second World War. Much has changed since 1899 when I was born in the room next to this one." Her voice was cultivated. and the Latin inflection on certain words was pleasant to the ear.

It was hard to imagine that this regal, white-haired old lady could be hiding his wife from him, but he was certain of what he had seen. She was clever, putting him on the defensive right away about Alessandro's death, letting him know he was not welcome, that he would not be allowed to presume on a family relationship that did not exist. He would not let her bluff him. Franco had seen Myra enter the house yesterday, just as he had; Marco had lied when he said that a beautiful woman never visited the countess.

This was his last chance to find Myra. He must go slowly with the old lady. Maybe she would let down her guard.

He brought out the locket, opened it and handed it to her. "This belonged to my wife, Myra. Her mother, Harriet Wellington, gave it to her. It was a wedding present to Lavinia from Alessandro. My wife planned to return it to the Rosettis and that is my wish also. Please, will you accept it?"

She looked at the picture of Alessandro inside the locket and didn't answer for what seemed like minutes.

"Yes, I will accept it," she said at last. The Countess

sighed. "You and your wife had no children, Signor Hornbeck?"

"No, we didn't," Beecher answered softly.

Beatrice Poldi entered the room with a tea tray and placed it on a table between Beecher and the Countess.

"I always have a small brandy at this time of day, Signor Hornbeck. Would you join me, or do you prefer tea?"

"Tea is fine, Countess. No sugar, please."

Beatrice Poldi poured and handed Beecher a cup of tea, then gave the Countess her brandy.

"Take something for yourself, Poldi, and join us," said the Countess. Beatrice Poldi poured herself a cup of tea and sat down on the other side of the fireplace.

There was silence in the room now, only the ticking of the clock and the faint ring of a china teacup against its saucer. A motor launch roared down the *rio* and left the sound of lapping water in its wake. The silence told Beecher more clearly than words that when his tea was finished, he would be expected to leave. He knew now that the Countess Rosetti had agreed to see him so that she could get rid of him once and for all. He had missed his chance yesterday, when the element of surprise had been on his side. Since then, she had prepared to meet him and had undoubtedly decided that it would be better to see him than to have him lurking about Venice, never knowing when he might appear again, unannounced. She obviously intended to tell him nothing.

"Countess Rosetti, I believe that you can help me find my wife. At this moment, I'm sure you know where she is."

"I don't understand what you are saying to me. You told me only just now, that your wife is dead."

"No, Countess. *You* told me that my wife is dead. I said nothing. I believed Myra to be dead until I saw her in Rome, less that two weeks ago. My search for her in Rome has led me here to Venice, hoping that if Myra were living in Italy, she had contacted you. You can imagine my shock when I saw her enter this house, yesterday. My gondolier also saw her. There is now absolutely no doubt in my mind that she is alive and that she was here yesterday."

"We had no visitor yesterday, except yourself. Is that not so, Poldi?"

"Yes, Teresa." Signora Poldi was not as accomplished a liar as the old lady.

Beecher forged ahead.

"I don't know why you refuse to tell me what you know. Did Myra ask you to lie to me? If she is alive and does not want to see me, she has only to tell me herself. I will never bother her again. Will you tell her that?"

"I can not tell her that. I have never met your wife. You must leave now, Signor Hornbeck."

He could sense her inner agitation, her fear, but there was no break in the front she was putting up.

"Poldi, I will have another brandy."

Signora Poldi hastened to replenish the Countess's glass. She fussed with the tea tray but did not offer Beecher more tea. She adjusted the pillow behind the old lady's head—that regal head with the white chignon, held in place by two jeweled combs. A stubborn woman with overweaning pride, thought Beecher.

"You must get your rest soon, Teresa," announced Beatrice Poldi, nervously.

"I do grow weary," sighed the Countess. This was no doubt planned carefully before his arrival, in case he proved tiresome and hard to get rid of.

Beecher made no attempt to get up and leave. "Countess Rosetti, why did you send for me, if you have no intention of being honest with me about your visitor yesterday? I can hardly believe that a woman of your position would bring me back here in order to secure a locket that is of very little value, merely a trinket." His remark stung her pride, as he intended.

The black eyes flashed. "I did not want it for myself!"

"Who then, Countess Rosetti? Could it be that my wife wants it back? It was hers you know, before she disappeared and made me think that she was dead. You may return it to her with my regards."

Beatrice Poldi crossed the room and stood in back of the Countess's chair. She put her hands on the old lady's shoulders, as though to protect her.

Beecher rose from his chair and stood in front of the Countess, looking down at her. He could see that her whole body was shaking slightly. Her hands were clenched tightly together in her lap, and her eyes were averted from him.

"Just tell me that Myra is alive, here in Venice, and that she does not want to see me, and I'll leave and never bother you again."

"I can not tell you that. It would be a lie." She looked up at him and he was amazed to see tears in her eyes. "Signor Hornbeck, please leave now. Go home—back to America. Your wife is dead to you. I can tell you no more. You must believe that she is dead. Venice is an unusual city, like no other. People often see strange sights in Venice, mirages. Our senses are not always reliable. They deceive us. You have only imagined that you saw the one you wanted so desperately to see. The poor dead woman is a figment of your imagination." This long speech, delivered with more emotion than he would have thought her capable, seemed to have taken all her strength.

"I'll leave now, Countess. Maybe your neighbors have seen the same figment that I did. It's a possibility. I can think of other possibilities as well, such as going to the police. I'll leave you now to your brandy and your rest."

He turned and left the room, not waiting for Beatrice Poldi, who hurried after him down the stairs. "Wait, Signor Hornbeck, I'll call Marco to take you back to your hotel."

"Don't bother. I'll walk or catch the *vaporetto.* If you'll get my coat." If he stayed another minute, he doubted that he would be able to control his anger and frustration.

Beatrice Poldi brought his raincoat. He could see that she was afraid. "I would not bother our neighbors, Signor Hornbeck. These adjoining *palazzi* are leased to Europeans. They have not yet returned to Venice for the summer season. Their servants know nothing."

Beecher had no intentions of interrogating residents of the Rio del Giglio tonight. He had just made the threat to see what their reaction would be, and it had aroused fear in both the Countess and Poldi. If there was no Myra, why were they both so afraid of what he would find out? He was suddenly sick of the whole thing. He had gone to the limits to find someone who didn't want to be found. For the first time since the whole nightmarish thing had started, Beecher wished that he had never seen Myra on the Spanish Steps. The thought tore at his heart.

Beecher stepped out into the rain and mist, and heard the massive door slam behind him. The pealing of a distant bell reverberated across the waters, sounding a death knell to all his hopes.

6.

Somehow, Beecher had made his way back to the Hotel Bellini. The entire evening was a blank spot in his memory and would remain so, a white page on which there would never be any writing. He had arrived back at the Bellini around ten o'clock on the *vaporetto*, but he didn't remember catching it or how long or where he had wandered after leaving Ca'Rosetti on the Rio del Giglio. He hadn't noticed when the rain stopped.

As he entered the lobby and crossed to the desk to pick up his key, old Renzo hurried up. "Signor Hornbeck, Maestro, do you wish Franco for tomorrow, with the gondola? He is free. You say to him that you wish to visit Ca' d' Oro, to see the Carpaccios and the Bellinis and also the Accademia. He will take you on a grand tour: the house of Gabriele d' Annunzio in which he entertained La Duse, the Isle of Torcello, the Riva degli Zattere where the artists and writers gather. The drawing you make of Franco, Maestro, he is so proud."

"It was only a sketch, Renzo. I'm glad that it pleased him."

" You are wet, Signore. Do you walk in the rain? Are you ill?"

"As a matter of fact, I'm not feeling well, Renzo. My plans for tomorrow are indefinite. I may be returning to Rome sooner that I expected."

"Signore, you have not yet seen Venice. Were you not happy with Franco?"

"Nothing like that, Renzo. I was very pleased with Franco and his gondola is quite—Beecher looked for the right word, that would assure Renzo—luxurious."

The old man smiled happily. "Yes, Signore, I know you would appreciate! I myself, advise Franco to buy the red carpet, the real leather cushions."

"Very elegant, Renzo. Now if you'll excuse me, I'm very tired. I need to get out of these clothes and order some food from room service."

"Remember Signore, dial five, Maria will help you."

"Tell Franco not to turn down any customers for his gondola tomorrow. I may call him later if he is free, or it may be necessary that I return to Rome."

Beecher ordered dinner from the ever helpful Maria, and after removing his sodden clothes, taking a hot shower and eating dinner, he had fallen asleep.

He awoke hours later. The room was filled with the pink glow of a dawn that only comes after rain. Like a somnambulist, he crossed the room and looked out over the balcony. The blue of the lagoon in the distance was covered with a canopy of heliotrope and jasmine, and the spires and ancient monuments of Venice rose from the water like spiky irridescent crystals. Between them, the square, squat *palazzi* appeared in the first light of dawn to be jeweled ivory casques, filled with their treasures, the art and relics of the Renaissance. They held no pleasure for him now.

He closed the shutters and returned to bed. When he awoke later, he would not remember going to the balcony, or what he had seen, a fairy city in a tale that would soon be over for him. He slipped back into a deep sleep and lay as one dead.

And then Beecher dreamed of the dark man. He wore the rough brown habit of a Capuchin monk, and his body was deformed and twisted. The monk stood on a high wall and struggled with Myra, who tried desperately to escape his grasp. The man's hood fell back, and Beecher saw the face of Marco. Myra was screaming, but Beecher could hear no sound. The monk held Myra around the waist; his other hand was entwined in her long hair. "You can have her," he called to Beecher. The voice was a thin wail, as unlike any human sound as a dream from reality. "You can have her if you will give me Cristina."

Beecher stood paralyzed by fear, his feet rooted to the ground. He tried to run, but he was unable to move his legs; he tried to scream, but no sound came. Cristina for Myra. He could not—.

It was gone. Over. Now he could see a long narrow room; almost like a tunnel with a light gleaming at the far end. A man was bent over a box. He was too far away for Beecher to see clearly what he was doing. Now Beecher was running, or rather moving with great speed along the tunnel, toward this figure. He had never seen the man before, but in the logical, illogical manner of dreams, he knew that the man was Dino Romano, the film director. The man was smiling and beckoning him forward.

Just then Romano turned and pointed to a large projection screen on which images moved and exploded into ever more bizarre shapes and colors, like some giant cosmic kaleidoscope. Beecher was totally enveloped in the light and sound.

"See me, Dino Romano," the man said, over and over again, like a broken sound track. His voice echoed through the tunnel, like a sound heard in some deep subterranean chamber.

Beecher woke in a cold sweat, the voice still echoing in his ears. "See me, Dino Romano," and Beecher knew what Caserta had meant, what the dying man had been so desperately trying to tell him. What had been eluding him for so long—what he should have seen from the beginning, rose from the depths of his subconscious like a miasma from the canals of Venice.

It shouldn't have surprised him that it would be this way. Life is so often like a strumpet, who defrauds and deceives us at every turn and then, when we are almost past caring, offers us the shining prize, implying that it could have been so easy if we only had known the secret password, the magic phrase.

The answer lay in Dino Romano's films. Caserta had known that Romano was dead, but what could still be seen of the dead man? His films, of course—Dino Romano's films. Beecher knew that he must return to Rome without delay.

Part IV - Finale

1.

Cristina met him at the Rome airport and kept her distance in a rather self-conscious way, as though to avoid a repeat of the incident at his departure for Venice when she had suddenly found herself in his arms. At first Beecher was disconcerted by what appeared to be her deliberate coldness, but then realized that he had really left her no choice. As long as he was obsessed with finding Myra....

That morning he had called her from Venice and told her he had seen Myra and had finally talked to the Countess Rosetti.

"Cristina, do you think Edoardo could get copies of all of the films that Dino Romano made in the last five years? Everything after 1985, and run them for me? I know now that when Caserta whispered 'see Dino Romano' he was trying to tell me that the answer is somewhere in those films. I don't know which one; I don't even know the name she is using, so I need them all. Cristina, I know I'll see Myra in at least one of Romano's films."

For a minute, there had been silence on the other end of the line, and then she had answered, "I'm quite sure it will be no problem for Edoardo. It will give him a thrill, just like the old days." It was difficult to hear—the line was crackling—but he thought he detected a faint note of bitterness in her voice.

On the way into the city, Beecher told Cristina about his stay in Venice. He told her about the second half of his dream, but not the first.

"Well, Beecher, you should know something soon," she said, narrowly missing a Vespa. "Edoardo was able to get the films. There are six of them. Four were shown only in Italy; the other two were shown abroad, as well. Edoardo went into action as soon as I told him. He engaged Tommaso, the young gardener, to drive Guido for the next two days, so he can devote himself exclusively to your project, with Guido's blessing, of course. Edoardo took off his chauffeur's uniform and put on his best matinee-idol, pinstripe suit and dark glasses and took off for Cinecittá to see his old friend, Sal Fioretti, who has charge of the film library. Edoardo called me at the gallery, just before I left to pick you up at the airport to say he had a projection room lined up for ten in the morning."

"That's better than I had hoped for, Cristina. How can I thank you?"

"Just let Edoardo know you're grateful. It will mean a lot to him. Working for Guido is often hard on his ego." They were lucky enough to find a parking place in front of Cristina's building and as they waited for the lift, she said, "I hope my roast hasn't burned."

Cristina's small apartment was an island of comfort and safety in a rough sea where Beecher had lost all his moorings and had been set adrift.

He leaned back on the sofa and stared into the fire. The warm spring days of last week were gone, and the chill and mist he had encountered in Venice had arrived in Rome just ahead of him. Rain fell outside the large arched window. He could hear it hit the tiled roof and drip off the drainspouts and the grotesque faces of the gargoyles that glared down at passers-by on the Viale Bruno Buozi.

The homey sounds of the clatter of pots and pans and the oven door opening came from the kitchen as Cristina prepared dinner. The smell of roasting meat filled the apartment, and the joyous strains of Mozart brought him back to the reality of a world where happy endings were possible. He was no longer anxious for tomorrow. He wasn't sure he was ready for any more revelations.

Cristina called from the kitchen. "Please light the candles, Beecher, and pour the wine; everything is about ready out here." She had the table set as before with her gold-rimmed china and Waterford crystal. Camellias floated in a silver bowl. She pushed open the swinging door between the kitchen and living room and brought in a platter on which a small standing rib roast sizzled in its own juice, surrounded by Yorkshire pudding and browned potatoes. "You can carry in the rest, Beecher. There's a bowl of peas and some rolls."

As they ate they chatted about recent happenings at the gallery. Guido had mentioned Beecher's proposed Italian series several times to Cristina with great enthusiasm.

"I haven't even thought about it, Cristina, since I left Rome," Beecher said. "Venice is an artist's paradise, but I can't think of painting with this other thing on my mind."

"I can understand that, but try to forget it for now. You can't do anything more till morning." She sliced more roast and piled it on his plate. "Beecher, you look to me like you've lost weight. Have you been eating?"

He shrugged, remembering Renzo and the tiny fish and the luscious melon with proscuitto. "Well, I haven't had anything to compare with this—I can tell you that." He reached across the table and took her hand. "Cristina, you have an instinct for knowing just what a body needs, as they say in Sparta. It seems that all you do is give, and all I do is take; *my* exhibit, *my* Italian series, *my* obsession with finding Myra."

Her face flushed. "You were thrown into this situation,

Beecher. You had no idea when you came to Italy that this would happen, just as I had no idea when I drove you to the Borghese Garden that day that I would become so involved in your life. Your search for Myra has brought back memories of Carlo, of that terrible time after his death. We were simply plunged into this, Beecher, and it's too late for regrets or the kind of polite little speeches that strangers make to each other. There's no point in our even discussing anything until you find Myra."

The Mozart had ended, and she got up and put on a recording of Brahms' second piano concerto. She went into the kitchen and brought out the dessert. "You mustn't laugh," she said, "but I tried to make you a cherry cobbler. It may not bear any resemblance to the real thing. I found the recipe in an American cookbook." She spoke rapidly, as though to hide her embarrassment, "I don't even know if our cherries in Italy are the same kind you grow in Indiana."

Tears stung his eyes. "Well let's try it and see," he answered rather brusquely. He couldn't let her see how touched he was. Rome was not the place to fall apart. It might take all the king's horses and all the king's men to get him back to Indiana again.

They sat in front of the fire after dinner and drank coffee and talked about painting and plans that she and Guido had for the Gallery. Beecher, told her more about Conner and Harry, about Sparta and his life on the farm.

"Has it occurred to you, Beecher, that you and I are alike in one respect. We both perceive ourselves as being rather ordinary characters from mundane backgrounds. and we were both drawn to opposites. Carlo and Myra had the exotic qualities, the charisma and fire we admired so much, but felt that we lacked ourselves."

"I guess so, I hadn't thought about it, but I suppose what you say is true. I never could understand what Myra saw in me. I guess that's why I'm having all these doubts now."

She looked at him with amusement. "You really mean that, don't you? That's where your charm lies."

"Oh sure. I'm considered to be the most charming guy in Sparta. But you *are* doing my ego good. Conner had almost convinced me that I have gotten so crusty that I must act fast, or my dog will be my only friend."

They both laughed. The sound startled Ottavia, who jumped down from Cristina's lap and hissed at Beecher. "Well, your cat doesn't agree about my charms. That's the first animal that's ever hated me." Ottavia glared at him with her cold, slanted Siamese eyes.

"Don't pay any attention to Ottavia. She hates everyone who comes here. She's jealous of me and is very neurotic."

"Are there many for her to be jealous of?" Beecher asked and immediately regretted it.

She was gathering up coffee cups and dessert dishes and headed for the kitchen, pretending she hadn't heard his question. When she returned she looked at her watch and said, "Would you believe that it's half past eleven? You look so tired and drawn, Beecher. I'm driving you to the Excelsior now." Cristina looked at Beecher with tenderness and then seemed to change her mind about something she was going to say. She went to the bedroom for their raincoats.

The steady swish of the windshield wipers almost hypnotized him, as Cristina drove through the dark city. The lights in the piazze and on the fountains became blurred halos in the rain and shop windows were ghostly and forgotten. Just as Beecher had decided that all the tourists must have made a speedy exodus from Rome, a nightclub erupted, spilling a crowd of loud, weirdly dressed young people out into the street. Cristina honked and barely avoided hitting one of them, a girl with pink spiked hair and a black leather mini-skirt. "We have them in London, too," she said.

"So far, in Sparta, we have been spared," answered Beecher. "So you see, living in the sticks does have some advantages. Mrs. Daily thinks a transvestite is a vest that's solid on one side and plaid on the other."

"That's wonderful," Cristina laughed. "You make Sparta

sound like Utopia, a place where there are still people who are innocent. Don't be offended, Beecher, but there's a little of that in you. That's what I meant about your charm."

"Please, let's not get on that again. I'm much more charming, now, in my citified clothes and my Burberry raincoat than I am as the amiable rustic, smelling of sweat and cow manure. You have the same idea that Myra did about the farm being glamorous. "

She had pulled up in front of the Excelsior, and Luigi hastened to open the door. Beecher took the keys from Cristina and opened the trunk. Luigi handed the luggage to a young bellman as Beecher leaned into the car to say goodnight to Cristina.

"Edoardo will pick you up here at nine. Just look for the cool dude in the sun glasses," she said. "He won't be driving the Lancia. Tommaso will have that. I would imagine he will be in a dark green Fiat."

"At the risk of sounding like a broken record, thanks again for everything. When I see you again, I should have some answers. Goodnight." He reached over gently and brushed a wisp of coppery hair back from her forehead.

"Goodnight, Beecher."

She drove away into the night.

2.

Edoardo picked him up the next morning in the green Fiat and drove him to Cinecittá, the enormous movie complex outside Rome. The chauffeur and former actor would have delighted in taking Beecher on a grand tour, but the artist declined.

They went directly to the projection room, where Edoardo introduced Beecher to his friend, Sal Fioretti, who brought in the film canisters and left Edoardo to run the projector. In this small dark room with plush velvet seats, Dino Romano, as well as Vittorio De Sica, Dino De Laurentiis and the great Fellini had viewed their million-dollar epics and Cannes Film Festival winners as well as their costly disasters.

Beecher sat through one expensively costumed colossus from 1983 with no success, but was able to dispatch the second offering in a hurry. It was an art film with a cast of four, that reminded Beecher of Rossillini's earlier *Stromboli*. After the four actors had all made their appearances, it was unnecessary to watch further.

It was Dino Romano's third film, *Filo d'Oro,* that gave Beecher his answer. The incredibly gorgeous face filled the giant screen: the enormous dark eyes under heavy, beautiful arched brows, the perfect nose and full lips, conjured up from the grave.

Beecher gave no sign of acknowledgement as he sat there in the dark while Edoardo watched the film, engrossed. For another twenty minutes she filled the screen, larger that life: first innocent, then seductive, angry, tearful. She ran the full gamut of emotion. She was not a great actress, Beecher realized, but she possessed a fire and seductiveness that would sway audiences, possibly had swayed Dino Romano.

The Italian voices went on and on, filling the room with sound that had become quite alien to him, as alien as voices from another planet. Just one more scene, Beecher told himself as tears ran down his face in the dark. Myra must have suffered terribly through the years. Why hadn't she trusted him enough to tell him? Didn't she know that he would understand? He took out his handkerchief and blew his nose.

"That's enough Edoardo. I've seen what I came for," he said.

Edoardo's expression registered shock as he turned on the lights and looked at the artist's drawn, haggard face. Beecher felt that he owed Edoardo some explanation, but he couldn't find the words. He merely said, "We don"t need to watch any more. Just run the credits at the end of the film." Her stage name was Angela Rinaldi.

After they returned to Rome, Beecher called Cristina from his room. "Can you meet me here at the Excelsior for dinner?"

"What time? Did you find out anything?" she asked anxiously.

"I found out. Not everything, but enough to put two and two together; enough so that the Countess will have to tell me the rest. Meet me in the bar at eight o'clock. OK?"

She would be there.

He took off his suit and lay down on the bed. Why hadn't he suspected? The moodiness, the guilt. Had Harry known? Myra had not betrayed him. She had not betrayed him, but she believed she had, he realized sadly. His dearest. How could he have ever doubted her?

At eight o'clock Cristina crossed the crowded bar to the small table in the corner where Beecher waited, smoking his pipe. The Brazzano emeralds in her ears and at her throat reflected facets of green fire, and the beams from the small lights recessed in the ceiling turned her coppery hair red against the black dress as she walked toward him.

"You decide what we should have," he said after she sat down. "You know that I'm no connoisseur. I was raised on sassafras tea."

"Don't pull that poor old hick routine on me, Beecher. You're a painter with an international reputation." She ordered two Camparis with ice.

The waiter looked relieved. He had caught the remark about sassafras tea and feared that he would be asked to produce some. Americans were strange people with strange tastes, but the Signorina was a different story. He eyed Cristina's figure appreciatively and shook his head as he left to get their drinks. That she should waste herself on such a one as this!

They had lingered over the Camparis and then had talked so much at dinner, that their waiter, Giorgio, had asked reproachfully if there was anything wrong with the Hotel Excelsior's famous green lasagna, when he collected their half empty plates. Perhaps they would like to try another entree? When they both refused the dessert cart and Beecher asked for the check, Georgio really showed concern. Cristina smiled as the waiter retreated with the check and Beecher's American Express Card. "Beecher, you are learning that all Italian waiters are really Jewish mothers in disguise."

They decided to walk down the Via Veneto. The rain had stopped and the air was warmer now and scented with flowers. Trees that were only budding when Beecher had first arrived in Rome for his exhibit were lush and green. Waiters at the cafes along the broad boulevard were setting out tables and chairs again and the *passeggiata* was in full swing. At the Fontana del Tritone, the pleasant-looking

American and the petite, copper-haired woman in the black velvet jacket stopped to talk for quite some time and then started back toward the hotel.

3.

The next day Beecher arrived in Venice at the Hotel Bellini. He stood at the desk and registered, handing his passport to Ricardo. "A mere formality, Signor Hornbeck. We are happy to have you back again with us so soon."

The waves made the same gentle lapping sound. How many dramas had Venice witnessed: political intrigue and upheaval, violence and assassination, love affairs that shocked the world, the deaths of poets and kings. And still the waves lapped, slowly eroding the foundations of this ancient city, in spite of all man's efforts toward restoration.

Beecher returned to the Rio del Giglio and confronted Countess Rosetti with what he had seen in the Romano film. When he asked her about Angela Rinaldi, she grew pale and ordered Poldi to bring her brandy. "You are very clever, Signor Hornbeck, but there is much at stake here. Harriet Wellington must come to Venice. Then the three of us will sit down together and talk."

"I can't see the necessity, Countess, of bringing my mother- in-law all the way to Venice."

"Promises were made in this room many years ago, promises that cannot be broken now. You must bring her here and then I will answer your questions—but not until Harriet Wellington is present in this house."

He could see that there was no point in arguing further, and so he left.

He called Harry in Connecticut. "This is like a bad dream, Beecher," she said. "As you know, when you called several weeks ago to tell us you were leaving for Rome with your exhibit, I was in Newport. Naturally, William told me when I returned..." Harry paused. "Beecher, can you ever forgive me?"

"I already have, Harry. You had your reasons, I'm sure. To call this nightmare a comedy of errors would be grotesque, but tragedy doesn't quite seem to fit either. The point is—can you come to Venice? The Countess isn't about to weaken and those were her terms."

"Teresa Rosetti, I remember her all too well. Apparently the years haven't changed her at all. I'll catch a plane out of Kennedy tonight if possible, if not, tomorrow at the latest. I'll call you back and let you know what time I'll be arriving," said Harry.

The Alitalia, DC-9 dropped out of the low-hanging clouds at Venice's Marco Polo Airport and touched down at the far end of the runway, a child's toy that grew larger and larger as it raced down the tarmac. The pilot employed the thrust reversers to slow down the plane, which came to a shuddering halt just short of the terminal. The stairway was lowered and passengers started to disembark. Beecher watched the small slim figure walk rapidly across the airfield. Harry was young-looking for her sixty four years and still moved with the grace of a girl.

She ran into his arms. "Beecher, you know I'd rather die than put you through this. Why didn't you call me in the beginning and tell me that you had seen her?"

"I didn't want to raise your hopes—your's and William's—before I had actually found Myra," Beecher answered.

"William doesn't know a thing, Beecher. He's never known. I'll have to tell him when I get home. I should have told you, but I didn't want to hurt you unnecessarily. It's incredible that you saw her—that you found out."

All the way into Venice in the *motoscafo* Beecher talked, and Harry listened to the whole story. Then he told her about seeing Myra a second time, here in Venice and how the old Countess and Beatrice Poldi had lied about their visitor. He even told her about the slip Marco had made. Beecher had planned to take Harry to lunch, but she insisted on going directly to the Rio del Giglio.

"I had late breakfast on the plane. Can we go there now, Beecher, and get this over with?" The same old no-nonsense Harry.

"I'll get a *motoscafo* when we dock at the Piazza San Marco. It will be much quicker than a gondola. The old lady is expecting us." Harry was traveling light, with only a small carry-on bag. William was in the hospital for tests and she must return to New York the following day.

"Beecher, I want you to know that I did beg Myra to tell you, and then it was too late. Lies always have dreadful repercussions. In this instance, you were the one to reap what we had sown." Harry suddenly looked old as she stared with unseeing eyes at the splendors of Venice that were spread out in front of her on both sides of the Grand Canal. The golden domes of San Marco were just coming into view ahead.

4.

Beecher and Harry were ushered into the hall by a subdued Beatrice Poldi. He was shocked to see the dark circles under her eyes. She led them up the stairs to the same salon where he had met with the Countess on his second visit to Ca' Rosetti.

Harry walked over to the old lady who was seated in the worn velvet chair and took her hand. "I had no idea, Countess, that we would ever meet again after all these years, and certainly not under these circumstances."

"Nor did I, Signora Wellington." She sighed and motioned for them to be seated.

The profound silence was broken only by the ticking of the rococo clock. Both women seemed to be lost in memories that Beecher could only imagine.

"I have lost my wife twice, Countess," Beecher began. "She was killed five years ago and then for these few brief weeks I thought that by some miracle, I was to have her back again. This is a second death.

"She was just as I remembered her, only more beautiful. That should have been the clue, but the beloved is always idealized in the memory of the bereaved, and Angela was more nearly like my memories of Myra than the real Myra would have been. Angela is the memory clothed in flesh, the essence and image of Myra. Both times I saw her at a distance and then only for a few seconds. A stranger would have guessed Myra's age at thirty when she died, instead of thirty eight."

Harry nodded in agreement.

"When I viewed Romano's film, and Angela Rinaldi's beautiful face filled that giant screen, I realized that I was looking at a much younger woman. She had to be Myra's daughter, as fantastic as that seemed.

"You, Countess, could have ended my agonized search for my wife if you had only told me the truth a week ago, the first day I came here. You must have known immediately that I had mistaken Angela for my wife. Why didn't you see me that first day and tell me the truth? Why did you lie to me when you sent for me? You and Poldi and even Marco lied."

The old lady glared defiantly at Beecher. She sat very straight, a small shrunken figure in black, clinging fiercely to the remaining shreds of dignity and pride that she had left. "Angela is all that I have left. I will do anything to protect her. You were not the first to come here—to try to take her from me. First there was Aldo Gionotti and then there was Caserta."

Harry interrupted at this point. "I think Beecher should hear the beginning of the story first, Teresa. Do you mind if I call you that? And please call me Harry. It's a little late in the day for formalities. After all, for the past twenty three years, you have raised and cared for my granddaughter."

Harry's granddaughter. Myra's daughter. Would that make Angela his own stepdaughter—the child he and Myra never had? Some of the implications were only now beginning to dawn on Beecher, whose mind felt like a scarred battlefield, where dreams and desires had battled with fears, doubts and frustrations for weeks.

Signora Poldi came into the rose brocade room with the

usual refreshment. The Italian didn't know much about making tea, Beecher decided, as he tasted the anemic mixture. The old Countess Teresa had fortified herself with a "small brandy", and Harry had joined her, turning to Beecher with, "Couldn't you use a little shot of this, Beecher?"

"Maybe later, Harry."

The clock ticked. A gondola filled with laughing, chattering Italians floated down the *rio*, below the open windows, and the sun fell in a golden shaft on the worn Aubusson carpet.

Harry put down her brandy glass and began. "As you know, Beecher, Myra was in school in Switzerland when she was seventeen. The school was located in the small village of Meiringin, near Lucerne. She had already been there over a year. William thought it was important—Swiss finishing schools and all that sort of thing. I had traveled that route, in my youth, because my parents had insisted, and found that it was not my cup of tea. Neither was it Myra's. I had convinced William that when Myra finished that year, she was to return to the States to complete her education. Unfortunately, that was a little too late. She went on spring vacation with some of her classmates and a chaperone to Lake Como. Lucerne is only a short distance from the Italian Alps. It was all supposed to be very wholesome and instructive: backpacking in the Alps, cataloging flora and fauna. But apparently while the chaperone was busy sniffing wild flowers, Myra got herself involved with a young Italian. Dino Romano was filming a movie at an old castle across the lake—some swash-buckling affair adapted from a story by Alexander Dumas. Beecher, you know what a romantic Myra was. He said he could help her get into the movies. Myra was stage-struck as a kid. She had visions of being an actress before she decided to study art."

Beatrice Poldi descended to replenish the brandy, and Beecher decided to have one. He swirled the golden liquid in his glass, took a sip to fortify himself, and turned to

Harry. "Tell me right now, Harry. Was it Dino Romano?"

"No, Beecher. It was Aldo Gionotti, a young actor who had a small part in the film. I'm giving you Myra's version, as she told it to me. She said that he was very handsome and swept her off her feet, to coin a rather archaic phrase. I don't know; I never saw him."

"Aldo Gionotti was handsome," said Beecher, "at the time Myra must have known him."

Harry looked at Beecher with surprise. "How could you possibly know that?"

"Anne Leone, his sister, showed me an old picture. Go on, Harry. The pieces are beginning to fall into place."

The Countess interrupted at this point. She had become agitated at the mention of Aldo Gionotti. "He came here too, perhaps three years ago. He said that he had found out that Angela was his daughter. He showed me a photograph of himself taken with Myra Wellington, years before. The resemblance to Angela was quite astounding. He told me of the, as you say, 'affair' during the filming of the movie. I gave him money several times, so that he would stay away from Angela—never to tell her that he was her father."

"But how could he have known?" asked Harry. "Myra went back to Switzerland. She never saw him again or wrote to him. He had no idea that she was pregnant. Only you and I, Countess, and Myra, of course, even knew his name."

"He didn't know about Angela until three years ago. He was at a film studio trying to get in to see Dino Romano when he saw Angela; she was waiting to see Romano also. He was astounded at the resemblance to Myra Wellington. He started a conversation with my Angela. She is too friendly, too trusting—I tell her often, but it does no good. He learned that she had been orphaned as a baby when her parents were killed; a steamer sank while crossing from Brindisi to Athens. She told him that she had been raised in Venice by her great aunt, Countess Teresa Rosetti. This is the story that I told her as a child. She believes that her parents were my niece and her husband, who did die, as I have described, only it was shortly before and not after her birth. Her birth certificate has been altered. I have friends in many quarters, Signor Hornbeck. Legally, she is Angela Rinaldi, daughter of Leila and Roberto Rinaldi, who died in 1964 when the *Hellas* sank in the Aegean sea."

It all fits in, thought Beecher. Caserta had said that he was the only one who knew "the truth about your wife—now that Aldo is dead".

"How did you finally get rid of Gionotti, Countess?"

"He became ill and died. I was glad. Angela was safe from him." She stared at Beecher with pride and not remorse. What had Pietro Reni said to Beecher that first day, driving into Rome—that an Italian would do anything to protect his family.

The Countess resumed. "Then a year after Gionotti died, the other one came."

"Do you mean Luca Caserta?" asked Beecher.

"Yes, Luca Caserta. He wanted money too, but this time I would not pay. I could see that he was afraid and that he was running from someone. I told him that I would not pay, that I had Mafia connections and that if he went near Angela, I would have him killed. Marco was able to get into his hotel room and slash his clothes and suitcase—a small warning. Caserta narrowly missed falling in front of a *motoscafo*. He must have believed me, as he returned to Rome and never came back. He left us in peace."

"Did you have him killed, Countess?"

"No, but if I could, I would have. Marco heard of his death on the radio." She smiled. Her face resembled a skull. How could I ever have thought she looked like Myra, Beecher wondered.

"He was killed outside my hotel room at the Excelsior. He was trying to get money from me for information about Myra. He must have seen the notice of my exhibit in the Rome newspapers and decided he would try to sell me the information about Myra's daughter. He was trailing me the day I saw Angela on the Spanish Steps, and he realized he better contact me quickly, before I caught up with her and found out for myself. He needed money desperately, to get out of the country, according to the police. I was going to pay him too, because I thought he would tell me where to find Myra. Zinelli told me that's how Caserta lived, by blackmail and selling information. Apparently that's how he died too."

"It became a tangled web," Harry sighed, "and all because of the lies I told in the beginning. I blame myself, much more than I blame Myra. She was young and romantic and in love with love and Aldo came along—a handsome young man in a courtier's costume on a white horse, literally. The setting was an old castle with a garden maze and a lake with swans. Can you see her, Beecher in that kind of a situation, at seventeen?" Harry's eyes were pleading with him not to judge Myra too harshly.

"I can understand, Harry. Go on."

"The girls went back to Switzerland, of course, and Myra didn't realize she was pregnant for some time. She called me crying; she was afraid and ashamed. It was late May, nearly the end of the term. I told her not to tell anyone what she suspected. I made some excuse to William and flew to Switzerland.

"The following week, after school was out, we went to Paris, where a doctor confirmed the suspicion that Myra was pregnant. She felt that her life was ruined before it had begun, that she could never face her father and her friends back home. That's when I came up with the idea that she and I would stay in Europe until after the baby arrived. I lied to William. We were supposed to be visiting various friends who were scattered all over. Actually we did travel quite a lot: Paris, Cannes, London, Edinburgh and finally, Rome. By the time we got to Rome, Myra's baby was due in eight weeks. It was then that I got the idea of looking up the Rosettis in Venice. It was just a hunch.

"Later I met the Countess Teresa and learned that she had just lost her remaining relatives, a niece and her husband in that terrible accident at sea, and was alone except for servants in this huge house. It then occurred to me that she might be willing to raise Myra's child, who would be, after all, the last living descendant of Alessandro Rosetti. Money was no problem. I told the Countess that I would support the child."

"You neglect to tell him that I refused your money. If I raised this child, I wanted to be sure that she had no ties to the Wellingtons. She never lacked any comfort, I saw to that, and I sent her later to the finest convent schools."

Beecher understood now why Myra felt that not being able to have children was a sign of God's judgement. She felt that she was being punished because she had given her baby away. As the years passed and she remained childless, she became filled with despair. "I understand her moods now, Harry," he said.

"Beecher, I pleaded with Myra to tell you. She planned to, when the two of you came to Venice to look up the Rosettis. She was going to tell you, and she hoped to see Angela for the first time since she had given her up as a baby. She hoped to convince Teresa.

"I had promised Teresa, in this room, twenty years ago, when I brought Myra's baby to her that neither of us would ever try to see the child again, and that we would tell no one, not even William. Those were her conditions." These two indomitable women looked across the room at each other. Harry dropped her eyes first, but not before Beecher had seen her tears.

"I feel that I have lived a lie all these years. The only way I have been able to stand it is that I knew the child was being loved and cared for and that no stigma would ever be attached to her name. Myra was happily married to you, Beecher, except for this shadow over her life. Maybe I did William a grave injustice to assume that he wouldn't understand or accept an illegitimate child. I've never felt happy or at peace with what I did."

"You seem to forget that I exist," said the old lady bitterly. "Only yourself, do you talk about, and your daughter. Angela has been my life and I have given her all the love of both a mother and a grandmother. Nonna Teresa, she calls me, grandmother, even though she believes me to be her great aunt. She is sweet and innocent still, at twenty-three. I, at first, opposed this movie business. The type of people she would be with frightened me. Dino Romano discovered her here in Venice in an amateur theatrical in the Piazza San Marco. He was here for *Carnivale*. But Angela was so anxious for it. She must spend most of her time in Rome, now, but she has not forgotten her Nonna Teresa and Poldi and Marco. She comes here often to see us. Unfortunately, you saw her arrive last week."

"Who did you tell her that I was?" asked Beecher.

"I told her that you were a reporter, who had come here to annoy me because of her movie career—that she must stay hidden until Poldi got rid of you. By the next day, when you returned, she had already gone back to Rome."

"Why didn't you simply let me meet her, that first day? I was no threat to either you or the girl, Countess."

"But you were, Signor Hornbeck. You had no children. Angela is the image of your dead wife. I remember poor Alessandro. I feared that you would lure her to America with promises of a movie career in Hollywood. She is all that I have."

"I promise you, Countess, that I will never try to influence Angela to leave you or Italy. This is her home. My wife gave up her child voluntarily. I have no claim on Angela. I should like to meet her. Perhaps I might be able to come to Italy occasionally and visit her—to get to know her."

"You could not meet her without telling her who you are—who her real mother was, and her father. Then she would know that I have lied to her, that she is not really mine."

Teresa Rosetti turned to Harry with pleading eyes. "Don't let him do this thing. You promised me. I kept my part of our agreement, all these years. Now keep yours!" Her hands shook as she grasped the arms of the chair. "I will soon be gone. Then you will be free to do as you like. But, I beg you to think of her. She is happier believing as she does."

"Beecher, I did promise. I can't go back on my word. Please don't see her, for my sake," Harry pleaded. "I believed what I did was best at the time, for both Myra and the baby."

"I'll abide by your agreement, Harry. I won't try to see her. I'll just have to accept the fact that she's from another part of Myra's life, the part I never knew existed. You don't have to worry, Countess. You have my word, but if you should change your mind, after thinking it over...."

"Signor Hornbeck, if you could see her without letting her know who you are; get to know her as an artist who has come to Italy for an exhibit, one who had admired her in the movies, perhaps," the Countess relented. "I can see that you are not like Aldo Gionotti, who was her father but cared nothing for her. He wanted only money from me. She may need you some day, for a friend, after I am gone. Go to see her on the Amalfi coast, if you wish. She is making a film there. I trust you. Think of some explanation for your friendship. She is a guileless child. She will believe you." Tears ran down the old lady's face and stained the ancient black silk shirtwaist.

Harry was crying silently into her glass of brandy. Beecher stood up. "You need never worry, Countess, about me doing either you or Angela any harm. I know how to keep a trust. We Hornbecks are not very colorful, but we do know how to keep a trust."

She looked up at him and smiled. "I believe that you do, Signore."

"Just one last question, Countess. Did you take the locket for Angela?"

"I did, Signore, for Angela, Alessandro's last descendant."

Fate, thought Beecher, has her own strange ways of evening things up. Alessandro had been buried and forgotten among Hartleys, in a cold alien land, but now his locket hung around the neck of this beautiful girl, who resembled him—his last descendant. She had grown up as an Italian, here, in his beloved Venice. Life had come full circle. The drama that had begun with Alessandro Rosetti and Lavinia Hartley so many years ago was finished.

5.

Beecher took Harry to dinner that night at Quadri, over-looking the Piazza San Marco. They dined in the eight-eenth century green and gold room beneath a painted Renaissance ceiling. Harry became slightly tipsy on the Barolo Mirafiore, and Beecher, losing some of his accus-tomed reserve, ordered a second bottle.

"Can't you see, Harry, how I thought I'd found Myra—that somehow she was still alive? It all seems like a dream now, even to me."

"Beecher, Angela is the very image of her. When you showed me that movie still after I got off the plane, I could hardly believe it."

"The more I thought about it, the more afraid I became that she had run away from me. Italy was just the kind of place Myra would have loved. I remembered her moodi-ness. Everything I couldn't understand before seemed to make sense. My fears and doubts fed on my own insecurity. I can see that now."

"Myra did love Italy. We stayed here in Venice the last eight weeks before Angela was born," Harry explained.

A string quartet was playing "Memory" from *Cats*. Beecher and Harry, two people engrossed in intimate conversation, were reflected in the giant gilt-framed mirrors of the restaurant.

"I took her to dinner often, here. We strolled in the Piazza San Marco and sat at Florian's and ate ices. No wonder you sensed her presence here, Beecher. I imagine now that I can feel it myself.

"Myra's labor pains started early and I panicked and sent for the ambulance. It was an enclosed gondola with a blue cross on its side and a funny-sounding little horn. We tooted down the Grand Canal to the hospital in that ambulance gondola, scared to death. Myra had a difficult delivery. The doctor spoke only a few words of English. I know it must have been a frightful experience for her. I have always believed that something went wrong during the delivery that prevented Myra from having other children. Perhaps it was only psychological—we'll never know.

"She was really such a child herself. She only saw Angela twice, in the hospital, but she did love the baby. I blame myself, Beecher. I should have convinced her that keeping the baby was the right thing to do.

"When it took guts, I didn't make the grade. Ever since, I've been trying to make up for it by campaigning for woman's rights, backing lame-duck candidates, even helping you catch Larry and Hal, but none of it made up for what I did, here in Venice, twenty-three years ago, when I gave my grandchild away." Harry began to weep.

Beecher reached out and took her hand. "Don't, Harry. I'll tell you what Conner told me. Part with all that guilt you've been carrying around. It's excess baggage.

"Teresa Rosetti lives for Angela. The child gave her life new meaning. That's important too. Angela has had a good life here in Venice. After all, her father was Italian. Now she has a movie career. I like to think that I made Myra happy—at least most of the time."

"Oh, you did Beecher. I don't see how you ever could

have doubted it. She loved you more than you'll ever know. You were the one for Myra; I knew that first time she brought you to Westport." Harry wiped her eyes and blew her nose.

"Harry, it's as though these past few weeks, I've been living in a strange dream. And I realize that I've been living in another sort of unreality ever since Myra died. I never really completely accepted her death until now. Conner was right about the painting in the studio—her easel and paints, her smock and straw hat. I'm ready to put it all away now."

"I'm glad Beecher. I've been worried about you."

They left the restaurant and walked through the streets of Venice. They paused by the Bridge of Sighs and strolled through the Rialto. When Harry grew tired, Beecher hired a gondola and they rode back to the Hotel Bellini. Beecher walked Harry to her room and opened the door for her with the gigantic key.

"Well I see, Beecher, some things in Venice never change," Harry said. "Tonight was a sort of sentimental journey for me—a bittersweet experience. I'm ready to close the book, now, on those chapters that were written here, so many years ago. Some things can never be recalled or changed, like those broken blossoms we saw tonight floating in the canal under the Bridge of Sighs."

"Goodnight, Harry. Call me in the morning. We'll have breakfast together and I'll take you to the airport." He kissed her gently on the cheek.

Beecher rode in the wheezing Rosa down one floor to his room.

The evening was warm and he sat on his balcony, smoking. The magic city spread out before him begged to be sketched, to be painted.

He sighed. Some day he would do it, but first he must send Harry back to William. Then he would return to Rome. Guido would be anxious to discuss the Italian series. Cristina would be waiting....

Beecher smiled and slowly relit his pipe.